Katherine V. Forrest
FLASHPOINT

Katherine V. Forrest
FLASHPOINT

NAIAD

1994

Printed in the United States of America on acid-free paper
First Edition

Cover design by Pat Tong and Bonnie Liss
    (Phoenix Graphics)
Typeset by Sandi Stancil

Library of Congress Cataloging-in-Publication Data

Forrest, Katherine V., 1939–
    Flashpoint / by Katherine V. Forrest
    p.   cm.
    ISBN 1-56280-043-4
    1. Lesbians—United States—Fiction.   I. Title.
PS3556.0737F58   1993
813'.54—dc20   93-4914
                                                              CIP

For Jo . . .

*Of a
thousand
cities*

Acknowledgments

I am especially grateful to the people crucial to me during the process of this novel.

To Montserrat Fontes for her perception and advice. To Michael Nava for his insight and moral support. To them both for the example of their lives and their splendid talent as novelists; for their friendship.

To Jo Hercus for honest overview and her loving support.

To Sherry Thomas, for input at key junctures, for the benefit of her experience and advice.

To Barbara Grier — again — an editor's editor.

The novel's characters and story are fictitious. Historical events are actual, as are geography and certain locales, as well as certain persons involved in historical events. But all characters involved in the story are imaginary.

Saturday
September 28, 1991

Where the Streets
Have No Name

QUEER NATION. Plastered across the breast of the ceramic flamingo decorating the front yard of Pat Decker's cabin.

Pat descended the deck stairs and yanked the flamingo out of the ground and flung it under the low-growing ferns fronting the windows.

Bradley Jones shook his head, and grinned at her. Warren Newman, standing next to Bradley on the pathway, rocked from foot to foot as if listening to a tune, then sang, "In-a-your-face, ever-y-place."

She snapped, "Easy to be in-your-face in San Francisco, young man. You can just save all your ACT UP stuff for Averill."

She turned on Bradley, aggravated by what he had chosen to wear here — jeans with trendy ladders in the knees and another raggedy hole for Christ's sake right next to his cock. Her anger growing that he would use her to prove his radical credentials to Warren, she jabbed

3

a finger at the discarded sign. "You try living up here with all these yahoos, Bradley. See if you want to advertise."

"Lots of Broncos and Subarus coming up the mountain," he conceded, stepping off the path toward her.

"Cowboys," she snorted, not about to heed his concession.

"Cowboys are my type," said Warren, moving ahead of Bradley to take her hands, his dark eyes softening with his smile.

She warmed a little to him, even though his pants were no better than Bradley's — cheap loose cotton with a silly black and white Egyptian motif, and the black T-shirt every gay man in the world wore these days.

Bradley slung a heavy, muscular arm around her shoulders and noisily bussed her cheek. "The cowboys up here have a two-hour drive to the beach, Patsy."

"The cowboys up here have guns." Unwilling to be mollified, she stood stiffly within his embrace. "I hear shots at night."

"Who doesn't? Who all's here, love?"

"You're first."

"How déclassé." He removed his arm as if taking care not to damage her. "What does Donnelly want?"

"I don't have a clue," she said, stuffing her hands into her back pockets. He was testing her, she judged. Finding out what she knew without revealing any of his own information. "Don't try to tell me you don't."

"I don't."

"Donnelly beckons and Brad comes running," Warren said in a snide tone that grated along Pat's nerves.

"Don't call me Brad," Bradley said with a weariness that suggested this was an oft-repeated order. "Great place, Patsy," he said, his survey sweeping over the trees and sky. "Gorgeous up here. And this air..." He extended his arms to expand his lungs.

Her view freshened by Bradley's appraisal, she raised her gaze above the cabin roof to the spires of fir trees. Smoke from the fireplace, mixed with the piney exhalations of the trees, seemed sweeter than incense, and she ached suddenly, fiercely, with a sense of impending and irreversible loss.

Warren said, "I hear you might sell the place. Why?"

She bit off the words: "Don't want it."

Warren's startled eyes glanced off her. "So...what's this with Donnelly? Think she might be sick?"

"Sick? Don't be ridiculous." Then, her pulse hammering in her throat, she considered what had not occurred to her to consider. "No," she decided. "She'd have told me."

"She'd have told me too," Bradley said, looking at Warren. "Sorry Patsy, we've all got sickness on the brain."

"I know," she said in chronic weariness. Her current life span was now at least twice that of most men she knew — some of them, obscenely, students she had taught.

She strode into the cabin as if she could leave the emotion suspended in the atmosphere behind her. In her wake, Warren whistled softly. Not in accompaniment to the song playing on the oldies station and not, she knew, because he had focused on the regal pines framed in the picture windows. He would be looking at the massive stone fireplace, dominantly beautiful in this room, the thick stone mantel darkened to deep gray from years of smoke and heat, the flagstones a pattern of tan and ochre fanning out from the fire pit. Age had burnished all the sheets of stone covering the entire west wall of this room. Age should be a burnishing process, she thought, not this leaden accretion of guilt...

"How long have you had this place?" Bradley asked, clearly impressed.

"Only since August. But the family's owned it from the thirties." She drew out her reply so that she could inspect him. "I remember coming here when I was maybe... four. That would've been in 'thirty-four." Bradley seemed no different, seemed to be in his usual robust health. But then she had seen him and Warren only three months ago.

"Where've you put us?" Warren eyed the steeply canted staircase against the dining room wall.

"In the den." She gestured behind her. "Bathroom's across the hall. I'll be bunking with Donnelly, she always liked the loft. Your neighbor's Averill. Averill and her latest... caddie."

"Caddie." Bradley weighed the word. "For just her clubs?"

Warren laughed, and Pat replied dourly, "Who knows? Fortune is fickle on the LPGA tour these days."

Bradley mock-sighed. "Only eighth on the earnings list this year."

"You know that's not what matters to her, Bradley."

At the sound of a slowing car engine she glanced out the window. "Discuss it with her yourself. She's here."

"Later." Slinging his duffel bag over his shoulder, he made his way down the hall. Shrugging amiably, Warren followed him.

The Sounds
of Silence

Looking down from the front windows, Pat watched Averill Calder Harmon position her BMW well away from overhanging trees. Birds might be fine as decor on a golf course but there would be no bird shit on that gleaming hunter-green finish.

The hand brake shrieked faintly, and Averill leaped from the car, her blonde hair a mass of dancing sprigs. She pulled two pieces of matched cowhide luggage from the trunk, dropped them to the gravel road, then turned and gazed off into the trees. Even from a distance — hell, Pat amended, even on a two-inch pocket TV — the woman radiated sun-kissed health. Butchy, but toned-down butchy, not like some other take-me-as-you-see-me LPGA pros. Attractive, she'd give her that. But nothing else. She hadn't seen Averill in . . . how long? Two years it had to be. Not nearly damn long enough.

Averill stood with her left hand cupped over her eyes as if to scout a path through the pines, the right hand closed and cocked as if around a golf club, the arm a pendulum. Setting her feet, she interlocked her hands and pantomimed a swing, then two more, as if threading a trouble shot to a green somewhere within the woods.

Pat shook her head. The woman's *existence* was golf. Even Donnelly had been a temporary distraction.

Pat's eye was caught by an embroidered orange-gold tree glistening on the breast pocket of Averill's white polo shirt, the emblem of the Mission Hills Country Club, home of the Dinah Shore golf tournament, one of the two majors Averill had won by the time she turned twenty-seven; and Pat became aware that she was an audience of one for this increasingly famous woman and her equally famous golf swing, a swing the press had dubbed "Harmony" during her first tournament win. Yes, dammit, the woman was magnetic. The networks loved her, the cameras doted on her all-American looks, the profusion of Huck Finn freckles across her cheekbones, the trademark curly hair, the eyes the cleanest clearest blue . . .

The passenger door slowly swung open. Pat stared at the woman who emerged struggling to extract another piece of luggage from the rear seat.

This was the creature who had Averill wound around her little finger? *This* was the woman that cautious, mistrustful Averill was terminally loopy over? She looked so . . . ordinary. The blue-checked blouse was cute, and there was a tad of style in the bright scarf, those were good fitting slacks on a nice enough figure, but such plain hair and really a smallish body, and the hips were pretty wide —

The woman looked up and caught Pat's greedily evaluating stare. Hideously embarrassed, Pat managed an abortive gesture of greeting.

Pointing to the absorbed Averill, the woman gave an exaggerated shrug, and her smile was so natural and spontaneous and filled with such kinship and connection that the sheer generosity of it conquered Pat. A Nancy Lopez smile, thought Pat. The tour's model of heterosexual virtue might have lost her dominance as a golfer but everybody was still in love with the Lopez smile. And anybody would fall in love with *this* smile. Even Averill Calder Harmon.

What's Love
Got To Do With It?

"Bradley, again — why exactly are we here?"

"We've been through this." He was tired of discussing it, even more tired of the polite irony camouflaging Warren's incessant needling. Right now he wanted his absorption of this surprising room uninterrupted, this room that might have been transported intact from his boyhood. But voice any of this and Warren would turn away in a wordless hurt that would require exhausting appeasement.

"Wall-to-wall dykes. Frankly, my dear, I'd rather be in Peoria." Warren fell back onto the bed. "Shit man," he said involuntarily, struggling in its enfolding depths.

"I can't believe it!" Bradley flung himself down beside Warren. "A featherbed!"

"Weird," Warren said, punching a fist into the yielding softness. "Like a water bed."

"Better," Bradley said, seizing him.

"You're crazy," Warren said seriously, and kissed him. He pulled quickly away as Bradley tried to take him fully into his arms. "Bradley, I don't get it."

"Hold still long enough," Bradley teased him.

"I can see Donnelly with you. I can see Donnelly with Miz Golf Pro. I can't see Donnelly with Pat."

Bradley shrugged. "All I know is, some women aren't attractive to men — but can be very attractive to other women. I have it on good authority from Donnelly that Pat's definitely in the latter category."

"Whatever," Warren said with a wave of his hand. "You don't like any of these women, Brad. Except for Donnelly."

"Pat has her moments," he said mildly, still beguiled

by the firm, sweet lips that had yielded too briefly under his.

"She always seems to have a mad on about something with you."

No more so than he did with her, he thought. He said, "Yeah, well, it's all part of the history." The quilt under his hand was ribbed silkiness and he picked up a section and traced one of its panels. A real quilt, hand-stitched, a haphazard design of colorful remnants just like the one his grandmother had once made. The one he had found in his sister's room the time he sneaked into that perfumed sanctum to snoop into its recesses in a compulsion to know the mysteries of femaleness... But he'd focused immediately on that quilt — tracing the stitches in the sturdy cotton, feeling his formidable grandmother's essence in the creation of every determined stitch in it, straining to imagine what it might be like to actually be a woman like her. A powerful matriarch...

"History?" Warren said. "You've got history with Pat, too? Your history with Donnelly's weird enough."

"Not weird for those days. Not weird for *these* days, for some people."

A memory of his brother boiled to the surface. This room, he thought, this room's fucking me over. He had managed not to think of the little bastard for months, ever since the phone call: *"Listen, bro, you come down with that HIV shit, don't you bother Mom about it. Have the decency to —"* *"Bruno, you listen, you —"* But rage had cut off his voice and he had slammed down the phone so hard the receiver had cracked.

Maybe it was seeing Pat. She had the same direct-from-the-shoulder bluffness as his brother. But his brother was popular, well-liked, while Pat seemed to have a permanent chip on her shoulder. "Pat would have made a good man," he said, and smiled at the struggle mirrored in Warren's dark eyes as he searched to attach this remark to their preceding conversation. If Pat were a man, he thought, Warren would be attracted to her.

Warren gave up the search. "I know you don't like Averill. What's Pat's beef with her?"

"Among other things she thinks Averill has a duty to come out. Thinks she can afford to be like Martina."

Warren reared into a sitting position. "*This* Pat who just tore down a Queer Nation sign? Give me a fucking break. Somebody has a *duty* to come out because she's a professional *athlete*?"

Bradley managed not to smile. Of course Warren would have a different take on this, as he did on everything.

Warren sat cross-legged in the cloud-like contours of the featherbed. "Nobody's got more guts than an athlete, they put everything right out for people to see, every failure right out there in public. Didn't you tell me this same Averill blew a three-shot lead one week, came right back to win some big tournament the very next week?"

"Some big tournament is right," Bradley said. "Just the U.S. Open. But there's guts and there's guts," he added. And, he thought, there's out and there's out. Even he wasn't totally out to everybody, it was too much work.

Swinging out of the bed, he examined a ship in a bottle on a scarred desk, knowing that unlike this bottle-bound ship, Warren was endlessly launched on this new subject. He tuned him out.

Wish They All Could Be
California Girls

"Pat, this is Angela," Averill said.

No last name, thought Pat. Typical stupid Averill. "Pat Decker," she said, taking the soft warm hand extended by the woman Pat had inspected from the window. "Welcome."

"Angela King," the woman said. "No relation to Betsy or Billie Jean. Or Martin Luther," she added.

Pat chuckled. Class, she thought, a classy cover of Averill's crass ass. "How about Don King?" she joked back.

So the woman wasn't a beauty, but she was fine-looking. Nice mouth, strong jaw line. So easy to look at that she must remember not to look at her too much.

"Both those men are — oh Bismarck, you're joking," Averill said, and giggled in embarrassment. Angela and Pat laughed with her, Pat amused by Averill's use of a state capital as a profanity. Averill had begun the practice as whimsy when an open mike had broadcast LPGA pro Lori Garbacz's profane opinion of an intrusive reporter to the nation; obviously the joke had become an unthinking habit.

"Lovely place you have here," Angela murmured. Her gaze was focused on the trees, not the fireplace, Pat noted.

"Nice," Averill agreed with a swift glance around. "Great fireplace."

Nice, Pat thought. Dogpatch compared to the houses, hotels and country clubs that Averill frequented. "You'll be down the hall," she said in abrupt dismissal, "across from Bradley and Warren. They just got here."

Averill made a face at Bradley's name. Then she took

Pat's arm with firm insistence. "Listen," she said, "what's this all about?"

Pat gaped at her. Averill always operated in a realm of pure economics, she wouldn't walk across the street except for a clearly defined benefit. Of all people, she would have made her attendance conditional on knowing exactly why Donnelly had summoned all their loyalties.

Averill's crystal blue eyes widened in all-out alarm, in obvious misinterpretation of the expression on Pat's face. *"What's wrong with her?"*

"Nothing I know of," Pat said, astonished by Averill's behavior.

Averill's face hardened. "Yes, you do, you —"

"Averill, she doesn't," Angela interjected smoothly, her dark eyes fastened on Pat in alert interest.

Pat jerked her arm out of Averill's grasp. "I don't," she confirmed icily.

"I'm worried, that's all," Averill muttered. "Let's freshen up, Angie."

Pat turned her back to her and marched into the kitchen.

Sixteen Candles

She set out potato chips and dip, peanuts, a bowl of fruit; then, Coke in hand, sat in her recliner and pushed the side lever to raise the extension for her feet. Except for some urgent requirement, mutual if cordial dislike might keep all of her guests in their rooms — until Donnelly arrived, if she was lucky. Tapping her fingers to the tune on the Oldies station, she inhaled the aroma of fireplace permeating the cabin and, faintly, furniture polish. She'd done a yeoman job, if she did say so herself, when Donnelly had given them all only a scant day's notice to assemble.

But Angela emerged from the hallway. "Do you have mineral water? Stay where you are, I'll get it," she said to Pat's nod.

After a few muted sounds from the kitchen, she returned to the living room glass in hand. "Averill's asleep. Amazing how she can just curl up like a cat in a patch of sun." She was looking around curiously as she spoke. "This house feels so ... settled in its pores. Has it been part of your life for a long time?"

"It has." Pat swallowed past inchoate emotion. "Are you psychic?"

Angela said gravely, "I doubt it."

"Make yourself comfortable," Pat invited, with every expectation that Angela would demur and return to Averill.

Placing the glass of mineral water on the coffee table, Angela kicked off her sandals and curled up on the gold corduroy sofa, tucking her feet up under her.

Another cat in a patch of sunlight, Pat thought. Angela's observation about the cabin still resonating, she mused, "This place has changed a lot over the years. But —" She pointed through the doorway into the dining room. "That paneling, it's original." There was also something different about that wall of glowing wood, but then it had been over thirty years since she'd set foot in this place ...

"It's ... lovely. It's ..." Angela was selecting her words. "It's like dark beautiful brandy you've kept in a cabinet for years."

Warmed by her, Pat said, "I remember one contractor offered to rip it all out, replace it with something lighter.

Mother wouldn't have him in the house again, said he
was a no-soul."

"I like your mother," Angela remarked.

Pat said with reluctance, knowing the revelation
would cause awkwardness, "I lost her in August."

"I'm so sorry. I'm sorry for your loss."

Pat nodded, looking away from her. "Eighty-four she
was, she had a long life." If not a particularly good one.

After a moment Angela asked, "This place, originally —
what else do you remember about it?"

Pat said tartly, "Freezing my tail off on the way to
the outhouse. Pine needles on the path in summer, snow
in winter —" A ripple of goose flesh coursed over her at
the memory of the cold silver stars, the heavy shadows
of the trees, the air freezing her nostrils, the ghostly
rustle of wind on the mountain. "It wasn't till after the
war we got electricity in, and inside plumbing. 'Forty-six, I
think." It *was* 'forty-six. *Happy sweet sixteen,* her back-
from-the-war father had said that icy October evening,
flipping the switch that illuminated every corner of the
cabin for the first time ever. *Better'n candles on a
birthday cake.* Maybe not, but a hell of a lot easier to
read by. Especially when it snowed enough to trap you
up here, when even a big car with balloon snow tires
wouldn't get you through the drifts.

Pat pointed to the steep staircase. "That's always
been here, too. Upstairs used to be just an attic."

An arctic attic. She and her sister in one bed under a
mound of covers, her brother in a bunk bed behind a
partition dividing the room, breakfast smells waking them
in the mornings, all of them emerging from the delicious
soft warmth of bed for the freezing dash down the
precipitous stairs to get to the wood-burning stove . . .

"Redid the attic in the forties, finally winterized the

place in the late fifties, got the furnace in. Then added the second bathroom, threw out the junky rugs, carpeted the floorboards wall-to-wall."

"Really nice," Angela said. "You've got a lot of memories here, Pat. My family could only dream of a place like this."

Pat was silent. This house had been her mother's territory. Her family had been thrown together here in ways far different from how they had lived in the house down the mountain in San Bernardino.

Angela said approvingly, "You never added a television set."

"Not for trying. We're in a shadow, even an aerial didn't help much. We got cable once, Mother took it out, said it made the place too connected with the city — radio music and the phone were plenty enough."

"Your mother was right, don't you think?"

"I do." This place had become a living, unchanging entity. Just like those ancient trees outside the window.

Time in a Bottle

The game was interesting, its object to take the curves on Highway 18 just fast enough so that the RX-7's tires would not squeal while at the same time she overtook and passed slow traffic without braking, and managed a few glimpses over the road edge at the hazy yellow expanse of San Bernardino far below. The mountainside itself surely wasn't all that interesting — dry yellow ground cover relieved by dark green shrubbery, and an occasional distant view, as she zipped around a curve, of the road snaking ever upward. Another season,

Querida Quemada thought, and this would probably be lovely, the landscape green and the bushes flowering. She tapped her fingers on the steering wheel in time to the Jim Croce song on the Oldies station, thinking that no aspect of the drive here had been all that interesting. All the communities she had sped past, nebulously familiar names on the Southern California landscape, Alhambra, Monterey Park, San Gabriel, Rosemead, El Monte, Covina, Pomona, Montclair, Claremont, Ontario, Fontana, Colton — *semejante,* differentiated only by the car dealerships along the freeway announcing the community they represented. San Bernardino itself seemed a monolithic sprawl across this end of the Los Angeles basin.

Twenty years in Los Angeles and she had never been here, never been on this road into the San Bernardino Mountains and the resort communities only an hour and a half east of the city. Well, not so amazing. In the limited world of her early years mountain havens of the privileged would have fit in with such mirages-in-the-desert as Beverly Hills and Bel Air. The town of Crestline, she had heard, was a more modest place than Lake Arrowhead which was only a few miles farther and two thousand feet higher up the mountain, according to the map.

The mountain was quickly becoming more interesting — more rugged and brush-covered. She glanced at her watch. She had plenty of time, she'd spin on up to Arrowhead, fill in one more gap in her knowledge, come back down to Crestline . . .

She shrugged, then smiled as the feather-soft caress of the fabric on her shoulders reminded her that it was cashmere. Camel-colored and beautiful, especially with her dark green pants. And her coloring. Yes, she looked good. Good enough to stand up and be counted with all the special people from Donnelly's past. What could be important enough to call them all together? Without confiding the purpose to any of them, especially to Double Q, Donnelly's own *mujer*? What could anyone do except to be here?

That'll be the Day

"How did you meet Averill?" Wrong thing to ask, Pat saw immediately as Angela looked down and took her time smoothing out a fold in the fabric of her slacks.

"In the tournament office at Palm Springs," she said. "She . . . had a special situation I was able to take care of."

She raised her gaze to Pat's eyes, and Pat knew she had been told the truth, and would be given no further details — but that Angela knew she could guess the details. And she could indeed guess. Reports of lesbianism on the LPGA tour had surfaced again in the press, as they did from time to time, and some reporter had been sniffing too closely around Averill.

"It's why I don't believe in outing," Angela said in confirmation.

With a smile, Pat tested her. "Even homophobic gay politicians?" Pat watched Angela's hand holding the tumbler of mineral water. Everything about this woman was graceful.

Angela smiled back. "I can make exceptions. I just think we need to encourage people to come out, and put emotional support systems around them so they can."

"The safer we make it, the safer some people feel

about staying in the closet." Carefully, Pat asked, "Averill's told you she'll come out?"

"Not in so many words, but she's so courageous I'm absolutely positive she will. When she's ready."

This lovely woman is so credulous. Pat said, "She's a famous woman, Angela. She's always been very, very cautious."

"She's been there all by herself. Never had any support."

Wait till you meet Donnelly.

"This ... Donnelly," Angela said as if reading her mind. "What's her real name?"

Pat blinked. "Her full name, you mean? I have to think." She chuckled at the absurdity of having to remember. "Her business cards always said 'C. Donnelly.' Candice. Yes, that's what it is."

"When will she be here?"

"Anytime. She couldn't be sure. It might even be late tonight."

Almost visibly changing gears, Angela asked, "How did you meet Averill?"

Oh hell. "After she ... met Donnelly. It's a long story," Pat said, shifting position in her recliner.

Angela's face seemed to pick up a shadow. "Believe me, the last thing I intend to do is pry."

Pat said, "It really *is* a long story." Uncanny how this woman could read her. She glanced toward the hallway. The house felt calm, as if it had absorbed the dissonant personalities contained within. "It's connected to how I met Donnelly. And some stuff before that."

"Averill should be asleep for a while," Angela said as she rose easily to her feet. "Why don't I get us both a refill?"

Desperado

Warren, wound into a tight fetal shape in the featherbed, slept. Bradley leaned back in the desk chair and scanned the room, letting it wash over him. A quintessential boyhood room, from the shoe scuffs on the legs of the desk and chair to the not-quite-scrubbed-out stains on the rough Navajo rug, to the dust-covered model airplanes and erector set constructions on the shelves, to the three old sports posters covering the walls.

Even in his deliberate ignorance of sports, he could call on enough cultural osmosis to identify two of the athletes in the posters. Joe Louis, 1940s-era hero from his own boyhood city of Detroit, posing with fists cocked, champion of the only sport at that time where his "skills" were accepted. And ballplayer Jackie Robinson sliding into second base in a fierce cloud of dust and defiance, an unwilling and angry and therefore perfect hero to break the color line. Bradley smiled at the Robinson poster. Would a similar fiercely burning athlete ever come along to break the homo line?

A caption identified another baseball player, in catcher's gear and poised to receive a throw: Roy Campanella. Bradley remembered him now, remembered his father's shock and endless carrying on that an accident had consigned this athlete to a wheelchair in his prime. Not so long ago the nation's press had gone into mourning over another sports star, some kid who'd snuffed himself out with cocaine, an event treated as Shakespearean tragedy, unlike the deaths of other superbly gifted young men in their prime...

Remembering Warren's fulmination over Pat's attitude toward Averill being in the closet, he reminded himself that sport was a symbolic stand-in and consolation prize for people's pinched-in lives. Like religion. He wouldn't worship at either intolerant altar. Unlike his father or his dipshit brother.

He looked at Warren. Interesting that he had not commented on the African-American athletes pictured in this room. Well, maybe not that surprising. Warren was totally indifferent to sports, and he was hardly race-identified, despite, or perhaps because of, his mixed heritage of an Afro-American mother and a white father. A wild weed, Warren called himself. A unique weed, in Bradley's experience; an outcast of several worlds and the uneasily accepted citizen of one, and completely separate from even gay reference points.

Again he gazed at the room. Whoever had inhabited it had not been here for many years, that much was clear.

He looked at his watch. He'd check the office in another half hour, see if they'd heard from Hennessey about the galleys. Christ, the book was going to press in only two more days. "You pretentious piece of offal," he muttered to Hennessey. Just because the silly prick read that Capote or Faulkner or whoever had revised his work even in galleys, he wanted to do the same thing and hang the expense. As if Hennessey could even tie the shoelaces of any decent writer. God, the delusions of mediocre talent.

Donnelly, get your ass up here, I have things to do. But he lay back, hands behind his head, and relaxed with his thoughts of her. How long had it been since they'd seen each other? They talked by phone at least two or three times a month, exchanging news and affectionate banter and gossip and memories . . .

He smiled remembering the last phone call and the mock-fight over how they first met. The only agreed-upon facts were that he'd been immersed in work on a term paper at a grungy table in L.A.'s vast downtown main library, surrounded by towering canyons of books he had assembled. She'd walked up to the same table, her own books and notepad in hand, and remarked, "You need somebody close by in case of a cave-in."

"Just leave me buried," he had grunted in reply.

She'd scraped a chair up to the table and snapped open a book and proceeded to ignore him.

Beyond this, their memories diverged. According to her, he'd asked her to go with him for a cup of coffee. He couldn't remember the logistics of how they'd ended up talking over coffee, but no fucking way he'd have asked her to accompany him anywhere, not when he was twenty years old and intimidated if not terrified by the very idea of Woman, and sure as hell he'd never have asked a thirty-year-old woman like Donnelly who had looked every bit as mature as her age back then, just as she did now.

Far more likely he'd looked dead with exhaustion — he was always an inch from collapse in those days — and she'd said something about him needing a coffee transfusion, and took him away with her. She'd always taken people in hand, then as much as now. Right from the start he'd felt safe with Donnelly. Thank God she had tucked him under her wing back in those good old days when he'd believed that if he just worked hard enough — well, fuck all *that* history.

It Never Rains In Southern California

"You gotta be kidding me," Querida muttered, her thought-stream interrupted by her entry into the mountainside village of Lake Arrowhead. A hotel sat in massive, dark-wooded splendor against the shore of an azure lake that stretched farther out than she had imagined. "A fucking Hilton Hotel," she marveled. A shopping mall adjoined the hotel, on the hill below. "Beverly Hills East," she grunted.

Following a highway threaded between towering pine trees edging the lake, she looked at the pseudo-chalets with contempt. These people came up here to get away from it all, and not only had they built structures just as rich and grotesque as the ones they owned in the city below, the houses were cheek-to-jowl with their neighbors, the one difference being that the residential lots were filled with pines instead of palms. Many of the houses looked deserted — and probably were, she speculated, their owners coming up here in summer to ply the lake in expensive speedboats, or to frolic in their expensive skis and ski clothes in winter. They would not be here now, in September. A landscape in transition from summer to winter would not be up to their standard.

She felt a keen disappointment that Donnelly knew somebody who owned a house up here. But then, Crestline supposedly was a more modest community. She shook herself, grinning in self-deprecation. *What's the matter with you? These are the gente you rub shoulders with every day.* Old Saunders had a place up here, she remembered. Could be any one of these monstrosities by the lake. Everywhere, people had to impress everybody everywhere.

Like A Bridge
Over Troubled Water

Opening her eyes to an expanse of window and a
hillside of pines, Averill reveled in immediately knowing
where she was. Good news/bad news: instant orientation
meant she was not on the road/the road was where she
wanted to be. She had long since surrendered hope that her
subconscious would adjust to life on the road, that a
new day could be born without her having to claw
upward through murk and panic. Even the embrace of
Angie's arms was not enough for her safe keeping. The
cause had to be the tension of competition; home — or
anywhere else when she was not playing a tournament —
never included the frenzied imperative to know *Where
am I?*

Soon this anxiety about Donnelly would be resolved,
she and Angela would be singing their way down the
highway to Buena Park for the Los Coyotes LPGA
Classic . . .

She sat up, stretched, rubbed her eyes. The luggage
sat half-emptied beside the bed. Where was Angela? She
heard murmuring conversation from the living room, two
voices. What was Angela doing out there talking with Pat
Decker? Well, so what if she was, that crotchety old
butch was nothing to be concerned about. Besides,
Angela didn't know any of the history. She'd come up
here willingly, no questions asked, she understood ties
and loyalties without having to have it all spelled out.
Angela understood lots of things without needing a whole
lot of discussion — thank God.

Sitting up, she looked around her at the plainly
furnished knotty-pine room. And fell back in renewed

weariness. She did not want to be in this boring place and especially not with these people. When Donnelly arrived she'd learn what all this was about, then get the Topeka out of here. Maybe find a hotel on the beach and burrow in with Angela. She could beg off some of her sponsor commitments, skip the Tuesday practice round and get down to Buena Park on Wednesday and use the Pro-Am for practice and hope it would be a good confidence builder.

She stirred in restless dissatisfaction. This very minute she should be playing the Safeco up in Washington. No. No, she shouldn't. Not after barely making the cut in Portland. What an abomination of a tournament, with that inquisitive snot of a reporter making things even worse. Just like the one in Palm Springs, the sticky situation Angie had gotten her out of. These days reporters thought they could ask anything, they could poke their slimy noses into everything.

She'd needed to take the week off, not touch a club. Her mental game had gone somewhere south of Rio, she'd gone absolutely stale, her fundamentals were in the toilet. Those five top-ten finishes this year were a mirage — she could have, should have, won three of them. She hadn't had a decent tournament since the Corning.

If she couldn't zero in on the key to her problems in the pressure cooker of competition at Los Coyotes, she'd do what she'd always done to right her game — call Judd Castain and have him fly to Buena Park to look at her supposedly flawless swing, then she'd stay at the practice tee till her hands and arms and back screamed from the work.

She stared at the green landscape with hostility. If she wasn't smoking her drives into the stupid trees she was

yanking irons into sand traps. How could you hope to
score when you were scrambling all over the place
needing to land nasty long chips or having to drop
ten-foot putts? At this rate she'd be a burned-out wreck
by the time she was thirty-five. Your concentration is
pure Des Moines, she told herself hatefully.

She lay with her hands behind her head trying to
calm herself. A break, she needed a break, that was all.

Donnelly. Irritably, she pulled the pillow down under
her head.

Why didn't Angela come back into the room?

What in Carson City did Donnelly want?

I Heard It
Through
the Grapevine

Crestline. Querida knew the town's name signified its
location at the tree-line of the San Bernardino mountains.
She took the Crestline cutoff, a road wound close beside
the rugged mountainside, and after one final hairpin turn
she dropped down into a forest of pines.

Ignoring for the moment the fork she needed to
travel, she drove on through the town, slowly traversing
perhaps a half-mile plateau of main road beginning with a
white wood-frame church, then an assortment of real
estate offices and several gas stations and repair garages,
a post office, used-car lot, hardware store, variety store,
an ice cream parlor, a few modest restaurants, none of
them fast food chains. All very small-town America. At
the end of the road she pulled into a large supermarket
parking lot to look at a small, glistening lake a fraction

the size of Lake Arrowhead. Lake Gregory, she saw from the sign. A lake/reservoir, and man-made, she suspected, looking at three aerating sprays of water arcing high into the air along its shore. Nonetheless it was pretty, its clear water filled with reflections from the pine trees on the surrounding hillsides. She pulled out of the parking lot, deciding to drive around the lake before she headed back for the fork in the road leading to the meeting place. The town had a nice feeling. She could like it here. Although neither in Lake Arrowhead nor here had she noticed any black or brown faces.

Goodbye Yellow Brick Road

"It all has to do with Donnelly," Pat said, doing her best to stifle rising laughter. The kitten had crawled out from under the sofa, had struggled up the side, and was now clambering awkwardly across the sofa back toward the unaware Angela. "I met her when she was with Bradley —"

"She was? Oh, so that's the connection. Averill didn't mention it."

I'll bet Averill hasn't mentioned a lot to you.

Pat let loose her laughter as the kitten tumbled from the sofa back and eagerly pawed the object of its attention — the fabric of Angela's pants. "Oh how divine," Angela breathed, scooping him up.

Enjoying the pretty picture of Angela with him, Pat said, "Somebody left him in the trash can across the street. Those people haven't been up here all summer. I just happened to hear him crying." She added, "He hasn't cried since I found him."

"People can be terrible..." Angela gently touched, stroked his dark fur. "What's his name?"

"Haven't named him."

Angela looked up at her. "You *are* keeping him?"

Pat sighed. "Well, I'm not keeping a good many things, including this place." *Don't ask for details.*

"Maybe I can persuade Averill..." Angela trailed off, smiling as the kitten curled up purring against her. "I think Averill should consider taking the cabin and him."

Yeah, sure. Pat continued, anxious to get off this subject, "Donnelly was at a family picnic, in a park in Glendale. Running everything, of course. Setting up tables for the food, setting up games for the kids and the adults too. I was there..." She hesitated, then filled in: "...walking my dog. I stopped to watch her. She needed one more player for touch football and she ran over and recruited me."

"Audacious." The kitten tucked against her, Angela had returned her full attention to Pat.

"You're right, pretty darn audacious for nineteen seventy-five. But that's Donnelly. She found out I lived only three blocks from her. And that's how it all started." A cold sensation passing over her, she looked away from Angela, gazing out at the pines. She would not clarify Angela's probable interpretation that she had immediately begun a physical relationship with Donnelly. It was all too easily condensed history as it was.

She heard a car come up the road, stop. "Company," she said regretfully.

With a Little Help
From My Friends

The light blue eyes of the woman in the doorway evaluated Querida. The handshake was firm. "I'm so glad to meet you, Pat," Querida said, and was gratified to see a softening in Pat Decker's stern face. An old-time butch, and great-looking, Querida marveled, gazing at the neat, artlessly combed back short gray hair, the chino pants and white shirt, and the face etched with life-experience like weathered granite. From the age of this woman, she probably belonged among those she'd read about — a lesbian trailblazer who lived without compromise when the price exacted was beyond modern comprehension. Much, Querida suddenly realized, like Grandmother Mary White in Mexico in 1936 . . .

Pat Decker introduced Angela King, who extended a hand and said with a smile, "Querida, your name is lovely."

So are you, Querida thought. "Thank you," she said. She liked the unpretentious clothing, the homely touch of the slightly protruding front teeth, the comfortably shaped figure. And the authentic smile. Pat Decker's lover, she had to be. They made a great traditional butch/femme couple. Pat Decker deserved no less than this fresh-looking, very nice woman.

A few minutes later, seated on the sofa, sipping a glass of Diet Coke, she divided her attention between looking around the cabin and out at the pine trees, and absorbing the information being delivered her way. She was the last to arrive, and, when Averill Calder Harmon came striding from the hallway into the living room, she saw immediately that she had married Angela King to the wrong woman.

"Angie honey, I missed you," Averill announced while surveying Querida with a glance and nodding perfunctory acknowledgment to Pat Decker's introduction.

So this was Averill Calder Harmon. Querida had known the name for years, from a knowledge of sports gleaned by exposure to TV news, much as she'd learned about products from commercials. When she was first with Donnelly, Querida had tuned in a televised golf tournament to see this woman who had been briefly in Donnelly's life and was still in continual contact. She'd inspected photographs of her in the newspapers and in Donnelly's personal collection. What had seemed a vague resemblance to Donnelly was, in person, quite startling. Not so much physically, but in intrinsic style she could be a blood *hermana*. The same open, direct look. Sensational eyes, though, more so than on TV or in the photos, and the incipient network of lines suggested not so much age as blooming health in the out-of-doors. She was no k.d. lang, but this one must draw dyke fans in droves when she walked down the fairway of a golf course. Pat Decker, Querida noted, did not seem particularly thrilled by Averill's entrance onto the scene. No surprise, given that Averill had taken Donnelly away from Pat.

She herself was impressed with Averill. That so visible and public a person would choose as her partner Donnelly, and then a non-artificial person like Angela, was admirable and did not fit Querida's image of the prima donnas of professional sport. She felt a touch of embarrassment over her pompous declaration to Donnelly that golf courses and tennis courts were for dilettantes who could afford to squander their lives, and professional athletes were paid performers in circuses sponsored by the rich as a vicarious substitute for their empty lives. Donnelly, of course, had simply laughed at her. Donnelly's relationship with Averill — although Donnelly had talked minimally about it — must have been a partnership of equals; Donnelly dealt from so much *granito* that she seemed a match for anyone.

"Pat and I were sharing memories," Angela said to Averill. "She's a very interesting woman."

"Sure." Averill smiled. Condescendingly, Querida thought.

"Hello everyone."

Bradley Jones had come into the room. Querida eagerly switched her attention to him. Until she saw photos of him she had imagined some fey little wispy fellow befitting a publisher of genteel books and a Donnelly-dominated marriage. This man was bigger than his photos and, in all objectivity, very masculine, very attractive. "So you were Donnelly's first," she said with deliberate impertinence as they shook hands.

He did not disappoint her as he returned deadpan, "So you're Donnelly's latest."

"And greatest," she said.

Bradley laughed. No one else did.

"I think I'll light the fireplace," Pat Decker said.

Querida thought: This could be a very interesting weekend.

Wake Up, Little Susie

"What in hell's keeping Donnelly?" Bradley growled. He lay sprawled on the carpet beside the coffee table indulging in a game of gin rummy with Warren instead of doing what he needed to do: evaluating the manuscripts stacked beside him.

"Lots of women between here and Sacramento," Querida mischievously suggested from the sofa. "Wrong," she added as Bradley selected a discard.

"She's still in conference with Governor Wilson," joked Pat from her recliner.

Flicking a glance at Querida, Bradley discarded the card he'd selected. "Gin," Warren said, laying down his cards. "Damn," Bradley said.

Perched on a cushion beside the fireplace, playing with the kitten while she watched Bradley and Warren, Angela laughed.

Smiling over Bradley's chagrin, Pat took her gaze from Angela to glance at Averill, who lounged in an armchair staring vacantly out at the trees. As per usual, Pat thought. On the several occasions she'd been in Averill's company, if someone's attention wasn't directly on her, she turned into a potted plant.

"So when did you know you were gay?" Querida asked Pat.

Pat was amused by Querida's transparent fascination with her, a fascination which contained the bluntly curious questions of a child. In comparison with the other occupants of the cabin, this young woman's company was relaxing. "I fell in love with a much older woman," she told Querida. "She was seven. I was six." As Querida chuckled, Pat reminisced, "A curly-haired, flirtatious, heartless little wench she was, too — took the candy I offered her like it was her exact due. At least I had a clear path to her — the little boys hated the girls, and no adult could even conceive of a six-year-old dykette. Those were the days . . ." she mock-sighed, gratified as the group, including Averill, laughed.

"I guess you had a hard time growing up," Querida suggested. She had pulled her stockinged feet up onto the sofa.

"Why would you guess that?" Pat teased, and Querida looked so sheepish that Pat relented immediately. "Okay, so I was born looking like a dyke. But age six to ten, I was one happy little hell raiser."

Well, life hadn't been quite that unfettered. Her father railed at her constantly over her "wild-assed" ways, while her mother took Pat's part with uncharacteristic vigor, contending that it was harmless fun and would end soon enough. For four glorious years she'd been a mischief-making tomboy, hellion ringleader of the neighborhood gang of boys, free to be anything she wanted to be, then...

"Then I fell in love with another little girl named Jeannette," she told Querida.

...Then there was grade six, and Jeannette.

She'd been too naive, too obtuse to pick up clues that her eleven-year-old, fervently vocal pining puppy-love for beautiful, aloof little Jeannette exceeded the garden variety schoolgirl crush. God forbid anybody in the religious establishment should ever notice you, and frog-faced, pinched-mouth Sister Jane Theresa did. And took her parents aside at a PTA meeting.

The fury of heaven and earth had broken over her head. Had the devil himself made her his personal playmate, her parents couldn't have been more aghast, her father bellowing the specifics: "You want everybody — *nuns and priests* — saying you're *unnatural? Queer?*" She did not know what his words meant, only that her character was so horrifyingly deficient that her father would no longer trust her mother to supervise her, he must now keep his own vigil and lash criticism on her and her equally inept mother about everything from the way Pat wore her dresses to the way she walked and sat and talked. Her mother said nothing, save one statement she had uttered with closed eyes: "Oh dear heaven, Patricia," turning away with a look of such pain that it was worse than her father's denunciations. Pain directed toward Pat would become ingrained on her mother's face, in contrast to the relieved approval she bestowed on her other two offspring. Pat's sister, older by four years, possessed, in Pat's opinion, the brains of a pork chop, but she was certifiably and redemptively boy-crazy, and Pat came to envy her and her brother Matthew so passionately that she secretly called them the prince and the princess.

"Deal the cards," Bradley challenged Warren.

"Of course, my dear lemming," Warren said. Tauntingly riffling the deck of cards, he sat cross-legged and looked, Pat thought, like a genie in his voluminous pants.

Pat said to Querida, "Imagine me trying to be a young lady."

I did try, Pat told her dead mother. You know how hard I tried . . .

Back then she could have been Margaret Mead in the way she studied the behavior, dress, and idiom of her pre-teen tribe. But her efforts at mimicry and to gain acceptance won her only contempt from the tribe, which infallibly judged her as the outsider she was. Less hectoring from her father turned out to be far from a relief: he acquired an air of embarrassment, even mortification, over his earnest, unfeminine, utterly misfit daughter, especially when she began to gain weight as if sheer bulk might wall her off from universal disdain. Pat sometimes looked at herself in photos from those days and ached for the odd, sausage-shaped girl forced into dresses and curls, the eyes bright and panicky, like someone peering up from the bottom of a well.

"That first little girl," Pat said to Querida. "I wish I knew what happened to her."

Surfin' Safari

That first little boy ...

Bradley arranged the freshly dealt cards into suits, and remembered the boy.

It was after school, around four o'clock, when he met him, on a day ripe with the color of late afternoon. They were both on bikes, the meeting sheer accident — they were aliens on new turf, Bradley out of his neighborhood, the other boy away from his as well — Bradley had never seen him here before. Pulling up to where the other boy stood beside his bike, Bradley placed his feet down on either side of his bike. "Hi," he said.

White-blond hair hung straight down over the boy's forehead like a sheaf of fresh spun silk, and curled up over the collar of his navy blue polo shirt. "Hi," the blond said in a low, firm voice, and looked at Bradley with wide open, very blue eyes.

And then they stared at each other.

Bradley pointed to a house under construction. Rain had come down hard earlier in the day, and probably for that reason workers were not there. "Want to take a look?" he asked, his heart thudding in his chest.

The boy got off his bike and walked it toward the house, Bradley following with his. They pulled the bikes into the entryway, out of view.

He and the boy picked their way into the recesses of the structure, Bradley's nostrils filling with the smells of damp earth and sawdust and plaster. No sooner had he led the way into an alcove well-concealed from the street when the blond reached for Bradley's pants, clutching at him.

Bradley held the boy away, and the boy looked at him, his eyes wild blue fright as Bradley gathered the fabric of the boy's shirt in one hand. With his other hand he opened the boy's pants.

And then nothing else mattered except the smooth firm silkiness in his hand, lying across his palm. So simple in its power, in the beauty of its setting between those pale thighs. His fingers gently closed around it and only then did he hear, startled, the ecstatic gasps of joy.

Bradley watched the boy surrender everything including his safety — his eyes shut so tightly that his lashes curled and knitted into themselves. His nostrils flared, his body surged as Bradley's fingers moved and squeezed, the tension building in the boy's muscles until he shuddered and a milky spurt arced onto the concrete floor.

The boy reached for Bradley and again Bradley held him away but only for an instant — to unzip his own pants. Then the hot, eager hand circled him, and Bradley almost swooned from the sweet ecstasy of that firm boyish hand upon him, and he came in the next instant, and the boy gasped again.

Bradley turned away from him and zipped up his pants, and walked away, directly out to his bicycle.

They pedaled off, Bradley without a backward glance, the blond boy, he was certain, doing the same.

He flew toward his neighborhood, the frenzy of his pedaling matching the frenzy of his thoughts. So now he knew what it was like to feel some other boy's cock. Big deal. The boy touching him, that was okay. Maybe the boy was one of those freaks who wanted to be a girl. Well, he might not know about that other boy but he did know about himself: he was okay.

During the four nights that followed, in his dreams he flew — down staircases, over open fields of white-gold wheat, in feverish wet dreams in which his joy soared free. On the fifth morning he rose knowing he would go back to meet the boy. He would let the boy touch him again, no more than that.

It had not occurred to him that the boy would not be there. Day after day he went back, in a mounting rage of frustration. Undoubtedly the boy had come back during Bradley's initial absence and had given up before Bradley's return.

From that day to this he had never stopped believing that his life would have been altered in some unfathomable degree had he found the courage, the self-honesty to come back the very next day.

What he regretted most of all was that he had not touched that silken white-blond hair.

If You Could Read My Mind

Okay, she wasn't born dykey-looking like Pat, Querida conceded, but her own growing up had had its own hazards.

In a sudden need for comfort she touched the women's symbols at her throat, her first gift from Donnelly. Donnelly had laughed incredulously at her name: "Querida Quemada? Your initials are the lesbian symbol!" And the two pewter ⚢s had arrived the very next day...

She loved the symbols and had yet to take them off, daring to wear them even to her sister Maria's wedding reception. If her mother and father disapproved of her *joyas* or her garb, they said nothing; they welcomed her to the wedding with their usual uncertain, wary affection, having long since relinquished all attempts at understanding their *extrana* offspring. Only her grandfather had given a sign of noticing, his glance seeming to pick out the symbols from an obscuring braid of gold chains as part of his survey of her white pants suit. His heavy eyebrows lowering in scrutiny, he had said nothing — perhaps in part because he would answer no question about the locket and chain he wore from her earliest memory of him.

Her grandfather observed everything; he had spent his entire life in vigilant observation, and not much wonder — in his youth he had been picked up and deported she didn't know how many times — he disdained to say — each time immediately returning, thumbing his nose at the INS *villanos*, refusing even to apply for amnesty during the period of eligibility despite the pleas of his family. Still bristling defiance at border guards and *fronteras*, at eighty-two years of age Miguel Quemada would occupy any land where he wished to live and at no man's behest or approval; his Latino identity resided equally in his genes and in his heart.

Sunshine on My Shoulders

Listening to Querida question Pat Decker, and to the jousting between Bradley and Warren, Averill knew she should make an effort to participate — it would please Angela.

Angela did not understand that being quiet was the real luxury. Anything you said in casual circumstances could be just as dangerous as if a reporter were present. Having always to be careful, to confine conversation to polite nothings cost far more than sociability was worth. People — including Angela — didn't understand what she had to lose, because they didn't have what she had to lose. No circumstances were safe, even these. Pat Decker and Bradley whatshisname had never done or said anything to her, but she knew they disliked her. For no good reason that she could see, except jealousy over Donnelly, and that wasn't a very good reason — Pat's relationship with Donnelly was a tapped-out vein by the time Donnelly strayed to her, and Bradley hadn't been part of Donnelly's life for years. Herself, she wasn't the least bit jealous of Donnelly's involvement with this Mexican girl. She didn't know anything about her except she looked attractive enough and bright enough to amuse Donnelly for a while.

Seeing Angela's perturbed glance slide off her, Averill sighed. All right, she mentally told Angela. In a minute.

She focused again on a squirrel playing in the trees. It *was* pretty here. Lucky Pat Decker, to spend at least some of her growing up time in this cool thick pine forest. No doubt swinging from the trees, diesel dyke that she was. Still, better to be here than wind-swept, broiling Mojave. But then if she hadn't been born in the California desert, the day would never have come when she'd found scrubby Oasis Golf Club only a quarter of a mile from her house, and wrapped her ten-year-old hands around a seven iron for the first time.

To this day she loved that cow pasture of a public course, those sun-blasted greens she always called browns. Endless challenge on the unforgiving terrain of that golf course — not to mention the shape of her future. She'd learned to bore shots straight and true into the shifty, gritty winds, to this day she was a deadly putter on lightning-fast greens.

The Ping. She'd shocked everybody at that tournament. Starting only her second year on the tour, but no way had it been a fluke. Never. God, the jolt of pure joy looking out that Tucson motel window on that Sunday morning and seeing the palm fronds straight out in the wind. Eight shots off the lead the day before, thinking she had a chance at a very decent paycheck if she played a good final round. That Sunday morning she knew she had one Raleigh of a chance to move into top-five money, the golfers ahead of her were none of them outstanding wind players, they'd be out there hoping to survive, that gale would blow who knew how many strokes off their game.

Hail Columbia, it had been *great*. Of all the video tapes in her library of all her tournaments that was the one, it was always fun to watch herself playing so relaxed, having the best and easiest day of her entire professional life, back when nobody expected anything from her. These days she had happy *moments* on the golf course when she pulled off a really terrific shot, but a whole happy *day* — forget it. There was just too much pressure all the time, and the galleries expected miracles. But what a gallery she'd had that day — charged-up and shouting, building and building around her as the fourteen golfers ahead of her all went to Harrisburg in a hand basket. The commentators, their voices edgy up there in their wind-swayed TV tower, saying again and again, "Averill Calder Harmon is pulling off a miracle." No miracle, just a confident sixty-eight right into that screaming desert wind to take her first tournament win and fifty-five thousand bucks and best of all, the qualifying exemption.

Same pattern the very next year. Alcott and Inkster had taken out ownership papers on the Dinah Shore these last few years but back then two old friends of hers arrived in Palm Springs to say howdy: heat and wind. Hundred-degree heat and forty-mile-an-hour gusts, and a final-round seventy-one on the murderous Old Course had cleaned everybody's clock. The gallery that day — *electrifying*. Every fairway lined with women. Women, women, women. That walk up eighteen a winner, the cheers a thunder in her head from all those thousands of women. Goose bumps everywhere, the sex current so high it was like heat between your shoulder blades, bathing you to the very roots of your hair . . . Ah, the Dinah Shore — that was the one she had to have again. By next April her game had to be in A-one tip-top shape so she could walk up eighteen a winner again, drenched in the outpouring from all those women . . .

She traced the calluses on her left palm. In plain fact, she wasn't playing all that bad right now, but she'd only won one tournament each of the last two years, and winning was all that mattered — just ask Amy Alcott or Patty Sheehan. Winning golf wasn't a matter of athletic ability, there wasn't a poor athlete out there. Winning golf was head music, it was all self-confidence.

And sometimes coaching. It hadn't been fair to lose Irene Walsh to cancer, Judd Castain could just barely tie her shoes as a coach, and neither one of them had been as good as dear old Gene Hollings. But Angela was here now as emotional support, and there were those five top-ten finishes this year. She had the will to win, and the ability was locked right there inside her, she needed to find the key back in.

She looked away from the trees, smiled at Angela, and said to Querida, "Do you get home very much?"

American Pie

Home? Querida stared at Averill, struggling to divine her reason for asking such a question, and what her own answer might be. The apartment in Brentwood? Her parents' house in Baldwin Park? With Donnelly, in Sacramento? Why was this woman asking?

"Jesus Christ, Averill," Pat muttered.

Querida understood. "I was born here," she told Averill. "So was my mother. My father was brought here as a baby."

"I didn't mean —" Averill stammered, "I was just thinking you must have strong ties to — you know — cultural —"

"Jes like my black mammy," Warren said, picking up his cards. "Makes it a point to get back to Africa every now and then."

"Oh Bismarck I'm so *dumb* — I didn't mean —"

"A Chinese friend's fifth generation American," Bradley said, arranging his cards. "White people still come up and ask if he speaks English."

"It's *okay*," Querida said to Averill, punctuating the statement with a laugh to lighten the atmosphere. Averill's remark was ignorant but not bigoted; she hardly deserved such face-slapping cruelty from the others. Even Angela, for heaven's sake, looked mortified. "It's okay," she repeated as Averill clasped her hands in distress. This woman, a physical goddess, seemed basically guileless, and Querida liked her.

"Overlook whatever you want to, Querida," Warren said, his dark eyes glinting, "but European-Americans pass as Americans and people of color are bad people turning this country into something it's not supposed to be. I had a Latino boyfriend, his parents denied him his own language and heritage to assimilate him into this culture. For what? Latinos learn English faster than any European immigrant, that's a *fact*, but there's all this English as the official language crap —"

"It's changing," Querida told him, energized by his anger. "Politics hasn't caught up, but business knows, they're already into industries that cater to Latinos, I can give you solid numbers, population projections — four to five million in California alone — "

"How do you know this stuff?" Angela interrupted in genuine interest, her first contribution to the conversation.

"From an economic model I helped construct. I work for Browning Consultants — I'm a junior economic analyst."

"Here," Bradley said, holding up his hand of cards, "go ahead, tell me what to discard."

"The five of hearts," she said with a grin, and turned to Averill. Now that she had this woman's attention she intended to capitalize on it. "I'm dying of curiosity. Your opponents on the tour —"

"Not my opponents," Averill corrected her with a smile. "My competitors."

"Okay, your competitors," Querida said, appreciating the distinction. "Is it true most of them are lesbians?"

"Columbus no," Averill groaned. Shaking her head, she did not elaborate.

Querida asked impishly, "Nine out of ten?"

Averill answered in a neutral, serious tone, "Probably about what you see in the population as a whole."

"Oh come *on,*" Pat scoffed. "We're over-represented and you know it — just like in nursing, therapy, teaching, the military —"

"Superior women do superior things," Querida agreed. "We're all family, so give us the skinny. Who are the dykes? I'm crazy about Julie Inkster —"

"She's married," Averill said shortly, and continued more amiably, "I don't talk about my competitors on the tour. I don't believe in it. I never gossip about them. I hope to Boise they don't gossip about me."

Angela was nodding, her eyes on Averill in admiration. "One thing I've found in being around the players," she said, "is they respect each other enormously. There's as much misconception about the touring professionals as about your nationality," she added.

As Pat got up to tend the fire, Querida sat back, accepting the close of this topic. She had other questions for this woman with the intriguing occupation of professional athlete, but they would wait until Averill's feathers had settled and she was open to questions she deemed less threatening.

Such irony in this whole business of nationality, Querida mused, gazing into the kaleidoscope of sparks and flames raised by Pat's poker. She herself expended so much effort in supporting Mexican-American causes and organizations, and yet the member of her family with the purest Latino blood was her hidebound, unregenerate reactionary of a grandfather who railed constantly at her — at all his brood, actually, but at her especially — for losing her heritage. The truth was that all his offspring, except for her, of course, had married full-blooded Latinos, while his own marriage to an Anglo six decades ago meant that their watered-down Latino genes came entirely from him.

That long-ago bride of her grandfather's was *el misterio.* Querida's grandmother, whom her own father knew only by name, age, and cause of death; a woman of whom no photograph existed, whose Anglo name — Mary White — was further reminder of her skin color. And whose excess of white blood cells had brought death from leukemia in Mexico at age twenty-four, a death so long ago — 1936 — that perhaps only Querida and her grandfather cared about the why of Mary White's reasons for challenging the iron-clad social codes of the time to marry a Mexican.

It could well have been a marriage of headlong passion. Miguel Quemada, the archetypal patriarch, was still classic-Mexican handsome: iron-gray hair parted straight down the middle, nut-brown skin that looked more weather-beaten than aged, lips that retained more than hints of considerable sensuality, and arresting roof-shaped eyebrows over unwavering dark eyes. Perhaps Mary White had found joy, however brief, with the vigorous young Miguel Quemada. But how had she fared as a stranger in his strange land? Had it been by accident or design that Mary White's widower crossed the border soon after her death, their son in his arms, to make America his own strange and hazardous land? It was all to remain a puzzle, because her grandfather would not answer the simplest questions about Mary White; she was on his proscribed list along with other private anguish he had removed from the world's inspection.

She loved her iconoclastic grandfather and was proud

that she seemed more his daughter than her father's — she possessed nothing of Pedro Quemada's features or his passive temperament, and her skin was darker than that of her brothers and sisters. Her nose was thin like her grandfather's, her ears delicate like his, she had his broad Mexican face and the shape of his eyebrows and eyes, and, according to her envious sisters, his "sexy lips." And, of course, his streak of stubborn independence.

Again she caressed the lesbian symbols at her throat. Warren was right. Her parents, like the ones Warren had alluded to, had considered fluency in English an essential requirement for the children they had borne on American soil. Her grandfather was the only one, including her mother and father, who spoke pure, non-mongrelized Spanish; she, like her sisters and brothers, knew Spanish but — a key difference — didn't think in it except for a few stray words.

Yet her grandfather was proud of her, his declarations of pride meant to be heard as proof of his acceptance that times had changed. She knew he had not changed, that innately he still believed women must work outside the home only if hard times warranted, and a wife surely must not be the family's prime breadwinner and distort the natural order of things by taking a good job away from a family man to become her own breadwinner. She argued with him constantly, but never about two subjects. Her own family's views on homosexuality were difficult enough; she could not bear to hear condemnation from his lips. On abortion his opinion consisted of one word and it never varied: "*asesinato*" — murder. The rest of the family, with similar conservative views, could not understand her passion on this subject, considering that she showed virtually no interest in the male sex or marriage. Little did they know that one day she might very well decide to have children —

There was a knock on the door, in a rhythm she recognized. She leaped to her feet.

That's What Friends Are For

"About time you showed up," Pat said, giving Donnelly a quick hug and a resounding buss on the cheek, then stepping back to surrender her to Bradley, next in line. Bradley bestowed a hug but no kiss; Averill surrendered her cheek and kissed the air; Querida delivered a brief but smacking kiss on the lips.

"*Yo te amo,*" Donnelly murmured to Querida. An arm around her, she said, "Good to meet you, Angela," and took her hand. Returning Warren's kiss, she said, "Sweetie, wherever did you get those silly pants."

"Michael Jackson's garbage can," Warren returned, adding a hug to his greeting.

Pat had picked up Donnelly's duffel bag and deposited it beside the stairs to the loft. Donnelly looked fine, she decided; she was the same strong, broad-shouldered Donnelly she'd always been, the eyes just as vibrant. Tired, she looked tired, that was all.

Returning to the cluster around Donnelly, she saw Angela scrutinize Donnelly with admiring curiosity, and noticed Averill's gaze moving down Donnelly's sweatshirt to her travel-wrinkled jeans to her beat-up loafers — combing her like a flea brush on a collie, Pat thought. The woman was still hung up on her.

"Okay, so what's all this about," Averill said heartily.

Provoked by the woman's thoughtlessness, Pat

snapped, "Give her two seconds to relax, why don't you."

As Averill turned on her, Donnelly said, "I'm glad you're here, Averill," and gently patted her shoulder. "Patty, I'd love a tall, cold one."

"Got one waiting for you." Pat headed for the kitchen, Donnelly striding beside her.

As Pat pulled a Foster's from the refrigerator and a pilsner glass from the cupboard, she noted in the bright light of the kitchen that Donnelly looked *very* tired, and, for her, a little grim. Could there be something physically wrong with her? "Long hard drive, honey," she suggested, casting a glance out at the dusk deepening the shapes of the trees to ink against a sky of gray-pink clouds.

Donnelly shrugged; she was surveying the cabin. "The place looks pretty much like you always described."

"Hasn't hardly changed at all." It was, in fact, eerily the same after all these years she hadn't been here. "Different carpet, new stove."

Donnelly asked, "How come your mother left it to you? Guilt?"

Pat poured the Foster's down the side of the glass, forming the half-inch-high head of foam Donnelly liked. "I figure she just wanted to piss off my father — nothing else makes any sense. And he is royally pissed, let me tell you. The lawyer who called me about the will said he pitched a monumental fit, wanted to contest it." Pat chuckled dryly. "Putting the cabin in Mother's name was just an indulgence, you know — he never dreamed she'd actually consider the place hers, much less leave it to the likes of me."

"I think you underestimate your mother."

"I think you overestimate her."

Donnelly always had the most expansive ideas about other people's largeness of spirit, Pat thought, watching her take a deep swallow of beer and then wipe the foam mustache away with the heel of her hand. Donnelly had lost her parents young, but she'd been damn lucky to have a mother who was the very independent widow of an Air Force captain killed in the final days of World War II. Sarah Donnelly had been a suffragette-throwback who admired people like Bertrand Russell and Virginia Woolf. Not much wonder the great calamity of Donnelly's youth had been the loss of that fabulous woman in a bus accident when Donnelly was fifteen years old. But after that she'd been looked after by her Aunt Charlotte, a spinster in the finest old-fashioned, feisty sense of that term. As far as Pat was concerned, Donnelly was a descendant of true female aristocracy — two splendid female role models.

"I think it was guilt," Donnelly said. "I think your mother might have been a lesbian."

"You think every woman might have been a lesbian," Bradley said as he and Querida came into the kitchen. "Averill wants to know if it's okay to smoke pot." Holding up his hands, he grinned as Pat stiffened. "Kidding, kidding, just kidding, Patsy."

"No hiding out in the kitchen, you two," Querida said. "We all want to know what's going on."

The affection for Donnelly mirrored in the young woman's eyes filled Pat with melancholy. So much past was gathered here in this place — did no one else feel it? Even Bradley — inhabitant of much of that past — looked oblivious. Did no one else feel caught in the headlight of onrushing memory? This new young woman in Donnelly's life . . . Donnelly being Donnelly, Querida probably did not know about Pat's first meeting with Donnelly, when that fierce optimism seemed like a beacon on a dark ocean...

"Okay, family, gather around the table," Donnelly said. "Let's have a council of war."

Bad Moon Rising

The tiffany lamp, its colored glass set aglow by a low-wattage light bulb, cast dark rich warmth over the circular maple table in the alcove off the kitchen. Bradley watched Donnelly take a seat, and the others arrange themselves according to their sense of ownership: Querida to Donnelly's right, Pat to the left, he and Warren along one side, Averill and Angela along the other. He felt a strange, acute apprehension.

"Listen up," Donnelly said, spreading her hands out on the table. "The big news is, Pete Wilson is about to veto AB 101."

"*Son of a bitch!*" Pat expelled the words so vehemently that Averill visibly flinched.

"He can't," Querida said with such conviction that Bradley, disassembled with shock as he was by this news, had to smother a snort of laughter.

"He can't do that," Angela declared. "People voted for him when he promised to sign that bill."

"What's a promise from a politician?" Averill asked rhetorically.

"He has to keep this one," Bradley muttered. First George Deukmejian in 1984, after the miracle of the first gay rights Assembly Bill in history to reach a California governor's desk, and all gay people daring briefly to hope — and his unsurprising but crushing veto snuffing out that hope. Now this. He knew protest calls had been pouring into Sacramento from the religious right, but that was just their gang-up-and-scream tactic ... AB 101 was a bill whose time had come, and Wilson had promised to sign it. He felt his resistance stiffening to Donnelly's news. A veto simply made no sense. "He can't make this huge a mistake," he said.

"What's the big deal here?" Warren asked caustically. "A one-day story in the newspapers. You're this bent out of shape when it makes no difference whether he signs it or not? It's up to us to get out and take —"

"He *promised* he'd sign it." Pat's fierceness drowned out Warren. "It's the *symbolism* of the bill that's important, don't you understand? His whole image is integrity!"

Bradley nodded agreement.

"He's about to compromise that integrity," Donnelly said quietly.

"Where do you get your information?" Bradley demanded.

"I can't say." Donnelly rubbed her hands over her eyes. "Somebody at his elbow."

Now he definitely did not believe her. This was opinion, rumor — not fact.

"Somebody gay, honey?" Querida asked in a subdued voice.

"You got it."

"I don't understand," Angela said. "*He promised.*"

"Political expediency won over symbolism," Warren sneered.

"You got it," Donnelly said again.

"Look, political expediency doesn't compute," Bradley argued. Wilson's fine-boned face, with its candid blue eyes and touch of austerity, filled Bradley's mind. A double-crossing veto did not fit with the fundamental decency he had sensed in this man. He himself had voted for Dianne Feinstein, but, believing Wilson's statement that he would sign a gay rights bill, had not felt unduly upset over Wilson's close victory. "It's a lose-lose situation. California's a liberal state — he won't gain any votes other than the ones he's got, and he'll piss off a lot of people who voted for him. His stock-in-trade is trustworthiness. Siding with the bigots will do a lot more harm than good."

"A one-day flap," Warren said. "It makes no difference anyway."

"Dammit, it *does*, Warren," Pat said heatedly. "I'm with Bradley and Angela. This is the most liberal state in the country, we *can't* have a so-called liberal governor vetoing a gay rights bill. Okay, supporting our rights is tough politically, but he's already stood up for us —"

"Standing isn't doing," Donnelly said wearily. "We worked so damn hard to push this bill through the Assembly, we lobbied everybody who has his ear to give him exactly your arguments. But ... the bulletin will be on the news. Pat, can you tune in one of the all-news stations from L.A.?"

"Hard to get much of anything up here," Pat snapped.

"I don't believe this," Angela said, rubbing her arms as if to rid them of goose bumps.

"I believe *you*, Donnelly," Pat said in a calmer tone. "But it wouldn't be the first time a so-called unimpeachable source ended up impeached."

Bradley remained silent. Much as he hated to agree with Pat about anything, he'd believe this when he saw it happen.

Donnelly's face conveyed only resignation. "I called

you here because I've got a lot more to tell you, and something vital for each of you to —"

"What," said Querida. "I'll do it."

"No, I should have realized that just my word on this wouldn't have the impact that learning it first-hand did for me. Let's sit tight till the news is released." She looked at her watch. "It's six now, that should be in the next two or three hours."

It won't come, Bradley thought. I can't believe the man will do this. Averill, he noted, had not uttered a word.

"Averill?" Warren prodded. "So how does the LPGA stand on this?"

Bradley swallowed a grin. Warren had also figured out that the woman probably didn't know AB 101 from a rutabaga.

Averill cast the chilliest of glances at Warren and said, "Donnelly, *this* is what you called us here to tell us?"

Her eyebrows knitting, Angela said, "If Donnelly's right, it's crucial to our lives as gay people."

"Of course I can see it's important," Averill said impatiently. "I just..." She trailed off, her crystal-clear eyes beginning to cloud.

Averill might be an idiot, Bradley thought, but in this case she was right. If Donnelly had called them all here — him all the way from San Francisco — just for gay politics as usual, he'd brain her.

"I can't believe he's going to do it, I just can't believe it," Angela said.

"You and a lot of people," Donnelly said. "Let's sit tight —"

"You sit tight," Pat said harshly. "I'll get us some dinner."

Lipstick on Your Collar

Donnelly picked up her olive-drab duffel bag and, accompanied by Querida, ascended the steep staircase to the loft. Fifteen minutes later she climbed back down — without Querida — and flung herself onto the floor in front of the fire Pat had just lighted, sitting with her back propped against the side of Pat's easy chair, arms circling her knees, staring down at her battered loafers.

Typical that Donnelly would not think that she needed to explain Querida's absence, Bradley thought. "Querida's lovely," he said perfunctorily. "A good sense of humor," he added.

She looked up. "A *great* sense of humor. She's got so much . . . potential."

All her lovers had had "potential," he suddenly realized. In retrospect it seemed she had gone onto a new relationship only after she had taken her current partner as far into self-awareness as she could. God knows he'd come out of his relationship with her stronger than when he'd gone in, and so had Pat. Averill was an aberration, someone Donnelly had promptly given up on like a sculptor abandoning a flawed stone. And yet she had not completely given up: Averill was here.

"Brad . . ." Her face was troubled.

She was the only one he had ever permitted to call him by that name. With Warren and Averill gone back to their rooms, and Angela immersed in a magazine, he used his own term of endearment to her: "Yeah, honey," he said.

"Wilson will veto that bill."

So much rage over the possibility boiled just below the surface that he could not answer her. His glance fell on her trademark footwear. "Those shoes," he said, "they look like the same ones you wore when I brought you home to meet the family."

Donnelly looked down at her shoes and smiled. "I still remember your dipshit brother going on about my name."

He laughed. The first words out of peckerhead Bruno's mouth had been, "Donnelly? Is that your first name?"

"It's what I like to be called." Her voice had been friendly but was that tell-tale, testy tap of a loafer.

Bruno turned to Bradley with his *har har har* of a laugh. "You gonna call your new wife by a *guy's* name?"

"Yeah. He is." And Donnelly, blessed Donnelly, had flipped him off, grinning her big open friendly grin. And mutton-head Bruno couldn't do one damned thing except stand there in shuffling, red-faced fury because his father was roaring his own *har har har* of complete approval.

Oh how his father had approved. Approved and approved of Donnelly. Grabbed Donnelly's hand and burbled how fine she looked and what a fine young woman she was, welcomed her into the family bosom with such alacrity, such eagerness — such *relief* — that Bradley never forgave him for so nakedly revealing the shame he felt for his oldest son.

That one gesture by Donnelly had settled his brother's hash but good. Bruno had remained off-balance, wary and excessively polite around Donnelly.

Not so his mother. Remote at best, wintry at worst, her silences in Donnelly's presence measured the depth of her dislike. His mother... always smelling of English lavender soap, with those vague, watery blue eyes that could suddenly focus with unsparing disapproval. She had couched her objections carefully, at first: "Bradley..." she faltered, those blue eyes at their widest, most disingenuous, "I think you need to give serious thought to the possibility —"

He had interrupted with a peremptory strike. "She's young enough to have children, Ma."

She had recovered quickly. "It's not that at all. You just can't have much in common with someone who... Bradley, she's just ten years younger than I am."

Well, he'd had one hell of a lot in common with Donnelly. It was his mother who hadn't, and her dislike, could it have taken form, would have been the shape of a cat in arched-back hostility. Donnelly was everything a woman was not supposed to be. Independent, fearless. Independent, bold. Independent, individualistic. Independent, confident. And worst of all, independent.

Donnelly had taken so much heat off him. Yet in some ways had put as much on as she took off. Just like Bruno had. Bruno, the stupid nickname assigned by his football teammates as a take-down from Broderick, one of the fanciful names his mother had laid on her children to compensate for the generic surname Jones. Football star, virility star, light of his father's eye, chip off the proud old block, Broderick/Bruno had fulfilled enough parental expectations to ease some of the pressure on Bradley. He himself was no slouch in the athletic department, but he couldn't measure up to his authentically het brother.

His life didn't revolve as theirs did around competitiveness and the constant striving to strut and demonstrate maleness, and so, as far as his father and brother were concerned, in the joyous celebrations of manhood, his psyche contained a big, very visible hole. For him the Hemingway-macho pose was simply stupid, the life and death symbols of the playing field unnecessary to his own life. Winning games was a hollow mastery, his heart wasn't in sporting competition, and he couldn't conceal his lack of zeal. Donnelly had known it from the start, hadn't judged him for it, didn't care. And for that he loved her.

His three aunts had loved Donnelly too. Her strength and self-reliance had thrilled them. But only to a degree. If she thrilled them, they did not accept or approve of her and they could and did look down at her in relieved censure; she did not fulfill their image of how women should behave. She was not a proper wife. Just as he was not a proper husband...

"Pat, can I help?" Angela called out to the rattling of pots and dishes from the kitchen.

"I could have someone set the table," Pat called back affably.

"I'll do that," Warren shouted as he came back into the room. "Have Angela do something more complicated."

"Can I—" Querida began.

"Only two of you," Pat interrupted her. "Kitchen's too small."

Nights in White Satin

Averill stood at the window wrestling with frustration. She should climb that staircase, follow Donnelly to the room where she had just retreated and say, okay, whatever the reason you brought me here, I respect that it's vitally important to you, now tell me exactly what you want so Angela and I can get ourselves out of here. But she couldn't. Not without infuriating Angela. And, maybe equally important, without permanently alienating Donnelly.

Money was what this figured to be. Everything was

about money. Write a check, help in the fight to right a wrong. Well, Donnelly had never asked her for a thing, so she'd write her a check all right, and for a size that would surprise her, even though it wouldn't be a tax deduction and she'd have to fudge with her accountant to explain it. She surely couldn't make a donation outright to a gay organization — she might as well walk down the fairway with LESBIAN written on her back. All right, she would wait for this business to play out, she had to.

Hearing Angela's laughter in response to some inaudible remark from Pat in the kitchen, she flinched. That particular intimate trill in Angela's laugh was hers and hers alone. She strained to hear the conversation, but the voices were pitched too low. Well, if she couldn't get herself and Angela out of here now, she could at least get her own self out for a while.

She turned from the window. Bradley, playing solitaire and humming along with the Moody Blues song on the radio, ignored her. She looked at Querida, who returned the look with a shy smile. Here was a chance to offer some additional reparation for that earlier faux pas about Mexico.

"Querida," she said, "how about coming into town with me, picking up some wine?" With Angela occupied helping Pat and Warren in the kitchen, she could go find something to bring back to drink, something decent.

"I've got wine," Pat called from the kitchen.

This place is so Tallahassee small, Averill thought in disgust. "Something special," she called back to Pat. "For a special gathering."

Pat did not answer.

"Sure I'll come with you," Querida said.

Darkness had fallen and the temperature had dropped sharply; Averill felt the chill keenly through the sweater she had pulled over her polo shirt. The clean smell of the pines, the fecund mulch of needles and leaves, had intensified in the descending dews of evening.

"Nice car," Querida said, slipping into the leather seat of the BMW.

"Thanks," Averill said, turning on the car heater and locating the oldies station with the Moody Blues song that was playing in the cabin. "Maybe I'm a wine snob, but I looked in the refrigerator, I wouldn't use what she's got to clean my clubs."

Querida chuckled. "I like a nice glass of wine myself," she said. "Champagne's my real sin."

"Mine too," Averill said with enthusiasm. "Let's see if they've got anything decent in this burg."

She was gratified to have anything in common with Querida. The woman was attractive, too — she'd give her that, and how could she not, with so strong a resemblance to Lucia? How odd, how ironic that this woman who was Donnelly's present lover should bring back one of her best memories, the first time she'd had champagne. In 1980, at the San Juan Open. That was the win — her tenth, an "easy" six-stroke victory, according to the press — when she'd felt the first sense of real accomplishment, in contrast to the mostly sheer relief of holding her nerves together enough to tough out another win. That was the tournament when she decided she'd actually done pretty well for a twenty-three-year-old pro only three years on the tour, that was when she accepted her laurels as a major player.

After she'd sunk the final putt and was danced around the green by her caddie, was dutifully bussed and patted by her competitors, was interviewed by the local TV and news media, she'd as usual called her parents.

"Half the neighborhood's here!" her father gloated from the west coast. "We're toasting you in —" His voice dropped in its awe, "*Dom Perignon*. We've been saving it for number ten."

"Wow, I'll have some too," she declared.

"You *do* that, honey," her father urged her, "and I mean it. Cut loose a little — you deserve it!"

And she did. She'd been inflexible in maintaining her training program, knowing that single-minded discipline was her only chance to remain part of a peer group where mediocrity was constantly weeded out in ruthless natural selection. Very early on, she had redirected her life into a regimen of strict diet which excluded not only alcohol but every fried food she'd grown up loving and had never stopped craving.

That night she'd released all discipline, let herself go sky-high with self-congratulation and champagne and fried-everything she could find on the hotel dining room menu. Buying extravagant quantities of Dom Perignon for competitors who weren't leaving San Juan until the following morning, she drank lots of it herself, reveling in its delicious effervescence and her own soaring intoxication. Until the wee hours, when she was left in the company of a comely Puerto Rican pro who had been in Averill's foursome the first day, and had subsequently missed the cut. Lucia Rodriguez had insisted on seeing the joyfully tipsy Averill up to her hotel room

If she had thought the early part of the night glorious, now, her inhibitions stripped away by inebriation, she discovered the glories of her own body in the warm hands of Lucia, whose tireless caresses fired Averill's body, whose silken tongue infused Averill with unthinkable, fiery pleasures. Breathing heavenly frangipani perfume, staring down into Lucia's dark gaze under the bold lights of the hotel room, she was shocked by her own aggression, by her appetite for the firm fragrant breasts, the supple, athletic body, the sugar-sweet skin, and, periodically throughout the night, the frangipani mixed with musk scent between her legs.

Lucia slipped out of the room just before dawn, leaving Averill in delicious, utter satiation. And with the realization clicking into place that, from the start, part of her drive to belong on the tour had been adoration of the athlete-goddesses with whom she consorted, brought to a gratifying height when she triumphed over them . . .

Growing up, she had had no time for boys, or even friends, in her obsession to learn golf, and if she did not know then that it would be her life work, she comprehended that she would not dilute her involvement in it for anyone. Later she had no time for relationships because she was building her success, and the demands of the tour took precedence over everything. *Married to the tour,* people said, half-admiringly, half-sympathetically, including her parents. She accepted the admiration, rejected the sympathy. She had won membership in a select sorority and in return for dedication, she had become one of the athlete-goddesses herself.

That morning what she most clearly understood was that she had unearthed in herself a powerful libido — and what had been unearthed was dangerous. She tore up the piece of hotel stationery on which Lucia had scrawled her number, consigning the night to the scrapbook of memories to be savored in secret. This foreign country had caused everything, and she didn't care who claimed Puerto Rico was part of America. Her parents were thousands of miles away, she'd been released from all complications and discipline and the gossipy scrutiny of other LPGA pros, and, not to put too fine a point on it, there was to blame what her father would call the native perversion of Puerto Rican Lucia.

Much as she had enjoyed Lucia, no way would it happen again. They were poles apart in culture, background, geography. Like one of those corks being popped off the champagne bottles, she'd just blown sky-high, and if she didn't do anything stupid, such as see Lucia again, she could always accuse Lucia — who had not an ounce of credibility compared with herself — of lying if she revealed their night to anyone. Besides, Averill told herself that morning, if she ever had time for the complications of a relationship, she could feel all those things just as easily with a man.

Since I Met You Baby

Taking advantage of Averill's cautious attention to the dark road that wound between thick, sheltering pines, Querida surreptitiously stared at the tanned hands on the steering wheel, the firm-looking breasts under the white pullover, the fine long planes of thigh.

Conscious of Averill's silence, uneasy in her presence, Querida knew her edginess had nothing to do with the woman's fame and everything to do with her sheer physicality. She was golden in her athleticism, sexual energy seemed to pulse just under her skin. The car felt drenched with pheromones. Donnelly had sexually enjoyed this woman, Querida thought with awe.

Querida found a question and asked it gratefully: "So what do you think about Donnelly's news?"

After a pause, Averill said quietly, "It's important to her, and that's what matters to me."

Querida nodded. This was her central position as well, but at a deeper level she was so *furiosa* over the issue that she immediately searched for an escape hatch from the topic. She asked, "Who's the woman player you admire most?"

After another pause Averill said, "I admire all of them for something. Patty Sheehan has a great swing, one of the best since Haynie —"

Glad to have an opinion she could interject, Querida said, "Nancy Lopez has the worst-looking swing I ever —"

"It works," Averill interjected. She added slowly, "She has the most incredible concentration, Kathy Whitworth in her great years, she had the same kind of focus..."

As Averill trailed off, Querida asked, "How old were you when you began playing?"

"Ten. I played tennis too, I swam — by the time I was twelve, golf was it." Averill was relating this history in a free rush of words. "I was on the boys' golf team in high school, won a full scholarship to ASU, left after a year —"

"A year?" This woman walked out on a full four year ride?

Averill glanced over at her. "It was one big decision, let me tell you. I missed out on a lot, and I still don't know if I did the best thing. But that first year at ASU I won seven tournaments, my team won the NCAAs, I was amateur player of the year and qualified for the U.S. Open — what was left to prove? I wanted to be on the tour. But nobody in my family ever went to college..."

Querida smiled, imagining her own parents' horror and histrionics had she so much as hinted at throwing away one of her scholarships. Unlike Averill's middle-class upbringing, her own childhood was burned into her memory as sheer physical deprivation. Her family had constructed self-respect out of never having worked in the fields, except of course for her grandfather; but while her father scratched out a living performing odd jobs, their poverty was so excoriating that she still remembered her astonishment at learning that other people possessed more than a few pieces of clothing, and that houses could actually be brightly lit at night.

Growing up in central California was being hot, wet and hungry. Or being cold, wet and hungry. A perpetually runny nose in winter, drenched in her own sweat during the suffocating days and nights of summer. So broiled had she been by the pitiless summers, so chilled by the pea-soup-fog winters, that she was fond of neither tanning nor sun, and to this day she loathed fog . . . To this day she was physically miserable in every season except for what passed as spring in Los Angeles, to this day *el jubilo* was her perfectly climate-controlled apartment . . . Proof, she always thought, of how unimportant emotional nurturing can be when physical well-being is lacking.

Her body to this day remembered its early ravening for food, its yearning for basic comfort, and she still ate with voracious appetite. During her senior year in college she had gone on an insatiable eating binge and her body puffed up, especially her belly; just as suddenly and inexplicably the obsession had melted away and so had the pounds. Her metabolism burned up calories, unlike Pat Decker's. Pat's form Querida thought of as comfortable; but other people, she knew, would be less charitable, corpulence being looked upon as somehow morally inferior. Her own mother was regarded with increasing condescension by virtually everyone around her as she added girth with each year of her life, like a tree acquiring rings . . .

The best memory of her early years was the school picnic when she was six. It had been held in a wooded area, she remembered vaguely, and the picnic table was loaded with food, and she had been urged by a faceless woman, in Spanish, to help herself. Wonderingly she had picked up a plate. And filled and refilled it. Helping after helping, until all by herself she had polished off an entire tuna noodle casserole and nobody had seemed to mind. Or even notice. And no, she hadn't been sick, but for years afterward an ingrained shame turned her away from any tuna-based dish. Still, during those years sometimes an aroma would trigger the richly intoxicating smells lifting off those wonderful platefuls of warm food, and one day twenty years later Donnelly had listened quietly to this memory, and said, "You must be dying to eat that again," and had prepared it. Now it was so much her favorite dish that her metabolism had to stretch to accommodate her intake; she had embraced that dish along with her lesbian-symbol initials and everything else that today she adopted with defiance . . .

Her escape to a different world would never have happened except for her field-worker grandfather, who had convinced his son to seek better work opportunities for his fix-it trade in Los Angeles. And so in 1970, when she was seven, Pablo Quemada had moved the family. And from there he had established the modest neighborhood business that to this day provided income from a cluster of faithful customers in Baldwin Park. And Querida had made her escape into the Los Angeles school system — into the world of scholastics, not to mention school lunches.

The move to Los Angeles had not been a cure-all, only a tiny glimpse of opportunity, and a tiny glimpse was all she had needed. Through some maverick gene she, unlike her brothers and sisters, was blessed with a special talent, although she sometimes wondered if what they lacked was the simple blessing of optimism. She suspected that she possessed the same orderly mind that her father applied to analyzing and repairing any sort of appliance, and she herself had re-applied it to mathematics, and beyond that, to economics. In any case, math scores had set her apart as a gifted minority, and then scholarships and part-time jobs had helped her through high school and college. Marching toward a future laid out for her like a vision of Oz, she had majored in economics, with a minor in business, and graduated cum laude from UC Santa Barbara.

During all those years, if she had felt any peripheral awareness of her isolation, it served to push her even further into study and work, even after she graduated from college and was recruited by Browning Consultants as one of their economic analysts. She told herself she was far too busy for any sort of emotional involvement, it was far more important that she succeed for the sake of her family's pride, and for the sake of their Latino roots. She was driven by the need to consign all those childhood memories to the realm of never-possible-again, not to mention using her visibility as a successful Chicana to help in the struggle to leaven the prejudices of the marketplace.

She said to Averill, "Your parents must have thrown a complete fit."

"Yeah, they were pretty upset at first, but they ended up sponsoring me my first year on the tour."

"Do they know you're lesbian?"

Averill looked displeased by the question. She returned to her careful tone. "They're very proud of me and I don't want to embarrass them. They don't deserve it."

Querida retreated to safer territory. "So, what's it like on the tour? What's a typical week for you?"

They had reached Crestline's main street. "They're all pretty much the same. Monday means travel, a couple of hours of pure practice when I get to the tournament site. Tuesdays mean a practice round and the practice range afterward." Averill's voice had regained its buoyancy. "Wednesday's the pro-am, we play with sponsors, local bigwigs, go to a sponsor dinner that night. I'm pretty cooperative about Wednesdays, I think it's good for the tour, but not all the girls feel that way. I usually work in some practice after I play the pro-am, Thursday the tournament starts, so there's practice before I tee off, and again after the round. Then it depends on how I play the next three days how much extra time I spend practicing."

"*Dios,*" Querida said, impressed. "I had no idea." She searched for more questions, feeling frustrated that she could not ask what she was burning to know: how many lesbians were actually on the tour, who they were, and if Averill had slept with any of them. "You were successful right off the bat, weren't you?"

"Oh Honolulu, not hardly." Averill was peering at storefronts along Crestline's main street. "I saved my worst round of the year for qualifying school. So I ended up non-exempt, meaning I had to qualify every single week in order to play the tour. My parents almost had a heart attack. They'd taken out a loan to sponsor me, and it was hairy, let me tell you. I cashed a decent check my eighth tournament, I had five top-ten finishes that year, and the next year I was exempt when I won at Tucson..." She pulled into the parking lot of the supermarket across from Lake Gregory, the small, pretty lake Querida had found on her drive up here. "This looks promising," she said.

Interesting, Querida thought as she got out of the

car. Except for that first disastrous question Averill had asked about Mexico, the woman only answered questions, she never asked them.

There is Nothing Like a Dame

"Nice job on that salad, Warren," Pat said, realizing that she had been paying exclusive attention to Angela.

Warren plucked several leaves of lettuce from the sink and tore them with a campy flourish. "We girls work *so* well together."

Angela flung a napkin at him, Warren caught it easily. "Darling," he said, "your butch act needs work."

"Children," Pat mock-chided, entertained by the two of them. Angela was clearly enjoying Warren, and Pat was finding that she did not mind his smart-mouth ways as much as she had before.

"I'd love to be a lesbian," Warren sighed. "I used to dream about waking up a girl in an all-woman world."

Dusting pieces of chicken in a bowl of seasoned flour, Pat reminisced, "I lived in a world like that. For three years. World War Two was hell for some people, for me it was a reprieve. People had other things to worry about besides hassling me."

Angela brushed Pat's arm briefly, a gesture that touched Pat to the quick.

She watched Angela gather up plates to set the table. Those old days *had* been good. That particular time always returned to her in bold strokes of memory — the huge black newspaper headlines, the rationing of oddities like nylon hosiery, the fervid patriotism and hatred for the Japanese, her histrionic classmates expecting an invasion of Santa Monica Beach at any moment. It had all blessedly combined to deflect attention from her, to screen her from scrutiny.

From the time she was twelve until she was nearly fifteen, with her sailor father collecting battle ribbons with his all-male fraternity on a destroyer-escort cruiser in the South Pacific, she had lived in an all-female world, she and her mother and sister running the house in contented, uncomplicated serenity, ignoring completely the one male in the vicinity, her brother. The war had brought peace to her, and the glamour and adventure others saw in the war had mostly escaped her until the mid-fifties when she saw the movie *South Pacific*. She envied her father then — well, actually she envied Lieutenant Cable sweeping the exquisite Polynesian girl Leah into his arms...

Dust in the Wind

Bradley again reclined on the carpet, this time near the fire. His just-turned-forty body was handling the floor, he thought, reasonably well. Instead of unboxing a manuscript, he again laid out a hand of solitaire and listened to the cheerful kitchen conversation.

So the Big War had given Pat a reprieve. If she'd survived because of it, her advantage for sure had been very different from how his boyhood had played out.

Meeting that boy on the bike had made all the difference, had served as a lighthouse warning beacon. From the time he was twelve years old he knew that he and that boy were unlike other boys in a crucial way, and he must at all cost learn a pathway to fitting in, and if he couldn't find a path, then the only method of excising his afflicted self was to remove it. Playing out the hand of solitaire, he smiled wryly at his memory of evaluating several modes of suicide, each method in some way too complicated or unacceptable. Thereafter the decision that he would go all out for baseball as an avenue to passing a few of the major tests of manhood, since he merely disliked the sport as opposed to football, the altar at which his father worshipped, and which his brother played with spectacularly brutal efficiency, and which he himself despised and loathed.

Scraping together just enough effort and ability to play a good-field, no-hit first base, he had also focused on his image as a student, concealing both his un-masculine hatred for mathematics and his equally unmasculine passion for poetry. He succeeded in establishing some turf separate from a peer group he wished with all his heart he could be a part of, but which he dared not come too close to, so that he could remain aloof from some of their more onerous and repulsive activities: pack-hunting for girls, drinking, fanatical obsession with spectator sports. His pugnaciously suspicious peers judged him as marginally okay — bottom line: not a fag.

He had Mitchell Howe to thank for that. For staking out a claim on such an extreme of behavior that compared to Mitchell Howe, he *wasn't* a fag.

Fey little Mitchell, with his soft dark hair and sensitive eyes, his wispy high voice and slender hips, pulling attention like a lightning rod, the prototype limp-wristed fairy. A top student, Mitchell Howe didn't even have the brains or wit to call himself Mitch.

Then that day when Bradley went into the cloakroom after batting practice to get his jacket. Mitchell was alone, leaning up against the wall, arms crossed over a collarless shirt open at the throat, one ankle crossed over the other in an attitude of waiting. Waiting, clearly, for him, Bradley saw in leaping panic as Mitchell's thin face lit up in eagerness and he left his post at the wall to saunter over and stand before Bradley. "What do you want," Bradley demanded as if the room were crowded with witnesses to the ax blows of heartbeat in his throat.

The pain and desolation in Mitchell's face increased Bradley's panic ten-fold. Mitchell raised a hand to conceal that pain and brushed the hair out of his eyes, saying to Bradley in his wispy voice, "I just...thought we might... maybe take in a movie —"

"You're nuts! NUTS!" And he fled.

That night, with desperate intent, he took a razor blade from the medicine cabinet. But again the prospect of his parents finding his bleeding corpse defeated him. So instead, for months afterward, to his brother's astonishment and his father's delight, he ran with the male pack and chased girls and got vomit-drunk twice, and made more jokes than anyone about fruits and queers and faggots. And was sick with misery and shame each time Mitchell Howe was sneered at and spat upon, and, twice, roughed up. Until Mitchell dropped out of school and left home, the mocking rumors had it, to go to San Francisco and be with the rest of the queers.

Bradley swept his cards into a chaotic pile. He knew his grief over Mitchell Howe was part of the anger that fueled his activist work in the community, but the knowledge never silenced the guilt; it served only to feed his hope for reparation, that Mitchell might look him up — especially now that he had acquired some renown in publishing, even if that renown was not in gay publishing. He had gone so far as to ask about him in San Francisco, Los Angeles, New York. Maybe Mitchell Howe was still alive and living happily elsewhere. Maybe he'd managed to be okay on the streets of San Francisco back in 1965. *Back,* Bradley thought balefully, *when I was fifteen years old and a lily-livered cowardly shit.*

My Eyes Adored You

"So how's the teaching business?" Warren asked Pat.

"I didn't know you taught," Angela exclaimed, pausing in her setting of the table.

You didn't ask, Pat thought.

"But then I didn't ask," Angela said. "What do you teach?"

"Geography," Pat replied with a chuckle she knew Angela would not understand. She answered Warren, "Let me put it this way — I can retire in another year, I'm counting the hours. The state's cut education so much it's a shambles."

"It's shameful," Angela said, looking at her with sympathetic expression. "Geography seems the perfect subject for you. It's so... definite."

"Exactly why I like it. It wasn't my first choice," Pat admitted. What was it about this weekend that was dredging up all this stuff she didn't want to remember? She beat down memory of another career she had pursued, consoled by the thought that if teaching was not her optimum career choice, geography, unlike other subjects, had proved invulnerable to male — or religious — revisionism.

"What did you want to be?" Warren asked, gracefully tossing salad between two forks.

"A journalist." She pulled the brim of an imaginary

fedora down over her eyes. "Pat Decker, foreign correspondent," she joked.

What she had actually wanted to do, at first, was simply go to college. Journalism was the career she had seized on because, even though she knew nothing about reporting beyond the romantic image of skulking about an exotic land in a trench coat, it seemed possible, and better than the drudgery of teaching, nursing, or typing. Then Mother had said, Fine, but learn to type, you'll need it for your journalism. And Father had said, We'll see, but learn to type. And she knew to the dismal depths of her that her parents were humoring her ambition, and any serious college money would be for Matthew, her prince of a brother.

Then came Matthew's sports-related injuries — the knee that needed reconstruction, the hip dislocation — and away went the money for his college, too. Not that he cared, college by his definition being for snobby rich kids and sissies. Said Matthew, her prince of a brother, Who do you think you are with all your airs, Fatsy-Patsy? He'd mocked everything about her back in those days, especially when she began to layer herself with girth as if it were armor.

She did go to college. Back when the California University system was still America's glory, and affordable. She'd ended up putting herself through, no one had helped, not even Jerry who'd promised . . . But God, that was a whole other story she didn't want to remember . . . Irony was, she did wind up, after all, with a teaching credential, and years later with the "drudgery" of being a teacher.

And she did learn to type, and if she hadn't used her typing from that day to this, she'd learned it for the best of reasons: Margaret McMinnville. To be in the same high school classroom with blue-eyed Margaret of the honey-colored hair and the lovely Scots burr and the fully ripened bosom at age fifteen and the wonderfully unfettered way with that willowy body...

After the trauma caused by Sister Jane Theresa's report to her parents, Pat had learned well. And so, with yearning as powerful as springtime for the seductive Margaret McMinnville, she sent a poetic note of flattery and tentative reaching out, composed oh so very carefully...

But not carefully enough. Margaret McMinnville's reaction had been to turn into Margaret McClam.

Then Matthew, her prick of a brother, found a trove of Margaret McMinnville treasures she'd collected...A bobby pin, a doodle on a scrap of paper, a sketch Pat had done of her, a note Margaret had sent her on a matter of purely school business, and worst of all, a poem Pat had composed. Still, none of it all that significant or incriminating, but her prick of a brother had dumped out her tin box of treasures on her bed and said, "Watch what you're doing, Sis." Any outrage at his invasion of her innermost being was drowned by his next words: "You'll be in the same manure as Miss Willows."

Miss Willows. Dismissed by the school. Pat's classmates had been endlessly hypothesizing with thrilled voices and faces over the rumored "unnatural practices" unimaginable to all of them.

Clearly, the blackest of disgraces had befallen Miss Willows and Alicia Powell, her star student, whom Miss Willows had been privately tutoring. Pat had been terrified that Matthew would tell Mother about her treasures. He didn't. Not then.

And now the news . . .

"*. . . on the hour, brought to you by your independent insurance agent. At the top of the news . . .*"

From the kitchen, the ceasing of conversation told Bradley that Warren, Pat and Angela were listening, too.

A chorus of boos and catcalls greeted the top story: the Clarence Thomas nomination to the Supreme Court would be reported out of the Judiciary Committee with a seven-to-seven tie vote, according to informed sources, and a close confirmation vote was expected in the Senate. President Bush had ordered major cuts in nuclear arms; also, the President was threatening to veto a bill extending unemployment benefits. Neo-Nazis had struck again in Germany.

"*Now for state and local news . . .*"

Devastating fires in Yosemite had been brought under control. The trial of Korean grocer Soon Ja Da was to begin Monday in Los Angeles for the shooting death of black teenager Latasha Harris . . .

"*Senator John Seymour has announced his opposition to AB 101, the gay rights bill awaiting a decision by the governor —*"

"The *stupid —*" Angela's voice.

"Hush up, honey." Warren's voice.

"*— statement released by Seymour contends the bill would invite litigation and stifle job and business growth. Gay rights activists and the bill's sponsor, Assemblyman Terry Friedman, immediately accused Seymour of pandering to his party's right wing. Calls relating to the bill continue to pour into Sacramento.*

"*Weather for San Bernardino and the mountain resorts will remain cool . . .*"

"The mealy-mouthed, slimy bastard," Pat hissed.

"What can you expect from a politician who looks like Pee-wee Herman," Warren said.

"... *concludes the eight o'clock news on San Bernardino's golden oldies station. Now, some vintage Peter, Paul and Mary...*"

Puff the Magic Dragon

Riding back to the cabin in Averill's BMW, thinking anxiously of Donnelly still awaiting the announcement of the governor's decision, Querida turned down the volume on the radio. Then adjusted it upward as Averill tapped out the lilting rhythm of the Peter, Paul and Mary tune on the steering wheel. "Love that song," she said.

"Me too," Querida said. "I was born the year it was popular."

" 'Sixty-three — right? I was six."

Querida searched for a means to capitalize on this new and agreeable vein of conversation. "Donnelly says she met you at a tournament."

Averill's chuckle was soft, amused. "Can you imagine Donnelly walking around a golf course following a tournament?"

"I can't. I sure wondered."

Even after they were lovers, Averill thought in renewal of an old hurt, Donnelly would rarely follow her on a round, and only after Averill underwent the humiliation of asking her. "I met her during a tournament at Rancho Park, but at a sponsor party. Some real estate bigwig she worked for bugged out at the last minute and she had to fill in. We were at the same table. She was nice as could be but you could tell she was mad as Carson City at having to be there."

How taken she had been by the smart, bold confidence of Donnelly's attire that night — a white tuxedo-style jacket over an open-throated, ruffled white shirt tucked into black pants, with a white bow-tie worn directly on the throat like a necklace. Her looks were interesting — not pretty, not handsome, but strongly pleasing.

By then, if she'd had to concede she was solely attracted to women, she felt fully in control of that attraction. And if her celebrity isolated her, it also presented a range of alluring possibility. Not, of course, fans. Lesbian spectators avidly followed the LPGA tour just as they gravitated to the professional tennis tour, the Dinah Shore being proof extraordinaire, but as romantic liaisons, they were out of the question — too dangerous.

Ditto the tour players. Cops, she had learned, often formed relationships with their own kind because only they understood the realities of police work. Golfers could easily adopt the same rationale. A relationship with a sister player would be a paradise of possibility and communion ... The tour women were athletic, gorgeous, admirable, so terrific that they didn't bear thinking about. Sure there were lesbian cliques on the tour — raunchy-mouthed Mattie Schroeder traveled with a whole coterie of adoring lesbian groupies — but she herself kept religiously separate from all that, and many women pros lived exactly the way she did, mostly isolated and in no visible relationship. The sport required too much work, travel and dedication, took so much money for minimal subsistence on the road from one tour city to another that some of the players, younger ones and those who gleaned only marginal earnings from their play, bunked together and lived as if they were members of a monastic sect. Maintaining a serious relationship was difficult until you were well established, and then success provided its own set of problems. Few players would ever choose to emulate Laura Baugh, who managed to periodically leave the tour to add to her brood of children then come back to shoot money-winning, if not tournament-winning, golf.

Averill Calder Harmon was Miss Congeniality to all her tour competitors, and she had deliberately staked out and cultivated a reputation for aversion to tour gossip, she had erected a veneer of obliviousness to the slightest hint of sexual overture. Despite constant temptation she had never given any of her peers the slightest suggestion of sexual interest, nor would she. To become involved with anyone on the tour would bring a drumbeat of gossip, would get out to Juneau knew where, would cause rumors in the press, maybe even get back to her parents.

Given all these problems and exclusions, opportunities for liaisons were still legion. A smorgasbord of sponsors, manufacturers' representatives and tour organizers pursued her — which was how she had first met Angela in Palm Springs, when Angela had shooed away that gay press reporter who had come on with all those insinuating questions. A very attractive and far more discreet young reporter in Portland had followed her from the Safeco tournament to San Diego before Averill's departure for Japan sufficiently discouraged her. And in Japan Averill had indulged in another "Puerto Rico" as she now referred to the ultra-safe liaisons in another country where she sometimes was able to take an additional week to further enjoy her bed partner's charms, leaving afterward with lingering memories but without complication or regret, just as she romanced and then abandoned the golf courses she played.

Utmost caution, that was the key, because if all public figures were victimized somewhat by celebrity, her own particular profession imposed the most stringent of codes. Entertainment stars like Jodie Foster or Whitney Houston could shrug off rumors of lesbianism, but scandal about Averill Calder Harmon would bring damage to her and collateral harm to the tour, which some in the press had already suggested was a secret nest of lesbians. Like the scandal of Billie Jean King's affair with Marilyn Barnett, exposure would fatally impact a money-making ability won dearly over the years. Gay rights radicals could not understand that tournaments did not appear out of thin air — sponsors financed them, sponsors with ultra-conservative business connections. Sponsors picked up the tab for everything from hotels and cars and clothing to clubs and bags and balls. To avoid controversy — and who could blame them for not wanting controversy? — they would leave in droves, and leave not only her but the tour.

If adulation over her presence on the tour had once thrilled her — and it still did, sometimes — she had become somewhat cynical, she had learned that people always wanted something from her, if no more than the status of being with her. She had grown accustomed to respect and deference, even timorousness from the people she came into contact with, but she was always, always on guard . . .

At the fund-raiser dinner that night Donnelly's lack of . . . well, respect, was intriguing. As was her directness. Eye-on-the-prize directness was visible all the time in the faces of pros like King, Carner, Mochrie, Alcott, Sheehan — all the great ones had it in full measure, and people in the religious life sometimes had it too, that unwavering focus and inner certainty. Donnelly had that look, but her openness and self-assurance had nothing to do with sport or religion; it was innate. So much so that her casual reference to herself in conversation as a lesbian seemed perfectly natural. Freed by an instinctive trust of Donnelly, Averill relaxed with her, went after her.

She'd had to. Had she not imbibed a few drinks at dinner, enough to give her boldness to ask Donnelly for an exchange of phone numbers, Donnelly would have gone on her way, despite Averill's overt interest. Averill had never thought it possible to be so immediately or so strongly attracted to someone. Nor had she thought it would ever be necessary to pursue someone...

I Can See Clearly Now

The creak of footsteps sounded over his head. Donnelly. She'd come to the top of the staircase to hear the radio broadcast, was retreating back to her room.

"Hey up there!" he roared. "Get your worthless tail down here!"

"Piss off, I'm taking a shower!" she screamed back. "I took orders from you long enough!"

"*What* orders?" he yelled.

"Yeah, right," Pat called amid Warren and Angela's laughter from the kitchen.

Bradley's resentment of Pat butting in was ameliorated by the welcome sizzle of food being dropped into hot oil. Picking up one of the manuscripts he'd brought out from his room, he settled back, watching the kitten wash its paws over by the window, and listening to the sounds of Donnelly moving around above him and then water running from her shower.

"I know Bradley was married to Donnelly," Bradley heard Angela say from the kitchen. "I hear you were once married too."

"For five minutes," Pat answered in the dismissing tone Bradley knew well.

But Warren said, "Did the poor fellow survive?"

"Barely."

Bradley grinned at the silence in the kitchen as the snarl in Pat's response squelched even Warren. That mysterious marriage of hers had always been off-limits. Donnelly knew about it, of course, and was as closed-mouthed as Pat. No surprise — to ask Donnelly for confidentiality was to lock your secrets in Fort Knox.

What the hell, the fact that he'd been married was well known, but it wasn't anything he ever discussed pro or con with even the closest of friends, and there had been one hell of a lot of pro about being married to Donnelly. He didn't care to imagine the continuing nightmare of the dating scene had she not given him the sanctuary of marriage. It had been bad enough with the few women he'd dated...

Right from the start, right from their first meeting, Donnelly had made him exuberant with hope that maybe he could really, actually do this thing.

His feelings of tenderness for women like Sarah... whose honest feeling and despairing love still haunted his memory... had never included physical response. Somehow he was drawn to Donnelly's boyish femininity, and his emotion toward her seemed to emerge from a rarer wellspring. Love, he had told himself, so this is what love is.

She was more entertaining than any woman he'd ever

known. Taking him to see movies like *Catch-22* and *A Clockwork Orange* and then arguing with him passionately about them, and even managing to drag him to baseball games where he found an amiable appreciation for the game now that it was no longer, for him, bound up in a heterosexual rite of passage. Any activity became fun with her. She loved to argue, and they had zestful debates over everything from feminism to Vietnam politics, debates no less fiery when they were on the same side of an issue. She brought her enthusiasm to his interests as well, concerts and the one athleticism he loved, hiking in the mountains and deserts of Southern California.

Best of all, for the first time in his life he belonged somewhere conventional. With Donnelly at his side he was fully approved of by everyone, everywhere. Life was fun. He liked Donnelly. Loved her.

Loved her enough that he could not risk a hint at the erotic masculine imagery that infiltrated his thoughts and appropriated his dreams. Still, if he dared not expose that particular aberrant self, he could reveal the feelings and secrets and pain and insecurity of his feminine side to this woman who derided his family's opinion that sensitivity or bookishness detracted from masculinity. And that put him ninety percent further than he'd ever been with another living soul.

While he worried about sex with her, she made his playing the role of perfect gentleman so easy that he willingly performed the simple physical moves any woman would initially expect; and holding her, kissing her, had produced pleasant enough feelings to encourage, even exhilarate him. Maybe he could do this thing, face the specter in the wings that taunted him to perform the act that really counted.

Three months into their relationship, although she had

neither done nor said anything to press him, he had to know.

On a hot Sunday morning — June of 1971, it was — he sat in the kitchen of her tiny Harper Avenue apartment drinking coffee while she swabbed the floor and shouted exhortations at the radio broadcast of the Dodgers game. His confidence recklessly high, he said, "Let's go somewhere, spend the night."

"Okay," she said without looking up from her mopping. "How about the beach?"

"Okay," he said, thinking this sounded more like a casual social transaction than a plan for an act of ultimate intimacy. But then she'd been at this dating business for a full ten years longer than he . . .

Whistling "Me and Bobby McGee" as the Dodgers defeated the Phillies, she packed a picnic basket. Tucked it into the trunk of her VW bug, and nonchalantly tossed an overnight bag in after it.

They spent the afternoon playing in the surf at Venice beach and devouring the contents of the picnic basket; that evening they pulled on jeans and warm sweatshirts and moved further up the beach where he roasted hot-dogs over a wind-blown campfire. She seemed in no hurry to leave the ocean, and certainly neither was he — his confidence had utterly evaporated. And so they sat watching the phosphorescent waves late into the chilly night on Santa Monica beach. Finally, Donnelly took him by the hand. Drove to Malibu and checked them into a cheap ocean-side motel.

Mumbling that he needed to wash off all the ocean salt, he took refuge in the bathroom, brushing his teeth and nervously scraping at his stubble with her blunt razor. When he emerged, Donnelly, stripped down to an ancient Beach Boys T-shirt, moved brusquely by him into the bathroom.

Clammy with panic, he got into bed and pulled up the covers, listening in dread for the end of the sound of the shower. When the bathroom door opened, the sight of her wrapped in a towel, her damp hair plastered darkly to her forehead, terrified him. This was impossible. He was a fool, he'd been a fool from the very start to think this would ever work, that he could actually do this.

She sat down on the bed. "You look awfully cute under those covers, champ," she said, and pretend-punched him in the chin.

He laughed. She laughed. His laughter hit a higher pitch. So did hers. His laughter became hysteria. So did hers.

Her face wet from laughter, she tumbled into the bed with him and suddenly she was lovely, her skin smooth and fine, her arms around him sweet and nice, her body warm and soft and interesting against his. Different. She was different. And nice, he told himself. She was Donnelly, above all else a beloved friend. He would try his best, it was not important what he felt, only that he please her.

To his delight he not only grew erect enough to penetrate, but friction allowed him to stay that way for much longer than he ever could during his masturbation fantasies of a male partner. Afterward Donnelly, whose composure was in marked contrast to his euphoria, of course misunderstood the reason for his joy, but that was okay, perfectly okay . . .

"Marry me," he said.

"Okay," she said. "Sure."

Again he thought they could have been conducting a casual social transaction.

A week later, in mutual agreement about no family involvement, they drove to Las Vegas, sent back telegrams of announcement, then went on to Utah for a few days' honeymoon.

After that first satisfactory night, Donnelly turned out to be affectionate, but passive and inhibited in bed. To his great relief. Much as he adored her, he could never have performed oral sex had she asked. And the thought of her doing that to him was equally repugnant.

Most nights he only returned her affection, and Donnelly seemed guiltily grateful for that, because, he suspected, he had so clearly demonstrated his sexual prowess.

It was all so utterly fraudulent — she placed blame for their tepid sexuality solely on herself, and he was relieved to have any reason at all not to perform.

Bizarre indeed that the couple who moved into the house next door would unwittingly help to solve the problem — the night he and Donnelly found themselves alone in the hot tub of these neighbors whom Donnelly had befriended. After the Martinsons took themselves off to bed, he and Donnelly horsed around in the swirling hot water, Donnelly making up for the strength inequality between them with agility. He had pinned her arms and was trying to dunk her when she wriggled a hand free and grabbed his cock. She ended up cheerfully jacking him off, and afterward he took her in his arms and accomplished the reciprocal act. From this the satisfactory sexual pattern of their marriage emerged: intermittently, in the nights afterward, they contented each other with the same practice . . .

If You Could
Read My Mind

"Fried chicken, oh Boise, my favorite," whooped Averill, shouldering her way through the cabin door, arms wrapped loosely around a paper bag filled with clinking bottles of wine.

Carrying another similarly clinking bag, Querida followed her into the bright warmth of the cabin shaking her head. Pheasant under glass would seem a more likely preference, given that Averill had bought eight bottles of champagne and eight more of chardonnay, six hundred and fifty-eight dollars on her American Express gold card without so much as a blink, except from Querida and the checkout clerk. Did Averill actually think the seven of them could drink all that between now and early Monday morning, the latest any of them could possibly stay?

"Big D's upstairs showering," Bradley said, glancing up and then performing so open a double-take at the bags of wine that Querida grinned back at him. He sat on the floor near the fire, reading a manuscript, one leg crossed over another at such an angle that she could look up the hole in his jeans into his crotch, had she been interested in looking.

In the kitchen Pat took in the sacks and remarked coolly, "When does the rest of the party arrive?"

"Anything we don't drink I'll take with me," Averill said airily, removing four bottles from her sack and proceeding to pry the neck wrapping from a bottle of champagne. "Saves time buying it down in Buena Park."

Pulling a corkscrew and wine glasses from a cupboard, Pat conceded dourly, "If the news comes in on AB 101, we'll be drinking toasts or drowning our sorrows."

"Only those who drink," Warren said primly, waving off Pat's offer of a wine glass.

"You might start," Pat growled. "You and Bradley can't smoke grass in here."

"I never smoke indoors," Warren said. "Nobody owns the outdoors — yet."

Pat turned her back on him to ladle cooked pieces of chicken to drain onto paper towels.

Sympathetically, Querida watched him stare at Pat, his hands visibly clenched in the pockets of his loose cotton pants. She and Warren were both outsiders, racially and generationally. Although she felt less an outsider than she used to, she thought, accepting a glass of champagne from Averill with a smile of thanks. Not like a few years ago when it seemed that she lived on a craggy outcropping no one else would find tolerable. No female friends, and only two male friends — Mike and Luis, entertaining and convenient escorts willing to accompany her with minimal sexual complications: they asked, she refused, and they always took no for an answer. Most men of her heritage, including these two friends, found her professional success daunting, and she made this into an excuse to avoid the courting rituals that had always made her feel inadequate and impatient. Anglo males were a different piece of work. The new consultant at work was typical, his initial interest and stereotypical illusions quickly stripped away by her assertive behavior.

Her professional peer group — exclusively Anglo — had, however, been forthcoming with a friendliness that extended beyond mere acceptance. But at a certain point they erected barriers, and that point was always where real intimacy began. The ostracism was too pervasive to be her imagination; she was unwelcome in the substantive realm of their WASP lives.

Querida took a sip of her Taittinger's. Champagne

reminded her of Denise. Champagne always did, always would. Denise Waterman — so blonde, so chillingly elegant and sophisticated and ultra-WASP that even the most predatory men stepped carefully around her. Thus the overtures from her had been disconcerting, extending as they did beyond the usual mentoring one might expect from a woman two levels above her professionally, and fifteen years her senior.

In a spiny combination of approach and withdrawal, Denise by turns had reached out in smiling friendship and then turned a diffident, apparently uninterested face to her. Querida felt subtly pursued, and in some ways angered by the pursuit. Any contact with the dazzling, intimidating Denise was disturbing; it galvanized her into recognizing her own isolation and loneliness — an unwelcome distraction from the need to navigate her way through the tricky political eddies of Browning Consultants. She suspected an equal isolation and alienation in the other woman, and that this odd dance of theirs was a somewhat prickly bonding of two women separated by a gulf of race and life-experience, their currency-in-common a vague sense of being under siege.

Then she was assigned to assist Denise in analyzing Riverside and Rialto locations for a clothing consortium exploring expansion out of Texas. In the midst of the compilation of statistics to devise an economic model, Denise invited her to discuss the project's status over dinner.

On a balmy Los Angeles night, on a palm-lined street in the Palisades, in a luxurious condo decorator-furnished in tasteful grays and pinks, Querida's nervousness gradually dissipated as Denise continually refilled their glasses with excellent champagne. They talked business comfortably, animatedly through dinner, and then had brandy out on a deck screened in by palm fronds bowing gracefully in the breeze. As Querida, relaxed to the point of feeling embalmed, placed her brandy snifter on the deck railing, Denise said, looking into her own glass, "So you don't have a boyfriend."

Disappointed, deflated by the question, Querida simply shrugged.

Placing her own brandy glass on the railing, Denise said, "Myself, I don't care for the species." Looking intently into Querida's eyes, she took Querida's hands in hers.

Querida did not resist; she was far too surprised — and entranced — by the desire revealed in the depths of Denise's gray eyes, too admiring of her courage, no matter its probable alcoholic fuel. Opened by her own alcoholic courage, and by the embrace slowly gathering her in, she felt safe and cherished in the gentle arms of the woman holding her, and from that moment she did not care about anything except the moment.

In the bedroom, Denise continued to shed her cool sophisticated image as if it were another garment. Kissing Querida softly, slowly, deeply, murmuring pleasure as she unhurriedly undressed Querida and herself, whispering her delight as her hands explored and savored Querida's yielding body, groaning in joy as her body merged in velvet warmth with Querida's nakedness. Her mouth exquisitely swelling each breast into acute sensitivity, her hand sliding between Querida's thighs as if it naturally belonged there. Her tongue inflaming Querida's nipples and her fingers fondling and teasing in the creamy wet as Querida's breath came in quick gasps, and then answering Querida's want, escalating the want to such a pitch that the floodwash of ecstasy was unlike anything Querida had ever known from her own fingers.

Afterward Denise's slow deep kisses arousing her again, this time Denise's mouth descending her for undreamed of pleasures from Denise's tongue and Denise's fingers inside her, Querida gripping the sheets, gasping from the ever swifter strokes, her body arching higher and higher, waves of ecstasy pulsing through her. Throughout the night, Denise, enraptured by Querida's response, wanting only that, her lovemaking unceasing, Querida coming again and again, riding eager fingers and writhing from that tireless, ravishing tongue . . .

"Querida," Pat said, "you look like you're really into champagne."

"Delicious," Querida said, and, relinquishing memory at its sweetest, lifted her glass in a silent toast to Denise.

Tears of a Clown

Listening to the chatter from the kitchen, the aroma of noisily frying chicken filling his nostrils, Bradley smiled. Warren should have been a lesbian, he so much preferred women to men. Maybe, it occurred to Bradley, Warren's rapport with women had much to do with being raised by a generously loving mother after the desertion of his white father. Unlike Warren's present Afro-American stepfather and three younger half-brothers, all of whom despised their in-your-face queer relation, Warren's mother still doted on him, still lavished him with affection, if not approval.

A woman's presence in his own life, Bradley reflected, had been a central event as well. The period of his marriage to Donnelly arguably contained the most telling events of his life so far.

Six months married and he knew that not even a therapist would understand the pressure that was building in him. In those days a therapist would have had him committed. Worst of all, being committed seemed like a good thing — he had to be some sort of monster to feel a clawing inside so intense it could burst through his gut. For the sake of everything he held dear — and Donnelly was most dear — he had to run the risk and find men like himself and release the pressure chamber his body had become. He had to do something because he was taking out his inchoate fevers on Donnelly, snarling at her over minor disagreements. She gave as good as she got, but he knew she blamed deficiencies in herself for his tirades, which made him withdraw in depression and self-contempt and guilt until the cycle began again. If he was picked up and arrested, he reasoned, that would be one solution to the problem: everyone would know, it would be taken out of his hands and Donnelly would be free of him and free to hate him; that in itself would release all the pressure.

And so he had sidled into the porno theater on Virgil Avenue to sit and watch men have sex on the screen, his semen soaking the handkerchief he held as the celluloid figures writhed in an orgiastic, abandoned freedom he had never known. His release came not from the sex acts he witnessed but from the sight of an emancipation he would never know, not if he valued his marriage, his career, his reputation...

The man, a bulky stooped shadow, sat down beside him, reached into Bradley's lap. Bradley got up and moved.

That time. The next time he permitted the urgent hot hand to clasp him, smothering his moan of ecstasy by clenching his jaw shut with brutal force. He did not touch his partner. Then or ever.

Inventing excuses to get into such theaters to release the demons he felt building up inside him became the rationale to save his sanity and his relationship with

Donnelly. She did not question his absences, undoubtedly suspecting that whatever he did during those times was responsible for his less frequent outbursts.

He went exclusively to porno theaters because the men he met were as secretive and desperate and self-hating and furtive as he. And shouldn't they be? He could not bear to see the men who approached him or whom he approached, to see himself mirrored in the pupils of eyes of men as frightened, as aberrant as himself. And so he operated in the darkness of movie theaters instead of in the bars.

Then.

That first year with Donnelly, his illusions about marriage disintegrated. There was no single moment of blinding revelation. Only the unfolding fact of what his life simply, essentially was: a stage performance. The place where he undeniably belonged was with the freaks in that outer circle of society from which conventional people averted their gaze. Conventional people did accept him; they were seldom as ill-at-ease around him as he was around them. But never was he unaware of his alien shape, never less than alert to the ambiguity of any remark addressed toward him, any enigmatic glance. If his masculine looks enabled him to pass, if he had become more adept at disguise since the days of Mitchell Howe, he was never without doubt that the truth of himself was beyond concealment. He was an alien with an antenna plainly visible to anyone who cared to look for it.

How else to explain such incidents as the one in the back yard with Donnelly's brother? Attractive as hell in those green plaid shorts that displayed his package, and brushing his boner up against Bradley while they cooked steaks together on the barbecue... What was he supposed to think? And Bill — seemingly oblivious Bill. The more flirtatious and physically aggressive he became, the more he'd layered it over with vicious homophobic bonhomie, every other word a sneering reference to faggots.

A year later Donnelly told Bill to go fuck himself "or get somebody to do it for you." Today somebody was doing it for him — Bill's long-suffering, sometime partner of sixteen years, who still patiently waited for Bill to return from his occasional forays into heterosexuality.

Bradley had known many other Bills since then, and no longer passed judgment. Looking back at his own marriage and the men he knew, gay or straight, it seemed that within most of them was imbedded at least a sliver of sexuality other than their primary orientation. How else to explain his own obscure but continuing attraction to Donnelly?

Bad, Bad Leroy Brown

"Jesus Mary and Saint Joseph!"

Hopping around the kitchen, shaking her hand from the sting of a grease splatter, Pat smothered the further curses she wanted to pour all over Averill. Her arrogant ass sashaying into the living room had distracted her from her cooking.

Querida seized her hand, held it under running cold water. "Catholic, I take it," she said, deadpan.

"Recovering." Pat took back her hand. "Thanks, it feels better." She took embarrassed refuge in activity, adjusting the flame under the frying pan.

Querida said, "Early as I can remember, I thought religion was a crock."

"Good for you. Wish I'd been that smart."

Me and the whole family, she thought. It had fucked her over and the family too, the whole lot of them trying to accommodate their lives to it, and what choice did they really have? The church had centuries of experience to figure out how to take over your entire existence, pounding the fear of God into you all day in school, everything from PTA on Monday to fish on Friday to Mass on Sunday, so much a part of you that to leave parish life was to abandon home and hearth and family. Good for strong souls like Querida who could walk away and never look back, but friends like ex-Mormons Janice and Rachel ached so much from loss of their church that they were like amputees suffering ghost pain for a missing limb.

At least her mother had managed to wriggle out from under total church control. Her mother, who spoke most disparagingly of two things: her husband's sexual appetite, and the church-mandated rhythm method of birth control. If just once I'd had the nerve, Pat thought, to break through that wall of non-communication to ask two things: the how of managing birth control back in those days, and about Monica Albert.

Her mother had to have learned birth control pointers from Monica Albert — how else had the Decker family been limited to three children? Monica, who would wander over with a twin tucked under each arm — wild-assed boys, a pair of little shits who Pat ignored even when she baby-sat them — to whisper gossip into her mother's thrilled ears, and her scandalized mother would gasp and laugh in a way that Pat never heard at any other time.

"You know what Monica told me *today?*" Pat's mother said to Pat's father as Pat stood concealed behind the dining room door. " 'I'll decide how many kids I want, I'm the one that's got to raise them. Father Gallagher and the whole bloody church can go hang!' "

"That strumpet's reserving her own hot little corner in hell," her father said, thick, emphatic cigar fumes reaching Pat. "And you'll be there with her if you don't stop listening to her rubbish." But her father was equally fascinated by the iconoclastic Alberts. If her mother admired and adored Monica Albert, envied her boldness and freedom, her father heaped ridicule on David Albert, gaunt and bearded, a marginally successful chiropractor decades ahead of his time with his holistic belief in low fat diets and exercise.

Whenever Monica, red-haired and dressed more and more like a bohemian as she grew older, would breeze in from next door, Pat would sneak into eavesdropping range. She and David had decided to live in an open marriage, Monica had told her flabbergasted mother one afternoon. And there had been other astonishing conversations, stuff Pat had had no understanding or concept of back in those days, like oral sex, which Pat had correctly assumed was a specialized form of kissing, but could not imagine beyond that. Like much of America in the mid-fifties, all she knew of sexuality — hers or anyone's — came from the pablum and gossamer of television and films, and pieties from the church, none of which matched the real life drama of the pinched-in lives she saw around her. Today's generation would never know the shocking impact of a book like *Peyton Place,* with its truths about sexual mores. If *The Well of Loneliness* seemed a relic of darker times, its existence had spanned decades of censure, right up until the seventies when it finally took its place on the shelf alongside other dusty *objets de scandale* as *Tobacco Road* and *The Tropic of Cancer* . . .

Staring at the dining room wall, lost in thought, Pat realized that she hadn't heard whatever it was Bradley had called out from the living room. Because she had solved a mystery, finally realized what was different about that paneled wall. Photo-portraits of her parents had always hung there, each identified by a ribbon-like decoration of ornate italicized print under the oval frame: *James Caspar Decker* and *Frances Methune Decker*. Her father, by his own admission, hadn't set foot in this place for years — so why had her mother removed those portraits?

The photos had been made just before the family had left St. Louis. Maybe, Pat theorized, they had symbolized her father's failure of imagination fully as much to her mother as they had to Pat. How else to account for living in, of all places in this Golden State, San Bernardino? Why dream of coming to California, and then choose a place so hot and dusty, so boring? And that had been in its best days, back before smog stained the skies and sometimes reached noxious tentacles all the way up here.

The one out-of-character thing her hollow-souled father had ever done was to buy this cabin which he'd picked up in a fire sale and then deeded over to his wife. By his lights, this one expansive gesture of his life had been a mistake. In Pat's view, this cabin had preserved peace in her parents' marriage and maybe sanity in her mother.

In later life her mother, Pat had discovered, had come up here into the trees and clean sweet air to read her romance novels and to feed the birds and squirrels until she was ready to come back down the mountain again and resume her life with James Caspar Decker. Her mother, her quiet, depressed, repressed mother, whom Pat was still trying to understand. Her mother, who had adored Monica Albert and hopelessly envied her boldness and freedom. It had taken years for Pat to see what had been in front of her nose: that her mother's descent into depression and silence had dated from Monica's death from breast cancer.

A heart attack had taken her mother, and a woman lawyer had stepped forward with a will that bequeathed this cabin to Pat, the terse legal language containing not a word of explanation as to why an estranged and disgraceful daughter had been preferred over a god-fearing husband and two conventional children...

Hey Jude

"Catholic, I assume," Bradley heard Querida say. *Catholic. Hannifan...*

A late Monday afternoon. He'd given Donnelly a work-related reason why he might — or might not — be delayed in arriving home.

After circling the block four times he'd managed not only to find a spot on Santa Monica Boulevard, but right in front of Motherlode.

He removed his suit coat and rolled up his shirt sleeves, then, partially concealed by a map, sat checking the street for auto and foot traffic. When the coast was clear, he got out and strolled in and up to the bar.

Releasing his breath in a long exhale, he made it a point not to look around until after he had ordered and received his Cutty Sark and water. When he finally glanced up he established immediate eye contact with a man of such ethereal beauty that again the breath was taken out of him. The slumberous dark eyes, the lips of poetic sensuality, the aesthetic face, the slender body Byronic in a flowing white shirt and black pants, belonged in a sculpture garden. He sat transfixed as the man picked up his cocktail and moved over to the empty stool beside Bradley, all the while holding Bradley's stare.

This is the luckiest day of my life.

The man said in a musical tenor voice, "Is it really?"

Bradley was not aware that he had spoken his thought. Smitten with embarrassment, and lust, he simply continued to gaze at the dazzling stranger.

With a gentle smile, the man took Bradley's hand in a warm, firm handshake. "It's my lucky day, too. The name's Jim."

"Bradley." He had never before given his real name, not even his first name.

Moments later they agreed to meet at the Tropicana Motel down the street, and that Bradley would stop and pick up some Cutty Sark.

By the time he entered the room he was grateful to have the paper sack to hold over his crotch. Jim, who lounged on the bed, turned toward him; and he too was hard. Bradley put the liquor on the dresser and moved quickly to the bed.

Always before it had been over in a few furtive, if ecstatic, minutes. But after the urgency of the first climax Jim became the slowest and tenderest of lovers, and Bradley responded in fountains of grateful rapture, his libido unleashed by the welcoming embrace of the man whose slender body lay so softly, delicately in his arms.

Hours later, thankful that his open-ended excuse to Donnelly covered so long an absence, he poured more scotch into the motel's plastic tumblers, and sat in the chair beside the bed. Both men had pulled on their pants; and it was time, Bradley ruefully knew, not to say adieu, but finis. He needed to take some small, real element of this beautiful, loving man away with him.

He said, "So what do you do for a living that you can come to a bar on a Monday afternoon?"

Seated on the side of the bed sipping his scotch, Jim reached for his snowy white shirt. "You first."

The mistrust game. But this man had given him the greatest physical pleasure he had ever known. This man had given him a measure of peace. He would give this man the gift of telling him the truth. "I'm a teacher. I get off early."

"I'm a priest. I do too."

"Seriously. I *am* a teacher."

"And I am very seriously a priest. Father James Hannifan. St. Basil's."

As he had in the bar, Bradley stared helplessly at him. This man, who had been in ecstasy with Bradley's penis inside him only a few minutes ago, a priest?

Hannifan pulled his shirt on over his hairless chest. "When you work in a candy store it's not unreasonable to suppose you might sample some of the candy." His face was tranquil. "A likelihood well understood by the establishment that employs me. They require that I be careful, quiet, judicious about where I select my candy and how I consume it." He added quietly, "They partake of the candy as well."

Bradley felt pummeled by his shock. "They do? All of them?"

The dark eyes glinted with humor. "Not all of them."

"A miracle." To cover his amazement, Bradley playfully reached over and clinked his tumbler of scotch against Hannifan's. "A beautiful angel from heaven. Who fucks and drinks."

Hannifan shrugged. "We all have to find our way through this life."

Intrigued by his *sang froid*, wondering if this was all a fanciful invention, Bradley asked, "Is this for real? Do the nuns do this, too? Are they actually raving dykes?"

"Not raving. But a good many of them are indeed dykes. Brides of an androgynous Christ. They'd sooner die than admit it." Hannifan mockingly pursed his lips. "The Sisters kneel and pray and fast and sing and revere one another, and struggle against 'particular friendships.'"

Bradley had been searching through his meager knowledge of Catholicism. "There's all this business about them being allowed in the priesthood," he ventured. "Why aren't they?"

Buttoning his shirt cuffs, Hannifan simply smiled.

"Well why not?" Bradley said with good-natured insistence. "Like you say, they're better at celibacy. They're moving into more and more all-male careers, like police work."

Hannifan answered seriously, "A big Irish cop comes to me for confession every week. Weeps about how much better it was when cops like him could break a few heads. Tell me, Bradley, you think people respect cops today like they did a few years ago?"

"Respect cops? A few years ago? Come on, Jim! In those days they broke heads like ours every chance they got, and right out in public. Anyway, all the guns and drugs — these are different times."

"No they're not," Hannifan said.

The expanded volume and decisiveness in his tenor voice seemed to preempt the topic. This was the self-assurance and priestly authority that would persuade and convince parishioners. For the first time Bradley believed he might, indeed, be a priest, and the knowledge was like the ground shifting under his feet.

As if sensing that he had brought the conversation to the edge of a realm that did not fully belong in this room, Hannifan raised his glass of scotch in a self-deprecating gesture and smiled.

But Bradley had only started on this vein of conversation. "Priests drinking, that's one thing." He gestured at the rumpled, damp bedclothes. "Talk all you want about a candy store, but this has to be the most sinful of mortal sins."

"Actually not, but Rome has no choice but to forbid it," Hannifan said easily. "The church's authority rests on its dictation of sexual behavior. Why else would people pay any attention? I mean, out of the Ten Commandments, civil or criminal law today takes care of most of them, and you don't need a church to simply worship a deity. Rome claims exclusive rights on ordering you to honor your parents, keep holy the Sabbath day, and observe certain sexual practices. It asks for a little protection money for the salvation of your soul — but not so much that you'd ever identify it as such. The truth is, most males need to be tied down to wives and kids and responsibility because without it we'd fight or fuck everything that walked."

Astonished to speechlessness by what he was hearing, and whom he was hearing it from, Bradley finally uttered, "But the guardians of our morality don't have to follow the same rules."

"They never have." Hannifan bent over to tie his shoelaces. "Faith, spirituality — side issues. Giving up all possibility for a permanent relationship is the price exacted for membership in the brotherhood. And you need to be judicious. You can't, for God's sake, touch boys or girls." Hannifan looked up and his dark eyes glinted with anger. "The ones who do that are draculas. Concealing themselves in the priesthood to commit an abuse of power that's an atrocity..."

Bradley could not sort through his reactions to discern what he thought abut the disclosures coming from this man. He knew he should feel relief or anger about all the Christian-based guilt and self-hatred he'd directed at himself; yet somehow he couldn't. He had heard anti-Catholic bigotry before and had been generally offended by it; but somehow nothing had ever seemed so profoundly anti-Catholic as what he was hearing from this ordained Catholic priest.

"So everything you preach is a crock. And you feel okay about picking and choosing what you believe."

Hannifan spread his fine, pale hands. "Bradley, everybody in this world chooses. Look, the church is no better or worse than any other political body or business enterprise. It provides an answer to a need, and works hard to persuade you that you need their answer. In return for certain dues, it supplies belief. And for some people the need to believe is quite passionate."

"Well," Bradley said as Hannifan unzipped his pants to tuck in his shirt, "one thing I know I believe in is passion."

"We worship at the same altar," Hannifan said, smiling. Pants still unzipped, he got up and moved over to Bradley.

An hour later, once more fully clothed, Hannifan said, "Same place, next Monday?"

"Yes," Bradley said.

He would find an excuse. A weekly staff meeting.

For months afterward he attended that same weekly staff meeting.

Once Bradley asked Hannifan why he had become a priest. "To wear the vestments," was the reply.

"I'd really like to know," Bradley said.

"That's the reason," Hannifan said.

The next Sunday morning, after Donnelly had gone off to brunch with some friends, Bradley went to the noon Mass at St. Basil's. Arriving moments before the Mass began, he sat in the rear of the elegant Wilshire Boulevard edifice which had opened a few years earlier amid much criticism of its multi-million dollar cost. The invasive smell of incense, the sonorous organ music, the soaring choir voices, the picture-of-piety altar boys performing their acolyte roles like a well-drilled Broadway dance troupe — all of it interwove with skillful seductive force, and dominating it all was Hannifan, poster saint in his purple-gold vestments and his strong rich tenor voice as he performed the ancient choreography of the Mass with vivid theatricality. Women parishioners on either side of Bradley gazed limpidly at the splendid Mass celebrant, a celestial figure more closed off from sexual possibility than they would ever dream. Marveling at the rapt adoration pouring over Hannifan, Bradley understood why Hannifan had become, and loved being — and would forever remain — a priest.

A few months later their relationship amicably ended. For Bradley, Hannifan was a pleasurable present, but had come to symbolize an empty future, even though Bradley could not at that moment see any other future he might hope to have. At their final liaison, both of them having admitted to having moved on to new sexual interests, Bradley allowed some of his own spiritual intimations to emerge.

"I could join a religion," Bradley told him, "if I could find one that didn't make me barf. The best thing you ever did for me was to show why religion is filled with so much hatred of . . . people like me."

"They know what's at stake. Our priestly reward for keeping the faith is they take care of us and cover our ass."

And they had. Bradley maintained a tie with Hannifan for years afterward, even from the Bay Area, and in August of 1983, when he called the rectory after not hearing from Hannifan for an unusual length of time, he was informed that Father Hannifan had been moved to "a convalescent home at the Salton Sea to recuperate from a severe bout of pneumonia."

Bradley had driven down the next day. Had sped through the Mojave and the beige dust clouds of a sirocco, knowing what he would find when he found Jim Hannifan.

Hannifan was sitting in a flimsy patio chair on a barren patch of sand outside a structure that looked like a motel cabin and probably had been before the church took it over. He was gazing peacefully off into the sand-swept desert landscape, his shapeless white shirt and pants flapping in the wind, his body wraith-like, a beard and sunburn partially covering his extensive Kaposi's Sarcoma lesions, looking, Bradley thought, like Christ must have looked after his forty days in the desert.

Seeing Bradley striding across the sand toward him, Hannifan struggled to his feet and embraced him with the tenderness that brought Bradley excruciating memory of their first time together in the Tropicana Motel.

"This is the luckiest day of my life," Hannifan said, his

arms around Bradley. Weeping in Hannifan's arms, Bradley held him, and continued to hold him.

Bradley sat with him for half an hour, awkwardly offering him news and gossip. Then Hannifan admitted he was tired and needed to lie down. "Thank you for coming, my love," Hannifan told him gently. "It's okay, I have no regrets, I'll be glad when it's over. Please don't think you have to visit again."

On February 28, 1984, Father James Richard Hannifan, age 37, died, according to the *Los Angeles Times* obituary, of respiratory failure.

The Air That I Breathe

Catholic she wasn't, Querida thought wryly, but with fags and dykes on the bottom rung of the pecking order, all it took to earn universal censure and *desprecio* was living in America.

Still, the morning after Denise — was she shocked? She hadn't exactly been living in a cave, gay-rights rhetoric was being trumpeted from the rooftops these days, but okay, she felt more than a little surprised. And more than a little stupid. She'd had the independence of mind to question something as basic as religion, yet never had it occurred to her to question something even more basic, her assumption that she was heterosexual — if somewhat deficient in the last two syllables of the word. Masturbation had always seemed to take care of what she wryly called, borrowing the term from the computer industry, "power surges."

Religious morality? The meek would never inherit the earth, and except for her grandfather, she had her *temerosa* family to prove it.

Her family. She could not be with any of them even briefly without choking back rage over their acquiescence to life as they found it. Only nephew Lawrence and niece Theresa, whose rebelliousness could neither be scolded nor beaten out of them, gave her hope. If it took such impudence, so be it. In the house where she grew up, if the renovations and up-to-the-minute appliances she had bought for her mother were, to her father, a reflection of his inadequacy instead of a source of pride in his daughter's success, so be it. Pedro Quemada could not give his child-worn, work-worn wife the ease and comfort she deserved in her later years, and Querida owed her no less. Her mother had conferred on her a name that meant "beloved," had encouraged her talent and ambition, and to this day warmly embraced her strange bird of a daughter and called her, with unfailing tenderness, *"mi Querida."*

She did not consider herself intellectual, or even marginally clever except in her own field, but she felt herself a stranger to her family due to — irony of ironies — education and money. If her family seemed resentful of the money that made cities all over the country accessible to her by plane, if they viewed her success with envy, all any of them had to do was voice a wish or desire and she would make it a reality — from the three-hundred dollar Raider jacket for Lawrence to the "pump" Nike shoes for Mario to the ruby graduation ring for Alicia. Still, some exotic component in her had spun her off into orbit away from their child-and-family-centered, authentic lives. To them, it was not much wonder she did not have a man — it was all part and parcel of her unnatural life...

She felt their surreptitious, judgmental inspection of her clothes, her accessories, her Sassoon-styled hair. She had tried to tone down her real self around them, but the family, comfortably intimate with one another, was elaborately courteous and formal with her. She felt the loss of them keenly, especially the gulf between herself and her two favorites among her brothers and sisters, sensitive Paulo and high-spirited Alicia. At holidays, family gatherings, she witnessed but seldom participated in the laughter, the fun, the family's sharing of parallel experiences with friends and neighbors, and she mourned what she had lost. Her family was a large part of her, yet it was as if she were on a train gone into new countryside, with a return track beside her, but no way for her to get off the train she rode.

That morning after Denise, she knew profoundly, if murkily, that she had discovered a country of her own. Denise had been an absolutely real and true unlocking of herself. She now had something to identify herself by, a place where she belonged, no matter how uncomfortable the place might be. Yet, gaining this knowledge of herself was overwhelming and schizophrenic. Whole new reasons had been added to her estrangement from her family, her heritage, and, certainly, her workplace . . .

And Denise . . . There was still Denise . . .

And now the news . . .

The group was seated at the circular dining room table eating dinner and listening somberly to the hourly news. Querida ignored the broadcast, a repetition so far of previous broadcasts; in her opinion, any decision on AB 101 would have been the top news story.

Covertly, she observed the other six people at the table, wondering if anyone else found it notable that while all three couples sat side-by-side, Pat, at the head of the table, had chosen to place Donnelly to her right, and Angela to her left. Aside from Donnelly, Pat was clearly tolerating the presence of the occupants of her cabin, but taking pleasure in Angela.

Bradley's broad shoulders were hunched over the table, his dark eyes distant, as if his thoughts had taken him somewhere well beyond the newscast. Warren's eyes also were distant, but with the vacancy of boredom. Averill was looking at Donnelly. A lot. Not staring, but flicking glances over her as if anxious not to be thought of as staring. Also, Averill was single-handedly working her way through a second bottle of Taittinger's, which had to be atypical and a symptom of distress. How could she play championship-level golf and be any kind of a boozer?

Donnelly, her gray-blonde hair several shades darker with dampness from the shower, sat quietly eating her dinner and listening to the news. Her black pants were crisp, the white denim shirt neat; and she seemed less tired and not as upset as when she had first arrived. She reached down from time to time to run a hand gently down Querida's thigh, a touch more of connection than sensuality. The woman had such amazing recuperative powers, Querida thought. Which had always been true of her . . .

**Will You Still
Love Me Tomorrow?**

A new hour of music began. Querida watched Pat smile as Angela selected another wing from the platter;

Angela had been eating Pat's cooking with relish. Maybe, just maybe table talk would now be something other than *la politica*.

But Donnelly remarked, "They've figured out it's sounder strategy to wait till tomorrow for the veto."

"Why tomorrow any more than today?" Angela asked.

"Demonstrations," Donnelly said, and consumed a forkful of mashed potatoes as if this succinct reply provided ample explanation.

"Queer Nation is on the street at a second's notice," Warren retorted.

"It's a great group, Warren," Donnelly said. "But if the veto's announced tomorrow it'll take all of you a day to pull a community-wide demonstration together, and that puts it to Monday — a work day. Patty," she added, "you always did make the best mashed potatoes."

Averill, Querida noted, had forgotten not to stare; her gaze was fixed on Donnelly's hands. Suddenly Averill raised her crystal-blue eyes to Donnelly's face and blurted, "Why don't you tell us what you want from us."

Donnelly held her gaze. "You need to believe me, first," she said, quiet affection in her voice.

"I believe you."

"Everybody here needs to believe me."

"Peoria," Averill muttered, and picked up her glass of champagne.

Querida watched Averill sympathetically. This woman wanted out of here, she was still in pain over Donnelly... How could Donnelly, fueled as she was by the belief that she had a discernible purpose on this earth, and so idealistic that she'd once worked with Moonbeam Jerry Brown — how could she have wound up with a self-absorbed woman like Averill for more than a night or two? The answer had to be, understandably, lust. Athletic deity Averill had to be the big blind spot of Donnelly's life. Well, not totally blind — Donnelly had come to her senses in only a month or two. But not entirely. She was still insensible enough to think that with another chance Averill could be the full sum of her parts. I'll bet the house, Querida thought, whatever it is Donnelly wants from her, she'll blow it all over again.

Donnelly smiled at Averill. "You know me." Her gaze encompassed the table. "All of you know me, you're the most beloved people in my life. If you remember the history we've had together, you'll figure out what I want."

Pat said tartly, "I'm the oldest one here, and damned if I know."

"I'm the newest one, and it beats me," Querida said blithely. She really didn't know.

"Bradley," Warren said, "she wants the ugly flannel bathrobe back. Give her damn thing."

Donnelly said through the laughter, "I *would* like to have it back. It's only a couple of decades old."

"Forget it," Bradley said, picking up his coffee mug as he grinned at her. "You took my favorite leather jacket."

"I always liked that jacket on Donnelly," Pat observed.

If looks could kill, Querida thought, watching Bradley's face stiffen.

"I liked it on her too," Averill said, and Pat's face became the one to harden.

"That jacket's my absolute *favorite*," Querida said, and fractionally dropped an eyelid as she caught the glimmer of amusement in Donnelly's chastising sideways glance.

"Being married to you was a real trip, Brad," Donnelly said.

Bradley smiled at her. "We're sure not in Kansas anymore."

Mack the Knife

Declining all offers of help with table clearing, Pat shooed the group out to the living room to drink their coffee around the fire. She felt so swept over by the past, so inundated by memory that she needed a few minutes separation from them to breathe, to regain composure. Plus, Donnelly's obtuseness to Averill's emotional and political vacuum irritated her beyond measure. And Angela's optimism that Averill would someday change her stripes was just plain soul-destroying.

So Bradley and Donnelly were not in Kansas anymore. They had no idea about being in Kansas. Their marriage couldn't hold a damn candle to hers, and if Donnelly knew the larger details, no one, not even Donnelly, could imagine the reality, could have any inkling how weird her marriage had actually been. And as for her marital "sex life" . . . God, poor Jerry.

But he had to take some measure of blame. She'd gone through high school with him on the far periphery of her vision along with every other male in her classes — why on earth he had decided, in her senior year at Riverside High, to start hanging around her, she would never know. She hadn't encouraged him, hadn't been the least bit grateful or even welcoming, even though his attention won her grudging points from her peer group. He was innocuous enough, and not too bad-looking if you overlooked his skinny body and weak receding chin; still, his limpid blue eyes and sweet smile could have attracted any number of girls.

"You be nicer to him!" her father shouted in exasperation after Jerry had invited himself over to the house and stayed for dinner and Pat all but ignored him. "You thank your lucky stars he's interested!"

She *should* have been thankful. Certainly she was

better off than her only two friends at school, like her, also outsiders, fish-lipped Catherine with her acne eruptions and pious devotion to Christ, and Frances, so albino in her coloring that her eyelashes were invisible and her eyes, the palest possible shade of blue, trembled in their sockets. No male at school came anywhere near those two, and Pat was certain that Jerry drew derision from his own peer group because of his interest in her plump, unattractive self.

Persistent, he'd been as persistent as a mosquito with his offers to drive her to school, to drive her to a movie, drive her anywhere. After his early morning work on his father's milk delivery route, any extra time was hers if she deigned to have it, and if not he worked on his car, a 1938 Packard whose innards he seemed constantly to be taking apart and cleaning and reassembling. He did not play sports or cards or any other game, nor did he read anything, even the newspaper. He loved radio serials and could rattle off an endless number of plotlines involving Hopalong Cassidy or the Lone Ranger. She liked him well enough — pretty much everybody liked Jerry, and she had no reason not to — but he bored her silly and she detested his awkward pawing of her.

The week of their graduation from high school, he asked her for at least the fiftieth time to marry him.

Annoyed beyond endurance, she snapped, "I've told you and told you I want to go to college."

"I been thinking," he said. "I got a dab of money saved, I'm gonna work full time with Dad and build his route till I can take some of it over. I figure if you go to school and work a little part time we can make it. You think about it, Patsy."

She endured his kiss, then went home and did think about it.

Jerry was okay, he was one of the few young males

she could abide being around... She dreaded her parents escalating their nagging that she further explore the thorny terrain of male relationships "for your own good." And if she got married, she would finally present her parents — her father especially — with something that would please them. She'd stop being a freak, she'd blend in with the great mob of young marrieds. She'd be invisible.

And Jerry had said she could go to college. She could go to college...

"Okay, I'll do it," she told him the next day.

Jerry's widower father, stooped from a shrapnel fragment lodged in his spine from his stint in the Philippines, scratched around in his head of thick gray hair and gazed up at her and his son in bewilderment, then said "Fine," and took no further interest. Her own father thumped Jerry repeatedly between his thin shoulder blades and called him son. Her mother was far less ebullient — perhaps, Pat thought, because she was looking at a family landscape made even more arid by this son-in-law.

The wedding was small and quiet; she and Jerry had few friends to invite. At the reception, as her father got more and more stupid with drink, her mother retreated first to silence, and finally to her bedroom.

Pat understood her virginal state to be a desirable asset, but otherwise was ignorant of marital relations. Her knowledge of male anatomy came only from the blueprints provided by her father and brother, and a few nude statues and art photographs. She wished she had not been so indifferent to the sniggering conversations of her boy-crazy classmates in school. Her mother offered no advice other than, "Be nice to him. Men have their ways, you'll get used to it."

In their Santa Barbara honeymoon hotel room, Jerry looked nothing like her brother or father nor any statue or photograph: the sight of his hairy, thin naked body shocked her to her marrow. His body against hers revolted her. And his penis, forced inside her for only a few seconds before the gush of ejaculation, was painful and loathsome.

No wonder her mother had not told her about this horror. Her mother knew she would never have married him or anyone. "Never again," she said, heaving him off her, sobbing with fury and betrayal. "Never ever again."

"It'll be better," he said. "It'll be okay, Patsy, you'll see."

"No I won't see," she snarled at him. "You'll never do this to me again."

She took the only revenge she could on her mother, who greeted Pat's return from her honeymoon with averted eyes and a fluster of nervous embarrassment. Pat ignored her, ignored all of her overtures to discuss anything about her honeymoon or marriage.

But she cut off a potential ally, because the wedding night wasn't the half of it...

Chariots of Fire

As Donnelly wandered off to the bathroom, Averill drained her champagne and placed the glass on the coffee table. Stretching and yawning, she offered, "I believe I'll toddle off to bed. Angie, honey?"

Angela sat before the fire, playing with the kitten, chuckling at its awkward swipes at the piece of yarn she teasingly dangled. "Go ahead," she said to Averill, "take your shower — I'll be right along."

Averill looked considerably less than pleased by her response, Bradley thought. Going to bed early seemed like a very good idea to him. Get this day over with and tomorrow, too, for that matter, and he'd work on forgiving Donnelly for calling him down here on a wild goose chase. She could be extremely persuasive — who knew that better than he did — and her confidence had always been more opinion-based than grounded in solid fact.

Wilson would not veto AB 101. This man was no George Wallace; the civil rights of an entire class of people hung in the balance, and those rights could no more be denied than the rights of African-Americans or women, no matter who disapproved — and there were still plenty of people who disagreed with the right of equality for either of those groups, too... The difference was, and here he could agree completely with Warren's cynicism, Wilson was smart enough to know that regardless of legislation, rights were still being denied African-Americans and women — these two groups were still impeded by the white male patriarchy of which he himself was a member — and gay rights would be no different...

"Turn in, Warren?" he said.

Warren sat cross-legged before the fire, watching Angela play with the kitten. "How about a little walk? Want to look at the stars?"

Meaning smoke some grass. He'd love to, but blackness filled the cabin windows; a pane rattled faintly in the wind. Mellow with wine, he hated to leave this room, warmed as it was by the crackling flames and the lingering aromas of cooking. But of course Warren hadn't had any wine. Bradley nodded reluctantly.

"It's cold as Madison out there," Averill said.

"I'll come with you, *caballero*," Querida said.

"Great," Warren said. "Stay where you are, Brad. Enjoy the fire."

His irritation at the diminutive of his name was

intensified by Warren's implicit challenge: why hadn't Bradley said a word to Donnelly for calling him Brad? Truth was, he wanted to hear the nickname only from Donnelly, the intimacy to be hers and hers alone. He was not about to admit that to Warren, or Donnelly, or anyone.

"Fine, I'll do that," he said, keeping most of the sharpness out of his voice. "Watch out for the bears."

"It's the squirrels that scare me," Warren said, shrugging into the jacket that had grass stashed in its inside pocket.

"I'll protect you, honey," Querida said, donning a leather coat.

As Warren and Querida left the cabin, a billow of frigid air in their wake, he wondered, as he often did, why he was with Warren. But that always lasted only as long as it took to remember Nicholas. And the first phone call almost ten years ago: "I'm sick, really serious shit . . ."

The horror of the plague, Bradley had once told Donnelly, went beyond whether he might have it. The full horror was realizing that in sharing the act of ultimate intimacy with another person he could be a carrier of death, as surely as if he ran down that person with his car.

Nicholas, gone eleven months later, claiming his current, dying partner had infected him with the virus, but had that been really true? Could Bradley have been his executioner?

Going for his AIDS test — and nothing to do with the rumors, the confusion, the dread about what caused this, how you got it, should you get tested, could you trust it to be kept quiet if you were tested; and nothing to do with Donnelly, who had demonically insisted "as the most loving friend you have in your life" that he be tested. He simply had to know. The exhilaration of relief soon evaporating, to leave a vacuum. And as Raymond died, then Hannifan, and the others, the vacuum slowly filling with eviscerating guilt and depression. He had done nothing different from his HIV-infected brothers; he no more deserved to live than they deserved to die.

Except for Donnelly, he hadn't told anyone. Warren didn't advertise his HIV status, either. He and Warren shared the blunted and deadened nerve ends of comrades surviving amid wounded and fallen friends on a battlefield, flinging their anger and their bodies into the demonstrations and the protests. But they were missing a piece of weaponry: the actual virus itself. To people with AIDS, and those who were HIV-positive, they were valued allies — but outsiders who could not possibly understand what it took to live whipsawed by hope and despair, the counting of T-cells and time, and the fatalistic planning of HIV-infected lives in a country that averted its eyes in casual, callous, hateful indifference.

Bradley knew very well that part of his attraction to Warren was that he would not have to watch Warren die. Above all else Warren was a very young gay man untainted by the suffering and anguish of Bradley's own generation. And Bradley had taken as his mission the easing of Warren's anger at Bradley's era for changing gay existence from life in the shadows to a brief liberated period in the seventies to these days of navigating in a minefield.

He had succeeded well enough that Warren had traveled beyond grudging some admiration to that same AIDS generation for its courage and fury, for being the first to embrace and nurture its identity and pride, for making possible ACT UP and Queer Nation and the world-wide gay rights movement. Warren had deferred internship as a therapist specializing in counseling people of mixed-race heritage to work at part-time jobs so that he could fight on the front lines "today, right now, when I'm needed." And Bradley, beneath the abrasive conflict of his relationship with Warren, was filled to bursting with loving pride in him.

Unlike his opinion of himself. He couldn't say that as a gay man or as a publisher he'd ever given his best to the fight. Way back when it counted, he'd lacked the courage, the sheer spiritual stamina, to go the way of someone like publisher Sasha Alyson, who had printed whatever gay and lesbian work he could find, and had crowned that achievement by forming a publishers' consortium — which had included Bradley — to distribute a free book about AIDS. He could not even lay claim to a tiny part of the firmament occupied by legendary St. Martin's Press editor Michael Denneny, openly gay from the Year One, it seemed, who had brought gay work into print when it was most desperately needed. Some of the writers Bradley published, some of his professional colleagues, still did not know — officially — that he was a gay man . . .

He had always perceived his niche to be that of a small-time, avant garde non-fiction publisher, and had led a fringe existence with creative marketing, cautious tending to cash flow, small press runs, and payment to most of his authors in copies and prestige. Over time his consistent publishing philosophy had gained him access to review periodicals, and he had acquired a minor celebrity as a publisher of cutting-edge, modestly successful books. Still, the National Book Award nomination three years ago had shocked him.

Paper or Plastic, Jason Bender's slender volume of savage Reagan-era insider memoirs, had given him cachet enough to attract new writers, and income predictable enough to share a small booth at the American

Booksellers' Association convention with other small literary publishers, not to mention opportunities to supplement his income by in-residence teaching assignments that did not necessitate returning to the field. Because he sure as sunrise did not ever want to return to the field of teaching ...

Most of all he was able to ease some measure of his guilt by accepting the economic disaster of publishing the poetry of AIDS. Out there in eloquent, anguished, tragic plenitude, it deserved permanent record, and publishers aside from himself were printing it, but after the first wave, led by Paul Monette, people with AIDS and their loved ones seemed to be the audience now, along with a few lonely reviewers who urged, begged, pleaded with readers to bear witness, however painful, to the extinguishing of the bright brief lives of an entire generation ...

I'll Never Love
This Way Again

She didn't want a shower, it was too cold away from the fire, only a masochist would want to come out of warm water naked into an icy room. It would be different if Pat Decker had put her and Angela upstairs — everybody knows heat rises — but the spiteful bitch had assigned only herself and Donnelly and Querida up there.

Anyway, she was too sleepy for a shower. Too lovely from the champagne. If Angela wanted to stay out there to atone for some perceived rudeness Averill had perpetrated, so be it. She'd just brush her teeth and get the bed nice and warm for when Angela's body would be next to hers. She loved Angela. Loved her. Angela

was so sweet and soft, gave such wonderful full-body
massages... It was beautiful to be naked in a cold room
if you had the warm naked body you wanted as a cover
for yours.

Like the first time with Donnelly...

She couldn't say she'd never forget that night,
because she couldn't remember whole parts of it. Taking
Donnelly to dinner near Rancho Park golf course, yes.
Wearing a white silk jumpsuit she'd chosen especially for
the occasion because everyone had assured her it was a
knockout. Making it her business to scope out the most
expensive restaurant on L.A.'s posh west side by listening
to recommendations until she heard not praise for food
but awe over cost. It had taken three phone calls to get
this woman to agree to dinner and she would impress
her or die trying. She'd heard of playing hard-to-get, but
no one had ever been that way with her, and Donnelly
hadn't been playing.

None of it had made any sense, including why she
felt so challenged by a woman worlds apart from the
glowing young athletic women she'd been involved with,
a woman, for Olympia's sake, fifteen years her senior.

She did not remember the look of L'Orangerie, the
table settings, the food, what she drank or how much,
she did not know or care about the size of the bill on
which she dropped a credit card. So admiring of
Donnelly was she, so aroused by Donnelly that they
could have brought food to the table raw, it would have
cooked on her fork.

It was not so much the woman's look — she had
arrived attired in dark gabardine pants and a ribbed
white turtleneck decorated with a large pewter women's
symbol hanging on a chain — but her composure. She
was the most self-contained woman Averill had ever

encountered away from her competitors on the golf course. One element, above all others, did burn into her mind — Donnelly's hands. Why, she didn't know. They were ordinary hands simply formed, with sturdy wrists; unadorned, with wide palms and long fingers that wielded cutlery with neat economy, hands that she wanted to hold and study, to trace the shape of every finger and examine every whorl of fingerprint. She wanted those hands to leave fingerprints on her, to leave palm prints . . .

If Donnelly felt any similar erotic current, she did not show it then. Amid general conversation, she seemed impressed enough with Averill's profession to ask questions, yet not so impressed that the questions ever left the realm of interest about her dealings with the press — *I'm as careful,* Averill told her, *as anyone would be in a pit of rattlesnakes* — and her essential career goal.

Her goal. Closing her eyes, Averill uttered, "*The Hall of Fame,*" confessing her ambition with the fervor she had withheld from the press, her competitors, even her parents. "It's the hardest, toughest achievement in sports, the one most worth having. You need thirty — *thirty* — tournament wins, including two majors. I've got two majors — the U.S. Open and the Dinah Shore — I'm only six wins away."

"You'll make it," Donnelly assured her.

"I'm thirty-two now. I don't have all that much time. With great new talents like Brandie Burton out there, it's harder and harder to win."

Donnelly went on to other subjects, tossing off pronouncements on culture and politics — George Bush, AIDS, Robert Mapplethorpe — and quizzing her for her own opinions, searching out answers beyond Averill's usual patter of safe platitudes.

Averill finally told her without a trace of defensiveness, "I really can't get involved in any of that stuff."

Donnelly did not take her seriously. "Of course you can. It's vital to your life."

She could not see that it was important, much less vital, but she did not want to displease this woman. "If I take a position and express an opinion about *anything*, and there's a reporter within earshot, it'll be printed."

"Well, maybe it should be," Donnelly said with a smile so disarming, so unexpected and so electric that the heat Averill felt must be similar, she was sure, to nuclear meltdown.

Donnelly offered to see Averill back to her hotel. Averill did not remember the cab ride to the Century Plaza. Only that Donnelly had followed her into the hotel room and closed the door behind her with a casual toss that evoked some dimly remembered movie scene.

Donnelly walked over to her and then stared into her eyes, as if she were caught by something — some portent. Her eyes still locked on Averill's, she felt for and opened all the fastenings in Averill's silk jumpsuit.

Averill had thought she knew her erotic possibilities. Until she stood naked in that cool room, her body touched only by Donnelly's gaze.

And then something seemed to break Donnelly's control, and Averill found herself pulled into her arms and there was the icy pewter symbol Donnelly wore, so cold that it burned into her skin, and the woolen texture of Donnelly's clothes, and then Donnelly pushed her down onto the bed...

Tearing at Donnelly's clothes and then the shock of Donnelly's body... and she felt Donnelly imprinting on her skin like ink sinking into paper.

Her body an arc in Donnelly's hands as Donnelly's lips first touched hers and then warm breath bathed her ears, her throat, hovered over her shoulders, her breasts, Donnelly's mouth grazing up her throat, lightly across her lips to explore her face, then Donnelly's mouth fully possessing hers, Donnelly's hands on her as if they would re-sculpt her body, and Donnelly's tongue inside her. Donnelly's fingers sliding into her. Wave upon higher wave of sensation rising to molten climax.

Needing to turn her hands and mouth on Donnelly, wanting to force moans from her. Astonished, frightened by the power of this woman to compel such primitive need in her...

That night she knew that for the first time she had ventured well beyond sex-as-performance. Donnelly made her feel like a goddess, the rite performed on her body elevating her into a new realm. As if she were making love, finally, with one of those impossibly remote Aphrodites on the golf course...

Before Donnelly, never had she entertained the possibility of an ongoing relationship. After that night she had no more compunction about ending Donnelly's fourteen-year relationship with Pat Decker than she would swatting a mosquito from her wrist.

Before Donnelly she was used to fending people off, not pursuing them. Before Donnelly, no one had ever left her... To have it all disappear, and to have been so *unprepared* for it to end... Never had she realized that she could actually lose someone. And happy as she was now with Angela, Donnelly still seemed unfinished business...

Save the Last
Dance for Me

   Leaning back against the wide trunk of a pine tree in the woods just off the road, Warren broke off humming the tune that had been playing on the Oldies station in the cabin and lit a joint, cupping his hands to shelter it, and offered it to Querida.

   She shook her head. "Don't even tempt me. I kicked cigarettes a year ago, I'm scared of anything that might take me back."

   "I hear you." He inhaled from the joint. "Glad you came out here with me." He motioned with his head toward the cabin. "It's tense as a Mafia meeting back there. Two years with Bradley — he's never once talked about his time with Donnelly. I'm the outsider here."

   "No more than me," Querida retorted. She jammed her hands deeper into her pockets, thinking she should have thought to bring gloves, and he must be freezing in his light cotton pants, and they both should have their heads examined for what they'd not thought to wear into this wintry country. The filtered lights of other cabins strewn over the forested hillside seemed to intensify the cold. "I'm just the new girl in town — I don't have a fraction of the history."

   "How long have you been with her?"

   "About ten percent of nine months." Querida grinned. "She's gone most of the time, but the ten percent is interesting enough."

   "She was married to Bradley what, four years?"

   "And Pat for fourteen. And Averill for maybe a minute."

   As Warren chuckled, Querida said, "Hey, I don't blame Donnelly for taking the minute. I'd take it myself."

Warren gave an exaggerated sigh. "Everybody's movie dream — the all-American golden girl. Or boy."

"Right." Leaning back against an adjacent tree and gazing up at the white-silver canopy of clouds and stars, Querida relaxed with Warren in comfortable silence, the pines stark inkblots around her, the cold air sharp with the smell of pine mixed with the aroma of smoke from the fireplace and Warren's marijuana. She did like gay men so much, they were so easy to be with, so brother-like . . .

Warren said quietly, "What in the hell is going on here?"

She shrugged. "Donnelly wants something important from us. She's turned more and more into a firebrand —"

"Who hasn't," Warren muttered.

What she would not say to this partner of Bradley's was that Donnelly had always possessed what all of her lovers past and present lacked: raw, out-in-front, pioneer-style courage. Courage like Querida's grandfather and grandmother. She said, "My guess is, she wants some major contribution of work or time or money, probably all three . . . Whatever she wants from me, she's got it."

"Big deal. I don't know the woman, but if she called me all the way up here to ask for something so fucking obvious —"

"Fucking obvious maybe to you," she said impatiently, "you're out there, you and Donnelly. You storm the streets, she storms the corridors."

Even in the darkness she could see the accusation on his face. "You don't?"

"Oh, I'm active . . ." She finished slowly, "More as a Chicana than a lesbian."

His shrug was eloquently dismissive. "I'm queer and I'm black."

She did not reply. She owed no further explanation to him or to anyone. She touched lesbian-feminist issues and Latino culture to the degree that she could, and that was a lot — a major donor to Viva! and the Mexican-American Women's National Association, even stupid MALDEF. Actively networking among Chicana women too, even though her functioning world was the world of whites. She worked with whites, lived with whites, and most certainly slept with them. Her three attempts at relationships with Chicana women had resigned her to the probability that they simply judged each other too harshly. Understood too well their vulnerabilities, their passive-aggressiveness and various other culturally induced tics. Or maybe she didn't care to look into a reflection of her own Chicana face, and the knowledge that all of her success was a mirage, all of it could be swept from her in the instant it took to awaken from a dream, and she'd be back wondering over electricity that could light up the night, she'd be living without hope and only the memory of what she'd dreamed —

Warren broke into the downward spiral of her thoughts. "What does Donnelly do in Sacramento? Is she, like, a lobbyist?"

She nodded. "These last months, she's been working her ass off shepherding the gay rights bill through the Assembly. She's a full-time consultant to gay political groups, AIDS groups, industry, and straight politicians smart enough to want a liaison to the community — she's connected to everybody, and I mean *everybody*. From Barney Frank to Urvashi Vaid to Roberta Achtenberg. When she's home, the phone rings off the hook —"

He asked abruptly, "Being with a woman like her, how can you be a Chicana before you're a lesbian?"

"I didn't say I was," she said sharply. "I said I'm

more *active* as a Chicana than a lesbian. Look, dammit, most Latinos in this country are a lot more Anglo than Latino. My own family is as patriotic as any American family ever could be, they could care less about Mexico or Latin America. We're part of the American mainstream whether mainstream America knows it or not—"

"Woman, I know all that," Warren interrupted in irritation. "You heard me when Averill said that horseshit about you going home. White Americans don't give a fuck about their European roots."

She said in a conciliatory tone, "Warren, the demographics I see in my work, they piss me off. Latinos are so passionate over American politics but we don't have a defined political identity, and worst of all, we don't vote. We have to vote, in big defined numbers. We're invisible, easy to stereotype—people don't know anything about us, we don't use the most basic means to tell them."

Grinning, Warren reached over and lightly punched her in the shoulder. "You're talking about the gay and lesbian community, right? The African-American community, right?"

She grinned at him. "Okay." She could tell he had warmed to her.

"Tell me," he said, "what do you get out of this absentee relationship with Donnelly? The woman's twice your age."

"We don't have the same hang-ups you silly boys do," she teased him. "What do you *muchachos* do when you're not young anymore?"

"Exactly the same," he said. "There's no such thing as an old fag. You haven't answered my question."

"You're right, I haven't. Put that damn thing out and let's get back, my feet are getting chilblains."

After one final, deep drag, he snuffed out the joint,

dropped it, scuffed it over with dirt. Sliding his hand into her jacket pocket, he tucked his cold hand into hers.

Why Donnelly, indeed, she thought as she trudged up the road linked with Warren, warming his hand in hers.

Last December at the Viva! party she'd learned all she needed to know in the first moments when Donnelly had come up and introduced herself: "Something about your face makes me want to know you."

Amused, immediately attracted to the confidence and aura of vitality surrounding this handsome woman, and wondering why she was present at an event celebrating Latino writers and artists, Querida had answered with, "What brings you here?"

Donnelly replied in a voice that penetrated the loud buzz of conversation and the energetic beat of the music, gesturing at the festive swirl of Latinos, Asians, African-Americans and Caucasians: "I like looking at the world the way it should be."

Donnelly seemed the freest woman she had ever known. Herself, she had always felt confined by the belief, in a non-religious sense, that her gifts were meant to be shared, although she still did not understand how a preternatural but less-than-genius bent for mathematics could be translated to extend beyond simple sharing of her high salary. But Donnelly knew exactly what she meant — and believed the same of herself, she told Querida that night over a late-night meal at a coffee shop on Sunset. And that shared knowledge was part of the glue around and through the attraction that took immediate and distinctive shape between them.

From their first time together, Donnelly in bed had been pure fun — and pure fire. To make love with her was to play with passion like you would play with matches. Teasing and laughing and play-wrestling each other until the fiery ignition point...

Donnelly was the first woman she had ever been comfortable with in every aspect of who she was, where she'd come from and what she'd become; they were well-matched in their essential strength of purpose. If she did not as yet fully know that purpose, she did know her goal: To stretch beyond the life of timidity and narrow conformity to church and society that bound her father and mother. To have the strength, like her grandfather, to lock away pain. To have the courage to risk.

Querida wondered if this had not, in fact, been Donnelly's gift to all of her partners, if her life-force had not provided all of them with a voice, and was the reason why all of them had gathered here so loyally and unhesitatingly.

Whatever Donnelly would ask of her this weekend, and whatever her own final purpose was to be, something within her was taking its form around this woman.

As she and Warren reached the cabin, that form crystallized as it had never had before: *I want to establish my own fronteras. Like my grandfather.*

Heartbreak Hotel

Her guests gone, thankfully, to bed, Pat tamped down the fire and was about to turn off the radio; instead she sank onto a cushion beside the dying embers and took the kitten into her lap and listened as the new song began.

Elvis. The day would never come when an Elvis tune did not bring back the bar days...and Elvis-worshipping Cindy. No one else except the Beatles would ever come along to be enshrined on Cindy's altar.

Could anything on this earth evoke memory more vividly than music? Blonde and femme Cindy Ralston, in tight capri pants and off-the-shoulder blouses, dancing with every butch in the bar, jitterbugging and snapping her fingers to *Heartbreak Hotel*. Curvaceous, vivacious, outrageous, the butches all said of her, a bright dream to all of them back in the darkness of the fifties. Nine years older than Pat but rebellious as a teenager, still testing all the waters, and not confused in the least by Pat's sexuality or her own.

Pat would never have guessed this high-spirited femme's age — thirty-five — nor her profession — registered nurse — nor, from the first moment that Pat caught her eye, that she would greet Pat's interest with equal interest. Exhilarated, beholden to whatever gods might be that such a belle would notice her much less want to go to bed with her, Pat made the first covenant of her life: she would spend every day and night making her happy.

She had met many women in the bars, had had flings and even a few serious affairs with some of them. Of them all, Cindy had been the most exuberantly lesbian. But then Cindy had previously been exuberantly heterosexual. Or had tried to be. Four times engaged to be married, backing out each time, and once, "Believe it or not, dear, I got all the way up to the church door, stopped, ripped off my veil, picked up my train and ran like hell."

"You're wonderful," Pat told her fervently. Had she had a scintilla of Cindy's guts she would have avoided her own ghastly mess of a marriage.

Rita and Peter, Cindy's parents. Rita Ralston, a tarantula of a woman trading on a lame foot and sanctimonious martyrdom to tyrannize a hapless husband and a glowingly healthy daughter. She'd welcomed Pat with clutching gratitude. Securely employed Pat seemed stable and calming — and surely a temporary influence in the life of her only offspring. Anything, Rita said, was preferable to Cindy shredding the family reputation "...in the kind of bars, Patricia dear, too *vile* to discuss in polite company."

Pat never mentioned that she had met and come to know Cindy at one of those bars, the Star. Wanting the conjugal exclusivity that would end Cindy's barfly existence, Pat found herself siding with Rita Ralston even if it meant abandoning the one public place, however abusive and shadowy and seedy it might be, where she was acceptable in the pants and shirts she loved to wear. In truth, she had never believed herself a legitimate part of a scene where aggressive toughness was the required stance to be butch, she had felt inadequate with peers she admired and respected.

Moving into Pat's tiny, tree-shaded apartment above Hyperion in Silver Lake, Cindy did modify her behavior — somewhat. "But Doll, I still need some fun, you know?"

Her tradeoff for the adventure of the bars was impromptu parties, some lasting over the entire span of her off-days, with an array of friends and acquaintances and strangers she collected along her charismatic path. Her evenings with Pat, she drank vodka gimlets and chain-smoked Kents and related humor-filled tales of the despotic doctors and cantankerous patients she worked with, and mocked her mother's constant nagging to give her grandchildren. As the evening wore on, she wove in wistful accounts of her childhood and childhood friends and her nursing school days, her failed heterosexual affairs before Pat's arrival on the scene including the flight from the church door, until Pat heard all the stories seemingly hundreds of times over.

Throughout those evenings Pat would nurse a glass or two of cheap wine and catch an occasional glimpse of wrestling or *Father Knows Best* or whatever had been tuned in on the minuscule black and white TV, patiently waiting for Cindy to wind down and come to bed with her and be stroked and loved to orgasm and then to sleep in Pat's arms. Each morning Cindy would bounce off to Hollywood Presbyterian Hospital crisp in her nursing whites, and, aside from a chronic cough, without a trace of the previous night's alcohol and cigarette consumption.

The real hangovers, occurring on Cindy's off-days when her drinking became non-stop, drove Pat completely into the Ralstons' camp. Cindy chafed under Pat's nagging: "You're getting worse than my parents." Too true. Unlike the Ralstons she had herself to blame for providing Cindy with no better than a fringe existence on society's extreme outer edge.

As Cindy's thirty-seventh birthday hove into view, her mother became despairing of her chances for grandchildren, "Time's running out..." her ominously uttered mantra. The actual nature of Cindy's relationship with Pat was, of course, never hinted at, the fiction maintained that the tiny sofa in the living room was Pat's chaste bed.

Cindy's fortieth birthday signaled a giving-up point for the Ralstons, who moved to a condo in Palm Desert, well out of proximity to their daughter and her disappointing life. In retrospect it seemed to Pat that from the day her parents left, Cindy began to find any and every excuse — tiredness, illness — to avoid sex, and she was stoned all the time, coming home from work stoned, denying she was stoned, and not a sign of alcohol on her breath. "What drug are you on?" Pat demanded. "Don't be ridiculous," Cindy airily answered her. As Cindy's moods became more erratic and her behavior more manic, she finally conceded that "Maybe I do a reefer once in a while in the basement john, all the girls do." Pat's fear was that Cindy either had acquired access to the drug supply at the hospital, or — a possibility she could scarcely contemplate — was pilfering painkillers from doses prescribed for patients.

Pat had no one with whom to share her agonies over Cindy, no one to consult for help or advice — no one who knew she and Cindy were a lesbian couple. By 1961, after five years away from the bar scene, the only friends she and Cindy had in common were Cindy's itinerant drinking buddies. Her own friends were work colleagues at Acme Building Supply where she had just become a service supervisor. Since the Ralstons knew their daughter's proclivity for intoxicants, had known it long before Pat had arrived on the scene, going to them with reports of fresh disasters seemed useless, even cruel. What could they say or do that would make a difference? When it came down to a choice between anyone's approval or what Cindy wanted to do, Cindy had always ranked approval a far distant second.

Afterward, Pat knew she would have hung in there indefinitely out of obligation and gratitude for what Cindy had once meant to her life. Except that widowed Lisa Snyder moved into the apartment across the hall and befriended Pat and swiftly sized up Pat's domestic situation. She told Pat succinctly, "Leave. Now."

And Pat began to dream of what life might be like with a woman who was not always half in the bag, who could actually listen as well as talk. Maybe even a life of solitude might be preferable. There was no suggestion in those days of a future with Lisa, but Pat gradually came to understand that there would be no future at all if she did not extract herself from Cindy.

And so, choosing a night before one of Cindy's off-days, she confessed painfully, reluctantly, "I haven't been good for you...we haven't been good for each other for a long time. I've decided to leave, it's time we separated —"

She scarcely managed to duck under Cindy's attempt to poleax her with a heavy glass ashtray, the blow paralyzing her shoulder.

Cindy screamed, "You fucking cheating bitch! I trusted you! *Trusted* you!"

She raged berserk through the apartment, flinging everything she could pick up, and then attacked with clawing fingernails that Pat escaped only by barricading herself in the bedroom.

She had been utterly oblivious, too focused on her own inadequacies in playing second fiddle to Cindy's real love affair with alcohol to see the full-blown depth of Cindy's needs, her possessiveness.

In cringing guilt, she surrendered herself to night after night of hysterical pleading and recrimination and abuse, determined that she would let Cindy vent all her fury and work through this. Then she would leap for freedom.

On a Friday night Pat came home from work to Elvis blasting from the stereo, and vodka and beer bottles littering the coffee table, and Cindy on the sofa necking passionately with another woman. As Cindy looked up bleary-eyed, the woman coolly extracted herself from her embrace and stood up — a swaggering, pint-sized caricature of a bulldyke, with slicked-back black hair, insolent black eyes and a smirk that blended perfectly with the black jeans and pointy, silver-tipped black boots she affected. The woman stuffed her hands in her jean pockets and issued a challenging stare.

"There was a time," Pat told her, pointing to the coffee table, "when I'd pick up a little shit like you and stuff you into one of those bottles." Turning her back, she stalked into the bedroom to pack as, behind her, Elvis began a new song and Cindy erupted into sobs.

Pat moved out that night, taking only her clothes, and cursing everything in her life she could not control, had never been able to control.

The new woman's name was Joan — "that creature" to Rita Ralston, who loathed her with fanatical dedication, sputtering to Pat, "My daughter is an ungrateful *beast* and she is unforgivably cruel to you. If she wants a man, why doesn't she..." And closed her mouth firmly, permanently on that particular subject. Pat knew what she meant. Pat might be butch, but Joan crossed the line into blatancy.

"You come and be my daughter," Rita declared, bombarding her with invitations for dinner and dangled hints of news about Cindy.

Pat could not reveal to Rita the facts of her parting from Cindy; that particular truth remained Cindy's to reveal to her own parents. Writhing in dishonesty and guilt — and because she loved Cindy and could stay close to her through the Ralstons — she dutifully trekked to Palm Desert once every several months and somewhere during the visit picked up kernels of news about Cindy who, according to Rita, was coming to no good. She'd left her job at Hollywood Presbyterian — "Fired, she can't fool me," and was living in the Simi Valley — "if you can imagine *living* in such a place" — and working in some other hospital — "a rinky-dink rathole of a clinic" — and staying with "that creature" and drinking and smoking more than ever and never coming out to see her mother and saying she wouldn't until "I make that creature welcome here and she'll *never* be welcome in this house!"

Two years after Pat's breakup with Cindy, Rita called

Pat. "Peter died three hours ago, a massive heart attack," she said quietly, and accepted Pat's shocked, stuttering condolences with eerie calm. Out of a wish to not inflict her presence on Cindy at the funeral of her father, Pat sent flowers to the service, and visited Rita a week afterward. Rita was still calm, and wholly diminished, and suddenly very old.

Rita soon moved from the Palm Desert condo to a trailer in Borego Springs. Over the next decade, as Pat's life became a period of quiet bachelorhood interrupted by a few brief liaisons, when her pets turned out to be more constant in their affection than her lovers, the relationship between herself and Rita became a dutifully exchanged series of birthday and Christmas cards and warmly worded notes, Rita's notes always containing an update on Cindy.

Then came the dark Christmas of 1974, just before she met Donnelly, when Pat did not send cards to anyone. And noted amid her baleful funk that Rita had not sent her a card, either. Over New Year's Pat sent an apologetic note. And a few weeks later received a brief reply in Rita's spidery handwriting:

Didn't send any cards out either. Sprained my knee and hip this November, very slow healing. And in October Cindy died.

Pat dropped the letter, and if a chair hadn't been behind her to fall into she would have landed on the floor along with the letter.

When she was able to, she picked up the phone.

"Rita . . . Cindy . . . What . . ."

"Oh, is it Pat? Lung cancer," Rita said in wispy, faraway voice. "Sudden. She'd been coughing worse and worse and she went in and it was way far along. They put her in the hospital where she'd been working, I visited her, she seemed fine, improving, they said. Then they called me. I think they over-medicated her."

Or maybe she saved the medication and over-medicated herself, Pat thought numbly. Had Cindy never even asked for her?

"Rita ..." Pat didn't recognize her own voice. *"Rita, why didn't you call me?"*

"Well, it was all so sudden, and there was only a small ceremony and bad enough that crea —" There was a brief, thoroughly deadly, pause. Then Rita rushed hurriedly into the breach. "It was the way Cindy wanted it, she didn't want anybody else there. Or to know," she added feebly.

Afterward, Pat never forgave herself for whatever banality she managed to utter before she hung up on Rita Ralston forever.

To this day she would never forgive herself for allowing Rita Ralston to keep her daughter, even in death, stuffed in the closet. For letting Rita escape with appearances and illusions intact. How many times had she imagined saying, "Your daughter was a lesbian and you know it, you know I was her lover every night of those eight years I spent with her. You had no right not to tell me she was dead. You had no right to act like the years I spent with your daughter were nothing."

She had had to content herself with never speaking or writing to Rita again. But of course, Rita had never spoken or written to her again, either.

Pat got to her feet to go to bed, the kitten tucked into the crook of her arm. Snapping off the radio, she said to Rita, "You bitch ... I hope you're dead."

The Lion Sleeps Tonight

Raised on one elbow on the bed, Donnelly had tuned in the Oldies station on the bedside table.

"You're tired," Querida murmured, reaching to her, cupping Donnelly's face in her hands.

"Not that tired." She slid her arms around Querida and turned her head to kiss Querida's fingers. "We haven't seen each other in —"

"Eighteen days. We'll be in L.A. tomorrow. Away from a cabin filled with your ex-lovers straining their ears to hear us."

Donnelly smiled. "The important thing," she said, tightening her arms, "is the ex part of the word."

"A distinction clearer to you than to them. War could break out any second."

Donnelly moved away to look at her. "War?"

She might have known Donnelly would be unaware of the tensions in this place. Her rational, optimistic eye always on the big picture, she could be perfectly oblivious to nuance. "War," she repeated, and ticked off on her fingers: "Bradley doesn't like Pat. Pat is barely civil to Bradley and Warren. Bradley and Pat don't like Averill. Averill disdains everybody. Warren is jealous of whatever he thinks Bradley had with you. Your ex-lovers are looking for a chance to tear out each other's throats."

Donnelly, chuckling, placed a finger across her lips. "Hush. The walls have ears."

Querida smiled. "Exactly . . ."

Hearing the radio from someone's room, Averill

murmured sleepily into Angela's hair, "We'll be in Buena Park tomorrow, Angie honey."

Angela sighed and curled around her for sleep. "The place isn't terribly soundproof, is it . . ."

"Whatsamatter, Brad dear?" Warren said as Bradley, hearing the radio come on above them in Donnelly's room, pulled away from his embrace.

The best tack in this name game, Bradley decided, was to ignore it. And best to ignore this sexual overture from Warren, rare as it was, because it came from the same taunting source. Adjusting his pillow, he said, "This place is made of Swiss cheese."

Warren's voice was sultry. "So's our apartment building, honey. That never stops you."

"Our apartment building is filled with other men, not women."

"Especially not ex-wife-type women."

"What does that have to do with the price of grass in Oregon?" He had chosen to match Warren's edgy sarcasm.

"Only that calling this particular woman an ex-wife seems more like calling your mother an ex-mother."

Bradley said coldly, "What in the hell do you presume to know about it."

"Only what I sense." The grin remained on Warren's face as if he'd forgotten to remove it; his dark eyes were opaque. "Did you come out to her or did she come out to you?"

Bradley answered grudgingly, "The latter."

"Were you surprised?"

"Look, just drop it."

Warren flopped onto his back. "Why, Brad?"

"I told you. The place is like a piece of fucking Swiss cheese." He rolled over onto his side, put an arm around Warren. "Just not now, okay? I'm tired."

Warren did not answer, but he tucked his head into the place along Bradley's biceps where he always did just before he slept.

Stroking a hand through Warren's hair, Bradley wished Warren would just stay away from this subject — it created turbulence in a relationship that contained enough roller coaster elements as it was. Warren loved him and he loved Warren — why go picking at scabs? Especially such painful scabs . . .

He closed his eyes, trying to comfort himself with Warren's body-warmth. It had been such incredible, astounding agony when Donnelly had turned to Pat Decker, and the pain hadn't had anything to do with the breakup of his marriage. His marriage hadn't been anything like the stories he'd heard about other gay men hiding out in a sham het relationship. Even though Donnelly could never possess the essence of him and she deserved much better, even though she must have felt the same way about her own marital deficiencies, their relationship had evolved beyond the surface connection of marriage.

Life in the Closet: an Ode, he thought wryly. Before he knew the truth of her, he had intuited a fundamental wrong about the two of them as a conventional couple, but Donnelly had covered up as well as he had. Better. If they had both passed as straight, marriage to so strong and willful a woman still cast doubt both on his masculinity and her femininity . . . Like being in a jungle with his face painted lavender, and with a wife whose face didn't fit in either.

But if they were the odd couple, they were acceptably odd to the world at large because they obeyed most of the heterosexual rules. To fully fit in with the heterosexuals, the production of children was the be all and end all... and he'd never suspected a thing when she suggested postponing this step. He'd felt only relief. And profound disappointment. He'd have loved a child, boy or girl, he didn't care which, to nurture, protect, cherish. But he just wasn't father material, he'd infect a child — not with his gayness but with the disconnectedness of his schizophrenic life. He'd hoped the same thing she did — that the clouds obscuring their future together would somehow lift...

Donnelly. He had supported her emotionally, but she was a woman adrift, and about that he could do nothing. Jobs came to her easily, and with her powers of observation, organization and leadership she quickly rose to positions of responsibility, but at some point she was rendered impotent, or there were sexual hassles, as if her male bosses would diminish, punish her feminine energy. Everything was pragmatism to Donnelly, and unlike him she could walk away from one job and into another without a look back, like an artist who never bothered to finish anything because the creation would inevitably be judged invalid.

Pat taking Donnelly from him had been devastating. Yes, he had had to see men on the side or he'd have lost his equilibrium, and over time God only knew what he might have done to Donnelly. But with the loss of her went a level of intimacy and trust and mutual support that he had never known with anybody, before or since.

Heterosexual marriage — fitting in, belonging, the inclusiveness — he had asked himself many times why had it not been enough, why it had not been worth settling for at the required price.

Being with a man was a powerful pastiche of wants

and hopes and inventions and wishes and unpredictabilities. A male relationship was invent your days, your partnership, your sexuality, your entire persona. It was feel your way with the male-to-male power shifts. And unless you bought into the judgment that the wholly different sexual and emotional dynamic of male-to-male union rendered it inferior, unnatural, tissue-disposable, it meant freedom. And he had finally — finally — stopped buying into the judgment. So why, unlike other gay men, did he not feel totally free?

Each morning of his life with Donnelly she had been his sun. And whatever the reason, he had never established that nourishing connection with anyone since. Maybe Donnelly leaving him for Pat Decker hadn't been Pat Decker's fault, but that didn't mean he didn't bear a brick load of antagonism to this very day . . .

Donnelly coming out to him, Warren wanted to know. No big deal, no dramatics, no fireworks. She had put it simply: *Brad, I finally understand some things about myself and I need to leave. I'm a lesbian.*

And he had said, *But you don't need to leave. I'm gay too.*

Oh my God, she had said as she embraced him, *everything makes such perfect sense now . . . But I still have to go. There's someone else. I've got some idea of a goal, finally, for my life.*

Warren sat up and asked, "Did you ever want kids with her?"

Ambushed by the question and his assumption that Warren had fallen asleep, he snarled, "Once and for all, shut the fuck up about my marriage."

Tears on My Pillow

Above the song on the radio Pat heard Warren's question, Bradley's snarling answer. Damn right he shouldn't talk about his marriage. All that misery for Donnelly before she finally found out about his lies, before Donnelly found her, they found each other. Misery must surely love company — how else to explain heterosexual marriage? Bradley and Donnelly had been a travesty.

Careful not to disturb the kitten which had curled up between her ankles, she shifted the pillow under her head, greeting the emotion that swept her with bitter familiarity, and grudging her concession that Bradley and Donnelly were no worse than herself and Jerry.

She might have been partly, just partly, to blame for her ignorance about marital relations — her mother had to hold a corner of that sack of guilt — but everybody, including her own mother, said a virgin didn't get pregnant on her wedding night. So who could blame her for attributing the non-appearance of a period to the nervous heebie-jeebies over living with Jerry?

After that obscene wedding night, the only reason she'd stayed with him, had cooked and cleaned for him, was that they were in a stand-off, he waiting patiently for her to come to her senses, she waiting for him to throw in the towel and join with her in quietly ending this farce so she could go to college and they could both go on to whatever else life held for them.

While they waited each other out, she missed her second period as well. And her third. In exasperation she consulted the unctuous nincompoop who was her family's doctor.

Dr. Jameson told her cheerfully, after poking around her stomach and vulva, "We'll have to wait for confirmation of the pregnancy test, but it's ninety-nine percent sure. Congratulations, Mrs. Eliott."

She'd always known the man was an incompetent fool. She reared to a sitting position on the examination table. "I can't possibly be," she informed him.

His Dr. Kildare face crinkled in a smile. "You are a married woman, Patsy."

There were a few things she hadn't bothered to tell him. "Look, I'm not staying married," she confessed awkwardly. "And we only — we did it once."

Jameson crossed his arms and contemplated her amiably. "I hope you don't believe that old chestnut about not getting pregnant the first time." He added in a kindly tone as hysteria bubbled up inside her, "Bride jitters are far more common than you'd think, Patricia. I have a daughter of my own to prove it. You better think again about what you really want to do."

She rode home on the bus in a maelstrom of panic. Whatever would she do? Abortion? Visions of eternal damnation in the hottest corner of hell, as promised by all the priests and nuns, loomed before her eyes. Never mind the hereafter, she decided, I'll go with the here and now. But how would she get an abortion? She didn't know anyone to ask. Her Catholic family? They'd help when the Pope turned Jewish. Free-thinking Monica Albert, where are you when I need you, she demanded of her mother's dead friend. She raised her eyes accusingly to heaven. All I ever ever asked, God, was just the chance to go to college . . .

She would abort herself. Somehow find out the way to do it . . .

But what if she died of hemorrhage, like Claudia Felstein? This, she decided in rising fury, was already the hottest corner of hell, she didn't need to die to get there.

By the time she reached the tiny house she and Jerry had rented, she was in a crazed, raging despair. Slamming the front door she screamed at Jerry, "Pregnant! You got me pregnant, you —"

"Pregnant? *Pregnant!*" He was so ecstatic he did not see her rage. So ecstatic she thought he would weep. He called both families, babbling the news. Her father was overjoyed. Her mother was reproachful: "I had to hear this from your husband?" Choked with fury at her mother's blame in all this, Pat could only shrug; if she opened her mouth she would howl.

But she told Jerry, "I still want to go to college, until I have this thing."

"Sure, get it out of your system," he offered expansively.

She retorted brutally, "This makes no difference, I'm still not having anything to do with you."

"I'll wait," was his rejoinder.

She understood with utter contempt the real cause for the delight of her proud husband. The truth of their marriage had been belied by a pregnancy which gave visible proof that Jerry Eliott had lead in his pencil. He was a real man.

For the next five months she took refuge on the campus of Cal State, in her classes and in her work at the college bookstore. At home she was sullen with hatred for the omnipresent Jerry and the creature he had forced into her — a parasite that took sustenance from her body and would soon cannibalize her entire life.

Mark Daniel. Seven pounds, six ounces. Born after a fourteen-hour escalation of pain so extreme she could scarcely believe it possible. When she awakened from her exhausted sleep, it was to a nurse placing Mark Daniel in her arms, and the feel of his fine hair, the sweet smell of his skin, seemed to bore into the very core of her exposed, vulnerable senses. Dark-haired and perfect, he burbled his joy at being in the world and in her arms. And after she took him home, he was still joyful over her protection of him, seldom finding any cause for tears.

I'll make a deal, she whispered into the warmth of his rotund body that first week of his life, *we'll do it your way for a while and then I'll find a way to go back to college.*

Two weeks after he was born, getting up for his 2:00 A.M. feeding. Reaching into his crib. Knowing in a heartbeat when she saw his still body, before she even touched him. Before even seeing his blue face. The scream from Jerry's throat, when she mauled him awake, surrogate for the one she could not emit from her own.

"I have to ask you these questions," the police officer told her, the expression on his lined, weary face hardening and softening with his wavering between sympathy and suspicion.

She answered the questions numbly, emotionlessly. But later when the harshly sobbing Jerry demanded of her, "Did you do anything. You didn't want Mark —" she flew at him, everything gone from her mind except the intention to gouge out the accusation in his eyes and exterminate him from this earth.

The day after the tiny white coffin was lowered into the earth, she walked out of the rented house, and her marriage, with the granite determination of forever.

Her mother said nothing. All her father said was, "I might have known this would happen."

Living in a cheap furnished room, working full time as a waitress, she'd managed after a couple of months to go back to college. She put herself through, her attainment of her goal sullied by the cancerous gnawing:

Had her wish for an abortion, then her resentment of her son while he was in her womb — her wish that he were dead — led to his death?

To this day there had been no equivalent guilt. No pain like that of her child's birth and his death. No one had any inkling, except Donnelly.

She buried her face in her pillow to blot her scalding tears. To this day she still knew in the core of her the feel of his fine hair, and his smell . . .

She lifted her head and howled into the darkness of the cabin, *"Turn down that fucking radio!"*

The kitten leaped from the bed. The radio was switched off.

Sunday
September 29, 1991

Stop in the
Name of Love

Sipping from her wine glass, Averill gazed out the window from her armchair, hoping for a glimpse of Angela who had gone off with Querida and Warren. She had no interest in being with them, in kicking pine cones or whatever silly juvenile thing the three of them would find to do. And her wrist had begun to ache in all this damp cold. Lifting the wrist to flex it, she glanced at her Rolex — won, she unfailingly remembered, for closest-to-the-pin at Firestone, hardly your pattycake golf course. Twenty after two... God, how the time was dragging. Would this business never end? She would give Donnelly till seven, no later, and she and Angela were out of here.

If for no other reason than because she was hungry. Toast and orange juice, the only edibles in this miserable place, and the orange juice barely passable Peoria from a frozen can. People were so stupid about what they put in their bodies. Bacon and eggs — you might as well eat a dish of nitrates and cholesterol. And lunch no better — greasy hamburgers and potato chips. How disappointing that Angela, who knew better, wolfed down the toxins just like everybody else.

Averill again flexed her wrist. The surgery on the tendon had been what, three years ago ... A complete recovery, all the doctors asserted, but it hurt enough for doubt to surface, even if Steinberg was the country's best sports injury surgeon. Not that she'd been hurt much overall, a little knee trouble, but not like some other players with their shoulder and elbow breakdowns. Blessed, she'd been blessed by inheriting Daddy's compact build instead of Mom's willowy frame. Everybody thought golfers — any athlete — should be big and tall, especially women, given the ratio of their strength to men's, but big and tall weren't advantages in golf, the legs and hips generated the power. A tall body meant more hazards in the swing — more elements to go out of whack.

The wrist ached just enough to taunt her about her professional life-expectancy. Not that she needed any reminding. Nobody had learned about mortality, how precarious a pro athlete's future could be, under stranger circumstances than she ...

Way back when she was fifteen. Oasis Golf Club, number thirteen hole, a narrow, punishing par five with a dogleg right. Her tantrum over the well-planned, perfectly executed second shot that bounced off a hard sand rut and out of bounds. Too furious to care about the groundskeeper, a slim, bearded young man in khaki shorts watching her from the shady intersection of greens sixteen and thirteen, she'd slammed her three iron against a scrub tree and then stormed on to card an eight and from there to play the next two holes execrably. That was when the man limped down the middle of number sixteen, making her wait on the tee, baked in early spring sun, raging with impatience for this nitwit to get out of her line. But he did not stop until his face, deeply sunburned through his beard, was inches from hers.

"What's the *matter* with you?" The disgust in his dark eyes seared her. "Anybody your age, a swing like yours, hit shots like you hit 'em, you got no complaints. *None.*"

Indignation replaced her aggravation at being accosted by this lunatic. "No complaints? This *dogpatch* of a golf course —"

"Kid, you got a lot to learn," he snapped. "This ain't Pebble Beach, it's a bone-dry desert course. Course condition's part of the game. Every sport's got some kind of wild card — like bad officiating in football. Real pros pull up their socks and go on about their business. But we're talkin' *real* pros here, not a head case like you."

Who *was* this jerk? "Look, you —"

"You look." He backed away, but only to shake a misshapen index finger in her face. "You're friggin' lucky, Miss Hothead. I had a big future in this game, got a leg and hand shot to hell in Vietnam. You need to work on yourself. Control your head, you'll own this game. Work hard enough, you'll be on the tour."

"Me? On the tour?" Her laugh was incredulous. He might as well have suggested that she drop in on Richard Nixon at the White House.

"For Christ's sweet sake," he muttered to himself, and then, hands on his hips, demanded, "You ever watch any pro golf?"

"Not much," she admitted. It was too hard to; her father watched televised sports including bowling, but golf on TV, he avowed, was worse than watching the grass grow.

"For chrissake whatever you do get yourself over to Palm Springs next week for the Colgate. That swing of yours — you can be as good as any of 'em."

He moved away from her, then limped back, stuck out a callused hand. "Hollings, Gene Hollings," he said, his grip brief but exceedingly painful. "Get hold of yourself and hit the ball good from here on in. Even with that triple on thirteen, you can finish with eighty-one."

And she had. And only later realized that since he knew her score, he had watched her entire round.

She had used her every wile on her father to wrangle permission to go with a group from the Club to the Dinah Shore. One look at Alcott and Whitworth and Haney and Carner and all of them, and their nerveless precision performance in front of all those spectators, had been like flame. Had told her what her future might be. From that time on she gave her life over to the resolve to one day play with those bronzed, beautiful, magical beings.

"Takes one hell of a lot more than talent to play this game," Hollings had told her when she went back and found him. "Takes knowing you're responsible for every single shot. Not the fairway, not the greens, not the golf course — you. *You're responsible.* That's what Mickey Wright always told herself and if it's good enough for her it's friggin' well good enough for you."

Hollings. Her first coach and her best coach. Dead six years later, he'd been dying of lymphoma the day she met him. But he'd taught her the greatest lessons, about using everything she had, and most of all, valuing every second of time given to her as a competitive player. So many golfers had greater gifts than hers, they thought they didn't have to work as hard as she did. She could only shake her head. They wouldn't see their mistake till their skills eroded, and then the train would be too far gone from the station. Martina was proof, Martina was a good tennis player who'd have ended up a good tennis player except she got smart enough soon enough to let two great athletes coach her, and Sandra Haynie and Nancy Lieberman had carved out the disciplined athlete and fierce competitor that was in her...

Herself, everybody always marveled at how she could stand over a putt on number eighteen with a whole tournament and a monster amount of money on the table, with thousands of people ringing the green and millions watching on television, and put the ball in the center of the hole. Everybody carried on about how she blew apart at the JAL Classic and came back the next week to win the U.S. Open. But she'd been playing good at New Rochelle, she'd lost her concentration, was all, and a week later got it back in full measure. A champion player — you heard the crowd when you had the game in the bag, otherwise you shut out everything, *everything* to focus down the channel of what you needed to do. You had to sight down it like it was torpedo alley and your very life depended on pulling out your total best. It was you and the golf course and nothing else.

People didn't understand. Out there on that proving ground, performing at that level, you didn't need anything else. You were playing a sublime game, no two shots ever alike, every shot needing to be planned, calculated, finessed. Strategy, strength, judgment, courage, patience, determination — it took it all, and it took more ferocious concentration than anyone could ever imagine, even the most dedicated amateur out there, and that's what separated the champions from everyone else. Championship golf was aggressive and cunning and gentle, it was strong and delicate, tender and artful. It was making love with the most capricious, unpredictable, endlessly fascinating lover, the most wonderful lover in the world . . .

She stirred in her chair. She just wanted to give Donnelly whatever she wanted and get the Topeka out of here, get back to what she loved. Donnelly could go on and fight her battle over this Assembly Bill she was so exercised about . . .

More Than a Woman

Pat tossed two logs onto the fire from the basket of wood she had replenished from the pile stacked under the deck. Smoothing goose bumps of chill from her arms, she glanced at her watch. Three-ten.

With Angela, Warren and Querida bundled up in whatever jackets they'd found in the guest closet, and outside strolling around the wintry landscape, peace had descended. But the cabin seemed empty in Angela's absence. Warren, Pat was certain, would now be trying to pass around a joint. She hoped Angela wasn't any part of that scene.

Watching Averill sit motionless in an armchair gazing out the window, Pat saw how easily Angela could be blinded, just as Donnelly was, by this woman's looks and money and fame. The woman, nothing but gorgeous in that royal blue jogging suit, had it all. But she was vacant as an elevator shaft. All this time, she had yet to display interest in anything but her wine glass, had yet to express the simplest curiosity about anybody's past or future, had yet to ask a question or make a comment beyond what was occurring at this moment in this room. Ask about her golfing career, though, and she'd rotate to you like a flower opening its face to the sun. With

Querida finally seeing she'd glean nothing about the tour beyond Averill's PR answers, the questions had all but ceased, and Averill had become, per usual, a potted plant.

Bradley, thankfully, had been quiet all this day, sprawled out on the carpet just like yesterday and writing on his clipboard, manuscript pages fanned out all around him in nice neat stacks. And he was decently dressed for a change, in normal pants and a white sweatshirt that looked clean if a bit scruffy. The only time he and Averill seemed to budge at all was when Donnelly, upstairs, raised her voice to somebody on the phone. She'd been conducting business by phone this entire day.

The phone. Everybody exclaiming over the two phones in the place because they were the old-fashioned black ones with a rotary dial. If her mother hadn't seen fit to change them, she wasn't about to, either.

Pat became aware that she was surveying this room just as she had a month ago when she unlocked the cabin with keys that had passed from her mother to her. Remarkable, she thought again, that so many things remained unchanged in all the years she had not come here. Like the pine cones stacked in the basket near the fire as kindling, yet no one ever used them except her mother, because everyone knew she had not simply collected but chosen them — for their beauty or oddity of shape; for color, or the lack of it; for pristine newness, or the distinctive stains of age.

For the first time since this cabin had become a part of her memory, Pat found herself, in a coalescing of unease, totaling up what she looked at. On the mantel, the ivory carving of a bird just launching itself into flight — the first object her mother had placed in the row of knickknacks she had accumulated over the years. Next the kitschy snow-filled globe of a skier coming down a mountain; then a fine glass boat speeding over a blue slate sea; then a stylized giraffe with its long neck raised over a fence. In Pat's absence, three other objects had been added: a tiny silver cage holding an even tinier monkey; a blank-faced woman in colonial garb imprisoned with her hands held in stocks; a miniature doll, dressed in lace, laid in a filigreed china box.

The three paintings on the wall had not changed: the woman in the golden robe was still seated on the rocks overlooking a cerulean sea; a ship with only its fat brown stern visible continued to hang, ready to vanish, over a dazzling horizon. And two women runners strained to break the tape as winner, their legs airborne in perfect synchrony.

Pat did not know how long she had looked at the objects, enveloped in her daze, only that Donnelly, in black jeans and a gray sweatshirt with a faded logo of some long-ago gay pride festival, came down the steep staircase into the living room, empty coffee mug in hand.

"Come here for a second," Pat said urgently. Ignoring Bradley and Averill who had looked up, Pat took her by the arm. "Look at the stuff in this room."

"It's quite interesting," Bradley said.

Her full-watt glare silenced and returned him to his clipboard. She gestured to the objects on the mantel, the walls. The answer seemed astoundingly clear — she needed Donnelly to corroborate it. Pat said to her, "Tell me if you think they mean anything." Donnelly moved to the mantel, touched a fingertip to the bird, the skier, the boat, the giraffe; she gestured to the three paintings. "Freedom," she said. Her hand hovered over the monkey in the cage, the colonial woman in the stocks, the doll in its box. "Prison," she said.

Numbly, Pat nodded. "It's what I see, too." Every one of these images placed in this house — the one possession

to which her mother held clear title — had so obviously
signaled her yearning for freedom, her despair . . .

Pain pressed in around her heart. Why had she never
seen clues to any of this before? Why had her mother
let her life fade to a close without ever saying a
revealing word to her own daughter?

As if Pat had asked the question aloud, Donnelly said
quietly, "If she saw her married life as a prison, the
direction of your life must have seemed a complete
disaster." Picking up the globe holding the skier, she
upended it, sending its snow swirling. "Maybe she never
knew what to say or do. Maybe she blamed herself.
Maybe giving you this cabin was the only way she had
of saying whatever she couldn't say to you."

Replacing the skier on the mantel, squeezing Pat's
shoulder, Donnelly went into the kitchen to get more
coffee.

Through blurred eyes Pat saw that Bradley sat writing
on his clipboard as if he had not heard a word. And
once more Averill had become a potted plant.

Holding the globe, upending it again and again, Pat
let herself remember the late summer Sunday when
Matthew first brought Emily home. The Sunday almost
exactly a year after the end of her marriage, when she
was going to college and living in a furnished room just
off campus, and had returned, by rare invitation, to her
parents' house for dinner.

With the backyard barbecue adding to the sweltering
temperature, Emily, fresh and cool in a pale rose
shirtwaist dress, bloomed against the desiccated horizon
of San Bernardino. How could this dainty young woman
with a tinkling laugh as light and lovely as a bird's trill,
with graceful little hands and feet and daisy-white skin
and a heart-shaped face softly capped by curly dark hair,
with a light sprinkling of pale freckles across her

cheekbones and those brush-stroke-fine eyebrows and pale delicate lips — how could this exquisite creature possibly be interested in her oafish brother?

"It's nice to meet you," Emily had said to Pat, giving her her soft small hand. "I've seen you several times in the library."

Pat had nodded mutely. How could she possibly have not noticed in return this enchantress?

After dinner, with Matthew gone to escort Emily home, Pat's father laughed over Matthew's left-footed shyness around Emily, not having noticed that his quiet wife had been uncharacteristically animated in the young woman's sweet presence. If Pat could not quite fathom her mother's behavior, she knew that lurking just below the surface of her brother's lurching clumsiness was the full capacity to trumpet ownership of Emily the moment the young woman allowed herself to be formally linked with him.

And if Pat could not for the life of her see what Emily saw in Matthew, neither could Matthew understand what Emily saw in Pat — because from that first meeting, having discovered that they shared a fondness for movies and long walks, Emily had pursued her for those activities, had befriended her.

Her brother for the first time treated Pat with deference. Emily's delight in her friendship with Pat — she spent more time with Pat than she did with Matthew — brought her that much closer to him. But he watched with vulnerable eyes, in unspoken disquiet. As did her mother, who took to phoning Pat to share her anxiety at how insensibly in love Matthew had fallen. The two of them needn't have worried. She was as careful around Emily as she would be around a hummingbird. Or a nun.

Emily was a smorgasbord of moods. Mischievous, fun-loving, filled with amusing stories of her new secretarial job at the local Ford dealership, she entertained Pat endlessly, relating her anecdotes with such droll exaggeration that Pat felt as if she had composed and rehearsed them especially for her. And sometimes Emily fell so broodingly silent that Pat would feel with dismal certainty that Emily had finally grown bored with her — until Emily looked at her again and smiled, and sometimes reached to her and stopped Pat's breathing with a brief, soft touch.

She so adored Emily that she virtually trembled in fear of revealing her feeling to her brother's beloved. If there was a chance to have Emily as a sister-in-law she must do nothing to frighten her, nothing to drive her away from her brother — or herself.

In the end, it didn't matter. It had never mattered.

Late one night — also a Sunday night — Emily came to her, in her furnished room. Entered the room, entered her astonished arms.

"Are you sure," Pat had falteringly managed.

In answer, Emily, eyes closed, raised her face and her pale, delicate lips for Pat's kiss.

And that night she became the sweetest, softest, tenderest, gentlest lover Pat had ever known. That night she opened every soft, warm, delicate, honeyed part of herself to rapturous fulfillment, to Pat's full possession, her endless adoration.

That night. The only night. The last time Pat would ever see her.

Two days later Emily vanished, without explanation, but with the promise to permanently banish herself from her own family if they revealed her whereabouts.

Matthew, his eyes as dull and dark as a slaughtered cow's, knew, without needing a shred of corroborating evidence. Pat's family all knew. And had not spoken to her from that day to this . . .

Pat walked outside the cabin, onto the side deck, needing to breathe. Bathed by the crisp air, she leaned on the deck railing and gazed into the pine trees stretching off to the peaceful distance. Her quiet mother had retired here, inarticulate with her own griefs. Longing for her own hopeless dreams, for freedom from the path her own life had taken. And she had sent the only message she could, by bequeathing the one possession clearly hers, to the daughter who had fled to freedom.

Stayin' Alive

Donnelly came out of the kitchen, coffee mug in hand. "The veto will be announced any time now," she said. Scanning the faces of Bradley and Averill for response, she smiled wryly and went on upstairs.

Bradley knew he had not absorbed her words. Still smarting from Pat's feral dismissal of him in front of Donnelly and Averill, he was angrier with himself than with her for his insensitivity, for barging into so highly personal an interchange with Donnelly. And for the memories surfacing about his own particular drama set into motion when Donnelly had left him ... but, probably, now that he thought about it, dating from well before then.

The first big shock had come five years into his time at Melrose High School in the Los Angeles Unified School District ...

To this day he was proud of the reputation he'd built as an instructor with excellent student-colleague relationships — Mr. Wonderful to his students, a young teacher with the kind of casual, daring irreverence for the sacred cows of literature that he knew adolescents would love, and in the process, few would particularly notice how much they were absorbing about books and writers and ideas.

He and history teacher Rothstein knew instinctively about each other, and protected themselves by ignoring each other. Norman Finlay, fortunately, seemed immersed in conveying his passion for music to his students, oblivious to both Bradley and Rothstein. Fraternization would have been death — would have given too much information to be added up.

From the start he'd had brush-ups with gay kids — as if he gave off some essence to them, like an oyster. The supplicants all boys with one exception, a plump, guileless lesbian suffering emotional assault from her peer group, they approached obliquely, edgily, but angling for any contact, anything to alleviate their anguish, their confusion. They were all of them emotionally brutalized, often caged like criminals by their families, forbidden all activities except school, given society-sanctioned beatings at home, peer-sanctioned beatings in the schoolyard — like fey little Mitchell Howe from his own boyhood. Sometimes they were forced, like Colin, to see priests or to endure treatment and drugs from psychiatrists.

To ignore their torment was to ignore someone torn and bleeding on a highway. Yet, what could he do? Refer them, God help them, to the dried up old prune of a school nurse? Talk to them? They were kids, they were jail bait. Any support, any positive advice aside from his usual mumble of "Things'll get better when you get older" would jeopardize his entire future. The fact was, if he *could* say something to them, what advice, what hope, what anything, could he give? If the best they could be told was to lead a secretive and furtive life like his, what did that do for them? The one and only empowering thing he could do was to preach tolerance in the classroom, in any unsubtle way he could — like choosing *To Kill a Mockingbird* as a major text in his literature classes. But for these nascent gay kids it was administering aspirin for gangrene.

He had been smart enough to sniff out Denny Coughlin, whose need to constantly show off his priapic heterosexuality to every female within eyeshot was exceeded by his hunger to tear out the jugular of anyone who hinted at uncertainty, insecurity, and, more than anything, Denny's ultimate aphrodisiac, fear. The fucking little prick was very careful around him, seeming to pick up intimations of Bradley's seething anger, seeming to realize that if he tried anything he'd get his swaggering little balls ripped off.

If Bradley knew better than to give the little shit any kind of unwitnessed opportunity alone with him, music teacher Finlay had not.

Poor trusting Finlay. A bachelor aesthete who'd locked himself away from everything except his teaching career and his books and his two Persian cats. He'd gotten himself maneuvered into "a counseling session" with Denny and the rest of the boys hadn't had the nerve to do anything but pile on Denny's accusations of sexual molestation and agree that Finlay was a strange-acting weirdo who looked at them funny.

Tied securely to the stake, Finlay called Bradley at home, which Bradley appreciated; it would have endangered him had Finlay singled him out at school. "I didn't do a thing," he whispered, "not a thing."

"Appeal," Bradley had told him in tight-lipped futility.

"You know it'll get into the papers. I can't do it to my family. Addison's telling me if I upset the parents, the district will..." He did not finish.

"Norman, what will you do?"

"I don't know. I can't teach again..."

Two weeks after Finlay was gone, Ronnie Galbraith, one of the gay students, hanged himself. In the two days it took for the shock to wear off and for life to continue as usual, there was no mention of Ronnie's sexual identity among the faculty or the student body, only subdued comments that "poor Ronnie" had always been "withdrawn," had acted "weird."

And shortly after that, John Briggs qualified Proposition Six for the ballot, an initiative that mandated the dismissal of homosexual teachers. Bradley couldn't argue, couldn't fight, couldn't so much as speak against it — not if he valued his career.

To hell, he decided, with fucking all of it.

His mother and brother had been incredulous. His father had gone berserk. *You got no kids, no responsibility, you finally made something out of yourself, you're pissing it all away? You fucking moron, you do this, I'll kick your ass all the way to skid row.*

Donnelly told him: "Whatever you need to do, Brad, I trust you, I support you."

In his last moments as a teacher, he said to his last class of fifteen-year-olds, a class which included Denny Coughlin, "You all knew Norman Finlay..." As he paused, they all watched him without so much as a fidget. "He had no way of defending himself, and now...now he's out of teaching and nothing will bring him back."

He repeated, "You all knew Norman Finlay. You all know his accuser. And the trustworthiness of his accuser." He looked directly at Denny Coughlin, whose pale blue eyes had narrowed into ice chips. "I know in my heart what was done to him was wrong. I wonder how many of you know in your own heart the same thing I know."

It had been intended as a rhetorical statement, and

he was astonished to receive a reply: a few hands raised, joined by a few more, until virtually everyone's hand was up except for Denny Coughlin's.

Bradley pushed on. "I wonder how many of you truly believe that he was guilty of anything other than being different."

Denny's hand waved in forceful affirmation, and he turned and glared until two other hands were raised in support and then quickly lowered.

"What was done to Norman Finlay is a crime," Bradley stated to his class of teenagers. "All of us who believed that and didn't speak up are accomplices. Including me. Including you."

"You're a dead man, fag face," Denny Coughlin said softly from his seat.

For the first time in his teaching life, for the first time in his entire life as a man, Bradley knew the exhilaration of being totally without fear. And knew that the feeling might never come again. He smiled at Denny, his smile widening and widening as Denny stared at him. "Not me, punk. Not today." And he stared until Denny got up and walked out, under the eyes of a peer group who regarded him with the pitiless judgment that only adolescents can render.

Leaving Melrose High School that day, Bradley understood that he had abandoned a crucial battlefield. Whether in his time on that battlefield he had ever made an iota of difference with anything he had ever said or done, he would never know. He was certain of only two things: that more gay kids would kill themselves and more Dennys would walk around freely, as sanctioned, card-carrying gaybashers.

The words Donnelly had spoken before she climbed the ladder finally penetrated: *The veto will be announced any time now.*

Bradley heard footsteps on the deck. Warren and the others had returned.

He looked down at the manuscript pages surrounding him. *I was forced to abandon the profession I loved. Donnelly has to be wrong...Wilson has to sign that bill. He has to.*

I Hear a Symphony

"Is something wrong?" Angela asked Pat.

"No," Pat answered softly. "Not really."

Querida, hanging her borrowed jacket in the closet near the door, had also noticed that Pat's face seemed altered by some emotion, but she did not know Pat well enough to hazard a guess as to what it might be. But Pat's pleasure at Angela's return had been transparent enough, and also the extinguishing of that pleasure when Angela went over and bent to Averill's embrace, touching a brief kiss to her forehead.

Even if Angela were not coupled with Averill, Querida thought sympathetically, no one could compete, not with what Averill had to offer. Too bad. If you could navigate your way beyond all the trappings, the woman was really pretty boring.

Querida sat on the sofa and watched Warren, perched beside Bradley on the floor, begin to scoop up all the manuscript pages. Bradley flailed in horror until he understood that Warren was only pretend-scrambling them; then he lay back on an elbow, grinning foolishly.

"Where's the kitten?" Angela asked, searching around her.

"Right here," Bradley said, sitting up to rumple

Warren's sleeve as Warren carefully restacked the manuscript.

"In the kitchen having a bit of milk," Pat replied.

Donnelly came down the staircase. *"Buenas tardes, mi belleza,"* she said to Querida. "Good walk, sweetie?"

"Hi. Yeah," Querida answered, wishing Donnelly would cool it right down till they got out from under the scrutiny of all these ex-lovers.

Donnelly sat beside her. "I forgot to ask, did you hear from Denise?"

Querida smiled. Speaking of ex-lovers. "Thursday," she said. "She's mulling over the latest company offer. Wouldn't tell me what it was, but she's pretty damn gratified, you could tell that from her voice. She needs to decide if she wants to come back to the company. I guess you know Hampton from Lambda Legal Defense contacted me about a deposition."

Donnelly nodded. "I think their involvement got your company off the dime."

Pat inquired, "What's all this about?"

"A story with a very happy ending, Pat," Donnelly interjected before Querida could answer.

Querida said, "A lesbian I worked with. She was in the closet, about a year ago another woman accused her of sexual harassment. The company fired her."

She paused, absorbed by the varied reactions of the people in the room. Warren with his shrug of what's new; Angela shaking her head, Bradley's lips tightening almost to whiteness, the creases in Pat's strong face seeming to deepen to crevasses. Averill did not react at all except to stare at Angela.

"She sued and won," Donnelly said, picking up the story. "No corroboration and no company policy, written or otherwise, just the same old crap, a company thinking a gay employee would slide quietly out the door." She continued with animation, "Not a shred of documentation the woman ever said anything to Denise or anyone else before she made her complaint —"

"None needed back in my day," Pat growled.

"Mine either," Bradley muttered.

Querida said, "All Denise ever did was trust this woman with telling her she's a lesbian."

"You see?" Averill said to Donnelly. "You see what can happen when you do that, when you trust anybody with that."

"You also see," Donnelly said to her, "what happens when we stop letting other people use it against us." She said to Querida, "Tell them about it."

Deciding to ignore the cross-currents in this room, Querida related, "A company lawyer interviewed me. Asked my opinion of Denise as a supervisor." She grinned. "I said she was fabulous, I was totally in awe of her."

Only Donnelly knew what she would not tell the rest of them, that this had all occurred exactly eight days into a love affair begun after her very first sexual experience with the fired Denise Waterman.

The phone call had come on a day Querida had been out of the office on assignment. "A word to the wise..." Denise's voice so low and calm that Querida knew she was under maximum control. "I just got canned. Melanie said I came on to her."

"*Melanie?*" Melanie, who had so often proclaimed the virtue of tolerance?

"I was so happy about... things, it just came out of my mouth that I was gay, I never intended it — but I thought I could trust her. She walked out of my office and right into Bible Bruce's."

Querida groaned. The born-again general manager. I'd trust Melanie too, Querida thought in consternation. She seemed so honest, so accepting... "Why on earth —"

"I asked. She said —" She raised her voice in falsetto mimicry: " 'It isn't right for people like you to get in the face of decent people.' "

Querida said faintly, "What about all this tolerance stuff?"

"I asked about that, too. Melanie means you can belong to any religion you want."

"Oh for —"

Denise said sharply, "Let it go, Querida. Protect yourself. Don't worry about me."

"You can forget about *that*," she had told Denise.

Querida said to her audience in the cabin, "The company lawyers wanted to know if she'd ever come on to me."

"Ooooh!" Warren said sarcastically.

"How did you handle it?" Angela asked. She sat on the cushions by the fire, the kitten in her lap.

"After I got over being so furious I could hardly talk..." Querida paused, feeling anger renew itself in a flame spreading across her nerve ends.

Thanks to Denise's warning phone call, she had worked through her panic, her paranoia — and had also consulted with several other women in the office.

"I asked Peterson if this was the same kind of homosexual witchhunt they did in the military." She nodded at Bradley's hearty chuckle of approval. "He huffed up and said they were just investigating an employee complaint, nothing more. So I said why the fuck didn't they investigate the two *written* complaints from the personnel secretary about Roy Costello, and I could corroborate that he'd hit on me, too, and there were all those other employee complaints about three other touchy-feely supervisors — and would he like to hear my own complaints about every guy who'd come on to me. Peterson got up and said thanks for my time."

"Hey, sister," said Warren.

Angela said, "It's easier now, isn't it. There's the city ordinance —"

"It has no teeth," Bradley pointed out. "A misdemeanor with a tap-on-the-fingernail fine."

"Still, it's there, it's a legal sanction —"

"It's taken a year," Querida told her. "The company let Denise go through all the legal shit, tried to pile her legal bills to the moon to see if they could wear her down. Lambda Legal Defense came in —"

"It's why we need AB 101," Donnelly said.

Warren asked, "What would you have done if Denise had actually gone after the woman?"

Fainted from shock and then murdered her, Querida thought. She said, "Anybody harassing a subordinate should be fired. But don't just go after gay people."

She still thought about Denise. Yes, she was happy with Donnelly, but Denise . . . What might have happened had their relationship not been so immediately stunted, had all of Denise's emotional resources not been poured into her rage at the company, into the bunker mentality necessary for a court battle with corporate America?

What happened to Denise, and to Denise and her, was a crime.

Chances Are

Focusing her gaze on Angela, Pat stroked the kitten.

All these memories dredged up in these last two days — she'd put everything behind her years ago, had gotten on with her life, as the popular jargon put it. But this cabin with the ghost of her mother hovering here, these particular people here, had opened it all up again. Not all for the bad, she would concede. The perspective of the years did alter the meaning of it all.

Like the dream last night. If you could call that flashing image from a past so long dead a dream. Those pale blue eyes filled with pity that came out of confident, triumphant contempt. In the dream Smithson had silently tossed down on his desk the necklace of her mother and a pair of trousers from her father, and said, *I have to give you these.*

Talk about dream symbols. Not even close to what he'd actually tossed down. Or actually said.

She could, all these years later, exactly envision his shambles of an office stacked with orders files. She had been called in there, told to shut the door.

He wore his suit jacket, a concession he made for only the gravest of occasions, and she had been puzzling about that when he said, "Dumb, Patsy. All you ever had to do was behave yourself."

Seated across from him she had said in genuine bewilderment, "Larry, what are you talking about?"

When he handed her a check and said, "Your severance pay," she simply stared at him in incomprehension.

He sighed, rolled his eyes. "I knew it, I knew it, I told Nate you'd do a Bette Davis." He reached into his drawer, dumped out onto the desk surface a photograph and a typed letter.

Numbly, she reached for them. He spread both hands over them. "Just look, don't touch."

That brought words from her in an angry gush. "Jesus Christ, what do you think I'm going to do with them?"

"Just look, don't touch," he repeated.

And so she got up from the chair and peered at the photo, leaned over to scan the letter. She was no further enlightened. "Okay, the photo's from the company Christmas party. The letter's from Betty's personnel file."

He tapped the picture with a blunt forefinger. "You got your arm around her."

Shit. Oh Christ. "Everybody's picture was taken that way. She wanted her picture taken with me. The letter's a formal acknowledgment of her help on the Benson account."

Betty had flirted with her, Pat had enjoyed the flirtation. Nothing more. She knew better than to ever have anything in the office, especially with a curious heterosexual woman.

She pointed to the photo and said in desperation, "Look, she's smiling!"

He shook his head and picked up the letter. "First paragraph, last line: 'Our association on this matter shows what can be possible.' Third paragraph, first line: " 'We have much potential as a team.' She says your letter gave her the creeps."

"I've never been the least bit—" She stopped to rephrase. "Every word in that letter refers to business. This is ridiculous. You're taking her word about this crazy accusation?"

He sat back. "Helen says it's true, you tried her, too. You know Betty, if we don't do something about it— she'll take this to headquarters."

The distance in his eyes was like watching a roadside scene vanishing in a rearview mirror. She was suddenly shouting as if it were the only way she could possibly be heard. "Betty's after my job! Helen hates my guts! They've cooked this up between them!"

He was only momentarily startled. He shrugged. "Another conspiracy, just like Kennedy." He raised both hands as she stepped toward him in outrage. "Look, you do like women, right?"

Never, never had she been asked the question. Never had she thought about an answer. Hadn't had to. She'd played the dress game, always worn their uniform, smart suits with skirts, stockings and pumps, the whole getup.

So what if she looked like a dyke. Walked like a dyke. In the macho building supply business, a dyke was an excusable presence in this 1970s world where businesswomen were despised, but mandates had come down from on high to hire them or else. Better to deal with a non-woman, as she was viewed, than some lipsticked fluffball that would make any of them look like an asshole if he actually had to pay attention and do something she said. At least Patsy Decker was a good old pseudo-boy. Amid this tacit understanding her being a dyke had been a non-issue. Until now. Now, suddenly, she had to dive into a bunker. Like a fool, she had trusted them. Like a fool, she had been ambushed.

"None of your goddamned business," she hissed through lips narrowed with fury at the betrayal of her trust and at her own naiveté.

He sat back, loosened his tie. "Look, Patsy, I'm not an unreasonable man."

In final price dealings with their suppliers, just as he was about to issue a ruinous ultimatum, he always loosened his tie, always sat back and said he was a reasonable man. "Patsy, for all I know, you could be telling me God's truth about Betty and Helen cooking this up." He spread his hands, a gesture she also knew too well. "But look at it from where I sit. Employees complain about you making a pass, I got no choice about this kind of... It's all over the office about you, even the customers know."

"Get Betty in here. I have a right to confront—"

He slammed a hand on the desk. "The hell you do. This ain't a courtroom. She made a complaint, it's all out in the open, you can't expect people here to want to work for you anymore." He picked up the envelope, held it out to her.

"Larry," she said, appalled by the finality of the white envelope with her name typed in black, "I've been here nineteen years —" Then she broke off. "God, that's it. Another three months, I'll be vested in the pension plan."

"That's bullshit!" he screamed. Another tactic she knew — false rage. He put down the envelope, loosened his tie further. "It's got nothing to do with the timing. Remember how Harrison had a heart attack a month before she retired? We still paid something to the family. You're a spring chicken, Patsy, you'll get another job easy —"

"This is age discrimination," she seethed. God, how she hated him. "Sex discrimination —"

"Not a chance." He snapped off the words. "For somebody else, it could be. Not you." And then he looked at her with the comfortable, pitying moral superiority of someone who owned the high ground without any possibility of losing it, and as if she were something under a rock exposed to sunlight.

"Let's call a spade a spade." He chuckled. "You'd be a hell of a lot better off right now if you were a spade. But the law don't cover people like you. Not yet and not ever, not in this Christian country. And that's all that matters."

He put the envelope on the desk, tapped a finger on it. "You get yourself another job, Patsy. We can work on why you left here and I'll give you a good recommendation. You raise any shit over this, I'll tell a different story. Now take this check and clean out your desk."

She said faintly, "I'm going straight to the EEOC —"

"Fine. Screw yourself. You decide. You give me crap, I'll give you crap. You'll never get a decent job in this town again."

She seized the envelope, stalked from the office, slamming the door.

And collapsed outside the office, sagging back against the wall, her legs betraying her.

And heard Larry on the phone. "The dyke just left. Make sure you watch her, see she cleans out her desk and gets the hell outta here." There was a pause. "Nah. Piece of cake."

She had not stopped to clean out her desk. One look at the secretary outside Larry's office, who sat with her face averted, had extinguished that possibility.

Two days later she had received a box filled with her belongings, with Betty's name as the sender.

The Way We Were

Pat stirred in her recliner. That Streisand song... 1974.

The year when everybody lost their jobs. Nixon. Golda Meir. Haile Selassie. Pat Decker.

The year Patty Hearst found herself picking up a gun and Pat Decker found herself doing nothing, except awaken each morning to exile from the place whose flow and pace had become, over nineteen years, her breath and heartbeat, whose walls and furniture and colors and smells were ingrained like her own fingerprints. No longer surrounded by people whose actions and reactions shaped and formed her days, no longer performing the work that both galvanized her and used up everything in her.

The year her energy lost its channel and each morning she could not believe everything was gone. Could not believe she was no longer in charge of a staff whose commitment and confidence and performance she had built, could not believe she would no longer organize and direct them, solve their problems and cheer their triumphs and meet their every challenge to her authority and ability. Could not believe she would no longer stride through the sales office that was hers, could not believe it had all been a chimera, that the staff whose loyalty she had painstakingly won over a period of years had accepted, in the span of a single day, and without missing a beat, her banishment.

Six weeks after her termination, she did come to believe it, at her first interview for another job, when she could not stop the tears leaking from her eyes. As an excessively polite, nervous personnel manager escorted her to the elevator and out of the building, she believed everything she had ever heard about job termination destroying self-esteem, self-confidence, self-control.

Her firing had been in September; by December she was an emotional and spiritual quadriplegic. Feeling Cindy's death somewhere deep in her bones even though the letter from Rita Ralston would not reach her until after the turn of the year, she spent weeks and months staring at the television set, existing on her savings, stirring from her apartment only to walk Sammie, her Dobie, and buy food.

Then that Sunday in February, when she had pushed herself out of the house to come to Griffith Park for Sammie's sake. Dissolved in tears, with Sammie at her feet whimpering his distress, she sat on a bench hearing a woman's boisterous laughter from a raucous picnic nearby, and knowing joy was gone forever from her life.

The woman came up behind her, startling her almost out of her wits. Clad in sweat pants and a sweatshirt, the woman blithely sang out, "The name's Donnelly," as if Pat's tears were invisible, "and that's our picnic over there —" She jerked a thumb over her shoulder, "— and we need one more person for touch football. We'll feed you." She leaned over to pet Sammie. "And this guy besides." She held out a hand to Pat, to pull her up from the bench. "Come on and play. You'll be good, I can tell."

And she actually had been. Until her stamina ran out — and she was in no worse shape than the couch potatoes she played with, including Donnelly's husband — she'd run full tilt, without regard for her physical safety, run as if possessed, until she and at least part of her rage lay exhausted on the grass. "You're a wild woman," Donnelly had gasped, collapsing beside her. "I love it."

That day she had taken the first step in putting aside the past. Spinning out a different future.

Thereafter the daily phone calls to and from Donnelly. Coffee in the evenings, visits over the weekends. Most important of all, the confidences, as she became able to talk first about Jerry. And Emily, and Cindy. Even Mark Daniel. And, eventually, her job and how it had been taken from her.

Months passed before she held hands with Donnelly, more months before their first kiss. No one, Pat was certain, had ever had so slow-dance a courtship as hers with Donnelly.

They had been considerate and gentle with each other in such equal parts that Pat understood only all these years later that while she had waited for Donnelly to put together her sexuality, Donnelly had waited with much greater patience for Pat to patch together her self-esteem.

All fourteen years with Donnelly had been a healing process. And she was still not whole.

To this day, the most enraging image she could conjure was accepting the severance check from that smirking bully and letting him run her out of a job and a pension rightfully hers, without any fight out of her at all.

How many times had she imagined taking that check and flinging it back into Larry's face, how many times had she dreamed of finding a way, some way, to fight back.

But there had been no way. Not back then. And not today, either.

How many people had this happened to who had descended into an abyss and unlike her, never emerged? Who scuttled themselves and their pain in drugs or alcohol or sickness or death?

Wilson had to sign that bill. He had to.

And now the news . . .

. . . on the hour, brought to you by your independent insurance agents. At the top of the news, Governor Pete Wilson has announced that he has vetoed AB 101, the legislation that would have outlawed job discrimination against homosexuals . . .

"Jesus," Bradley whispered.

Sucking in her breath, Pat felt hair ripple from the back of her neck across her shoulders and down along her arms.

. . . a lengthy, four-page veto message, stated, "The test

of fairness to be applied to the bill is whether there is evidence of discrimination so pervasive as to warrant state government imposing so widely a burden so oppressive to so many innocent employers . . ."

"*Innocent employers!*" Warren screeched. "Can you believe this shit?"

"Hush," Donnelly commanded.

. . . concluded his veto message by stating that adequate laws exist to protect homosexuals against job discrimination. In other news —

"*Liar,*" Donnelly raged over the voice from the radio. "The hypocritical, lily-livered, back-stabbing *coward.*" She added in a tone that matched the coldness in her eyes, "If he thinks this ends it, he's dreaming. He'll regret this day . . ."

Amid her own chaotic rage, Pat felt a sliver of gratification that Donnelly, expecting this news, was as shaken by the actuality of it as the rest of them. Even Averill looked distraught, her gaze shifting between Donnelly's thundercloud face and Angela's head-shaking distress. Querida sat with her head bowed, fists clenched whitely in her lap. Bradley's face was blank, the light in his eyes seeming to have shrunk to a pinpoint, as if he had pulled the news into a private place deep inside him. He brushed Warren's consoling hand from his arm like a mourner allowing nothing to penetrate a shell of grief.

"We've got statements ready for the media," Donnelly said harshly, and added to Pat, "I wish to hell you could tune in something up here besides this goddamn horse and buggy station."

Pat barely swallowed her scream *You invited yourself*

here, I didn't, knowing her fury would be misdirected at Donnelly. Striding to the radio, she muttered through clenched teeth, "I'll try picking up one of the news stations from L.A."

. . . Saturday Senator John Seymour announced his opposition for the same business-related reasons —

"There, right there," Bradley said as the crackling voice on the station faded.

"Am I an idiot?" she snarled. She had momentarily lost the station as she tried to fine-tune it.

. . . learned from an unidentified source that the governor had decided last week to veto the measure. Other aides in Wilson's office said the veto was announced Sunday to avoid having it released at the same time a new statewide opinion poll comes out tomorrow. The results of that poll, according to another source, will show 62 percent of Californians in favor of the governor signing the bill, and 29 percent opposed . . .

Bradley groaned, buried his head in his hands.

. . . little hope exists of overriding the veto. We hear now from the author of the bill, Congressman Terry Friedman:

"The bill was fine-tuned as much as it could be. It was amended to remove any objectionable provision and was left simply as a statement of fairness and treating gays and lesbians as other groups who are subject to discrimination. I'm not saying I'm giving up. I just don't know what else to do."

Friedman also expressed disappointment that the governor would cave in to right-wing extremists and fundamentalist religious groups and he called the veto a victory for the bigots in Wilson's party. The governor,

Friedman said, had an historic opportunity to do something here and failed. This is John Peterson, reporting live from the capitol.

We go live now to Veronica Johnson in West Hollywood...

Thank you, Gary. Leaders in the gay and lesbian community are expressing outrage at the governor's decision. Here now is Torie Osborn, executive director of the Los Angeles Gay and Lesbian Community Services Center.

"For Governor Wilson to cave in is absolutely cowardly and outrageous. There was widespread support for the bill, it was a simple job discrimination bill..."

"Go, Torie," Donnelly said softly.

... and now a statement from John Duran, co-chair of the Lobby for Individual Freedom and Equality, which helped sponsor the bill.

"Pete Wilson is a political coward —"

"Right on," said Warren, raising both fists.

"... wherever he goes, we will be there to remind him of his veto. Demonstrations? Wherever he goes..."

"Viva, olé," said Querida.

Director of public information for the Los Angeles Gay and Lesbian Community Services Center, David Smith, has also stated that the governor has just sold out every single gay and lesbian Californian, that the veto is a mistake for which he will pay —

"Enough," Pat said, reaching to the radio.

"Wait," Donnelly pleaded.

"Enough." She changed the station back to music. Donnelly might be a masochist, but she was not.

Just One Look

I just don't get it." Angela looked baffled, angry. "I don't *get* it."

"Let me tell you what I've heard," Donnelly said. She paced the room in her agitation. Bradley looked away from her in order to concentrate on her words.

"Wilson initially delayed acting on the bill to give the religious right a chance to fire off all their usual ammunition, have them think he was giving their views serious consideration. But he fully intended to sign the bill. Then he started getting pressure from his closest political advisors, and topping that, a call from the White House — from Bush's Chief of Staff."

Bradley listened with rapt attention. The entire room was still.

Donnelly stopped pacing, stood with an elbow resting on the mantel. "My hearsay understanding is, John Sununu told Wilson that given Bush's re-election, which right now does look like a given, Bush's hand-picked successor for the 'ninety-six presidential election is Wilson. *But.* He's stone-dead if he puts his signature on a gay rights bill. Dead with the right wing, dead in national Republican politics."

Pat said, shaking her head, "He *wouldn't* be dead. Even George Bush can't be dense enough not to see the changing climate in this country. By 'ninety-six the Republicans will need to run somebody who's a moderate."

"Pat, they don't see it that way at all," Donnelly said. She looked around the room, her intense blue gaze settling briefly on each of them. "The Reagan wing is still in charge of grassroots Republican politics. They loathe Bush for breaking his promise about no new taxes, they think it's taken this election away from being a lead-pipe cinch." She ticked her points off on her fingers: "The economy's stagnant, they're not sure we won't still be in recession next November. They need an overriding issue like they had in 'eighty-eight but they can't get away with another racist Willie Horton ad like they did last time. You follow me so far?"

"Keep talking," Bradley said tightly.

"So, the quote, moral decay of America, unquote, is another way to play the haves against everybody the haves consider inferior. It's a way to play the race card without identifying the card, to keep the religious right in the fold and still rabid. They couldn't have a Republican governor sign a gay rights bill because this time the moral issue starts with us. They're mapping out a strategy that marches right over our bodies, that identifies us as the moral worm eating out the heart of America."

"Jesus," Pat said, "from the Reagan eighties to the Nazi thirties."

"Not if we can help it, and we can. There's a meeting in Los Angeles in about two weeks. A secret meeting. With some names you know, like San Francisco Supervisor Roberta Achtenberg, some you don't, like David Mixner, who's very important to us. This veto is extremely damaging, coming out of a liberal bastion state like California, but these are people in a position to lay the framework for a national strategy to survive, to come together politically like we never have as a community, and behind a presidential candidate who's in our corner."

"And who might that be," Pat said sarcastically, "Tiny Tim?"

"More and more Democrats support gay rights,"

Donnelly said mildly. "Jerry Brown, Paul Tsongas. Any of you know much about Bill Clinton?"

"A nonentity governor from a nonentity state," Angela said in a deflated tone.

"A no-chance lightweight," Warren scoffed.

Donnelly smiled. "He'll be announcing his candidacy in another week, and it's all but certain he's the one we'll be lining up behind."

"*Him?*" Querida said. "That apple-cheeked guy who made the longest, most boring speech in history at the last Democratic Convention? Not Jerry Brown? You worked for him, you love the guy."

"I do. Jerry is brilliant, he has wonderful ideas. But he has an image he can't recover from. He's not electable. Clinton, let me tell you, is gifted and brilliant," Donnelly said, "with an astonishing grasp of the issues facing this country."

"Have you met him?" Warren asked in interest.

"Yes. And Roberta knows him well. She's so convinced, so committed that she'll be organizing his California campaign."

Bradley looked impressed. "Quite a gun in his corner."

Pat said heavily, "He doesn't have a snowball's chance in hell. He doesn't have a prayer."

"Maybe not. Probably not." Donnelly shrugged. "Look. We have to plan beyond next week, next year. None of the Democratic heavyweights — the Cuomos, the Bentsens, the Gephardts — are getting in the ring, they figure somebody else can be the sacrificial lamb for George Bush. If Clinton navigates the primaries in a decent fashion, he'll be on the national scene. He might even win the nomination..." She paused as Pat snorted. "Stranger things have happened, Pat. Whatever you think of Jimmy Carter, he came out of nowhere, a nonentity governor from a nonentity state. More likely, Clinton can position himself to be our nominee in ninety-six with a big chance for the White House, and in the meantime we'll have a voice in the primaries defending us. And if the day comes when he gets to the White House, we'll have a president who believes in ending discrimination against us."

"Donnelly, you are such a dreamer," Pat said.

"The scenario seems not impossible," Bradley said thoughtfully, "even for this election. Bush's health is a wild card . . ."

"I'll tell you what, Bradley," Pat said. "If Mr. Flap Mouth Clinton even wins the *nomination,* much less the election, I'll meet you on election night and roll a peanut down the middle of Castro Street, *with my nose.*"

"You're on," Bradley said. "If *any* gay-friendly candidate wins the nomination, the Castro will be the place to be on election night anyway."

Stand By Me

"All right, Donnelly," Averill said. "Now. What do you want from us? Out with it."

"Out with it, right," Donnelly said with an attempt at a grin as she moved to the sofa. "First off, knowing and loving the four of you, it was important for all of us to be together, really important to me. All of you gathering here means everything to me."

As Bradley watched her arrange herself on the sofa, hitching up the sleeves of her sweatshirt and then sitting cross-legged with a hand clasping each knee, he felt his insides begin to unclench for the first time since he had heard the news broadcast. Of everyone else in his life, he had always been most comfortable with her. The bluff, warm honesty, the unconstrained physicality, the simplicity of her — it was easy to see how he and these three other lovers had been swept up in the generosity of her devotion, her sheer largesse.

"We've come such a long way together," she said. "I confess I called you because mostly I just plain needed you. I knew this would be one of my worst days ever, I needed to have you around me. You're the people I love."

She paused, and Bradley followed her selective gaze as it settled first on Querida. Sitting beside Bradley on the floor, she leaned casually back on her hands, forsaking her expensive-looking houndstooth pants to the carpet. Pat, settled in her brown corduroy recliner with an ankle crossed over a knee, was next, and then Averill, slouched in her armchair as usual, at her usual post by the window, her usual wine glass dangling from a hand. Then he felt himself under the warmth of her gaze. Then Warren and Angela, on cushions beside the fire, who looked on politely, attentively, like children understanding that they had been invited to a gathering of adults. Donnelly's gaze had lingered, Bradley thought, no more on one individual than another, including Querida.

Donnelly said quietly, "For all of us, coming out's been a journey at our own speed. I've always believed no one has the right to judge that speed — to ask anyone to come out. Until now. Now it's absolutely vital that everybody in this room think about coming out, and coming out now."

Since she surely did not mean to include his already-out self in this statement, Bradley again shifted his attention away from her.

Pat was first to speak. "Who on earth wouldn't know I'm queer?" she joked.

Querida said reflectively, "It's really no secret about me... I'm not officially out, especially to my family, but it doesn't matter — I could hardly be more on the outs with them anyway."

Bradley resisted sliding a fatherly arm around her. Querida had grown on him. The expensive clothes seemed cheerful, unabashed materialism more than pretension, and she was an engaging young woman in her bold, unorthodox, innocent way.

"Well, I'm not out to anybody," Averill said in a tone flat with anger, "except for the very select few I thought I could trust. I have a lot more than just myself to consider. I can't be out."

"Yes, you can," Donnelly said. "We all have more than just ourselves to consider."

Anger spread over Averill's face. "No one has a tenth of my problems. We had this conversation before, Donnelly."

"No conversation, Averill." Donnelly's voice was cool. "You informed me how you intended to live." Then she directed a glance of inquiry at Bradley, who had yet to speak.

He said, "You blew me clean out of the closet, remember?" Her return smile, its affection, told him that she did indeed remember those two tumultuous weeks after he quit as a teacher, when she had announced the major change in her own life, beginning the final demolition job on both of their conventional lives by coming out to him.

He should have known what she would do next, this woman who saw only the forest and never the trees unless they were pointed out to her, this child of a father she had scarcely known and an independent suffragette mother long since dead. Released from all the constraints of family-tied loyalties and guilts, Donnelly had been her own consistent, honest, optimistic self in thinking she was doing everyone a favor, especially him, by going to his family to explain that the end of their marriage was no one's fault, especially his. And outing the two of them to his parents had been, by her lights, only the proof of it.

Less than an hour later, veins popped out in his father's neck and temples that Bradley had never seen before: *Like a goddamn fool I hoped. I might of known it was too goddamn much to hope you'd stay married and work all this out, I might of known after you went and quit teaching you'd be too goddamn selfish to consider your mother or anybody else on this earth but your own goddamn self. What kind of pervert did you marry that she has to announce to the world she's queer and needs a divorce from her fag husband? Give us a chance to raise our heads in this town — get the hell out of our lives and stay out, the both of you.*

He had. Gone up to San Francisco and found his community and his honest life and his life's work in publishing. And Donnelly, years later, had finally emerged the activist she had always needed to be, was born to be.

Had Donnelly ever spoken a word of remorse about severing him from his family? He remembered that she had looked abashed for maybe a second, for as long as it took to again lift her gaze up from the trees to the forest: "You're better off, Brad. Better for you, better for them they know the truth, who you really are."

Better off? Well, his father still did not talk to him. *You know how stubborn he is,* his mother had said any number of times. *When did your father ever budge once he made up his mind?* His mother did talk to him, and often. At one point, whenever she could sneak away from his father and call him collect. These days she talked by phone in front of his father, and visited often, and his father paid for the phone calls and the plane tickets. His brother had dropped in by phone too, once, with that wonderfully sage advice, "*Listen, bro, you come down with that HIV shit, don't you bother Mom about it...*"

On balance, thinking about all of it over these past two days, he was glad Bruno had called. Never again would he care about Bruno's opinion of him, or whether he would ever again see a brother — or a father — who were such complete and utter dickheads...

Fire and Rain

Donnelly raised both hands, not for silence but for attention. "Now listen, really listen to me. Averill, don't close me out, just hear me. The bigotry behind this veto, it's the same old manure — demonizing us and then sanctifying it with one or two out-of-context passages from the Bible, never mind all those other passages in the same book that everybody ignores. Fair-minded people aren't in our corner, they don't know who the hell we are. The activist part of our community is all they ever see —"

"And what's wrong with that," Warren demanded.

"The same thing that's wrong with thinking radical feminists represent all women. Activists have dragged all of us into a better world, but they're a fraction of who we are. Straight people have so few of our faces to look at, they're like visitors to earth judging all the foliage by a few pine trees."

As Warren remained silent, chewing over this response, Donnelly added, "Activists — and the religious right — are defining us totally."

Bradley flicked a glance around the room. No one moved except for Averill, who looked as if she could not speak until she had finished choking on whatever was in her throat.

Donnelly said, "Tell me what sense it makes to fight for civil rights if we all stay in the closet."

"Catch-22," Angela said softly, as if timid to speak up. "We're in the closet because we don't have civil rights. And we don't have civil rights because..."

"More and more of us are coming out," Bradley offered. "Some of us have been out there a long time."

"I may not wear the word dyke across my chest," Pat said, "but I hardly have to. I call that being out. Way out."

Donnelly shook her head. Her gaze encompassing only Bradley and Querida and Pat, she said, "You're out in your community, to your gay friends. Except for a carefully selected person here and there, how many straight people know you're —"

Averill slammed her hands down on the side of her chair. "This is all so fucking *easy* for you to say when it's *my throat* you're trying to shit down."

"Hello?" said Donnelly, looking astonished.

"Averill!" Angela gasped.

Bradley gaped at her. *Hello, toilet mouth.* Was it the wine? The woman had totally lost it, state capitals and all.

"This is a setup, a fucking *charade.* This is all about *me* coming out. I'm the big fish. You want *me* to be the sacrificial lamb people can piss all over —"

"I thought Norma Desmond had an ego," Warren said *sotto voce* to Bradley.

"— you sit up there on your fucking sanctimonious pedestal, you never understood when we were together, you don't understand now —"

"Averill, wait a minute —"

"I listened, you listen. You're not in the spotlight like I am —"

"Yes I am."

"You don't have the press on you like blood-hounds —"

"Yes I do."

"— asking every disgusting filthy question they can think up, you don't have a big career to smash to smithereens —"

"I know all those things, Averill. The LPGA tour is a business, just like any other. The people you revere want you to hide just like any other —"

"They want me to be *private!*"

"Not private. Hidden. Ashamed."

"I'm not ashamed! I don't shove my personal life down other people's throats, that's *all.* What right do we have to be so completely selfish? To do this to our families? Our —"

"Selfish?" Querida said heatedly. "*We're* selfish? When other people kick us out of our jobs? Tell us we're sick? Perverted? An abomination?"

"Right, Querida," Angela said firmly.

Averill looked startled by the interjections from this quarter. "What's *wrong* with simply being discreet?" Her voice had lost some of its rage. "Nobody but a few fanatics listen to that religious shit —"

"Especially if your own church happens to be the golf course," Donnelly observed.

"So what if it is," Averill retorted. "I'm a member of the tour, I uphold its standards, I've taken on obligations, responsibility, I take my commitments seriously —"

Warren said, "Step right up, folks, get your internalized homophobia —"

Averill said furiously, "You stay out of this, you — I'm *sick* of all your labels. You ACT UP jerks think everybody owes you something, you never had a career anybody can take away from you, you —"

"You're right, Miz Pampered Pro Golfer, all we're doing is dying. I never had a goddamn thing handed to me, you —"

"Back off, Warren," Donnelly said sharply. "This doesn't involve you."

"The hell it doesn't." He jerked a thumb toward Bradley. "Tell him all about the closet, why don't you. He's so shut off he might as well be in jail. He hates being gay, he's still living back in the days he was married to you."

Bradley stared at him, thunderstruck. "Where in the fuck did you ever get such crazy crap?"

"Man, how long have I been pounding on you, trying to find a way in? Did anybody except your ex-wife ever find a way in?"

Bradley shot back heedlessly, "You should talk about being closed off. You might as well wear a chastity belt."

"You get sex —" Warren's voice rose, "you take it and go, man, like I'm a whore. You're as self-hating as this woman who doesn't have a clue beyond her stupid golf bag —"

"Stop stop *stop*." Angela's eyes were squeezed shut in anguish. "Everybody *stop*."

Whole Lotta Shakin'
Going On

As silence descended Angela said, "You're all getting crazy and you're all ganging up on Averill. It's not fair. She's right, her being out isn't the same as your being out. Coming out for her is coming out on a stage —"

"I'm glad somebody sees that," Averill said aggrievedly.

"I'm with Angela," Pat said angrily, and plunged in with her own long-held bitterness: "But only because you've got no room delivering lectures about the closet, Donnelly." She jerked her head toward Averill. "Not when you left me for the biggest closet case of all time."

Averill hissed, "Don't you call me a closet case, you diesel dyke, you couldn't hide your butch dyke ass in a closet if the door was twenty feet wide."

As Angela uttered "*Averill!*" in a horrified gasp, Pat quickly recovered: "You wouldn't have the brains, you wouldn't have the *guts* to come out of your closet if it was leaking shit down around your ears."

"Stop this," Donnelly said, "stop it *now*. Pat, I left you for myself. For the exact same reason you left Cindy —"

"Don't bring Cindy —" Pat managed to utter, bludgeoned by this personal grief being dropped into a roomful of strangers.

"She's part of it. Listen to me, Pat. And you too, Averill, and Bradley and Querida. You're all four of you jailed in your closets."

"Say what," said Bradley, his attention still fixed on Warren, who was staring defiantly back at him.

"Oh please," Averill said sarcastically.

Pat said with equal sarcasm, "Okay, I'll wear a DYKE T-shirt."

Querida did not speak, and Donnelly turned to her. "Querida, who do you respect most on this earth?"

"My grandfather. Of course."

"Bradley?"

His dark eyes narrowed in thought. "A pretty short list. One or two professional colleagues."

"Pat?"

She quickly sorted through the question. "Same as Bradley. Professional colleagues. In particular, Virginia Uribe — the head of Project Ten."

"Are any of you out to any of these people?"

"I can't be," Querida said.

Bradley shook his head.

"No," said Pat, recalling in a flash of memory the seminar she had attended along with other teacher colleagues open to learning greater sensitivity to gay and lesbian students. Listening in silent hero worship to the easy-mannered woman who had begun the first counseling program in the nation for lesbian and gay high school students and had reaped unremitting thunderbolts for her trouble. Pat had not further identified herself to Uribe, whose warm, dark-eyed glance had lingered on her, and who made no visible sign of recognizing a lesbian sister nor any attempt at approach.

There's enough grief just being a teacher, Pat had told herself afterward, grief enough seeing the brief lives of ex-students Frederico and Danny and Anjelica extinguished by AIDS...And the benevolent, grandmotherly Uribe looked every bit the part to counsel teenagers, while she herself...

Donnelly said, "You're not out till the people you respect know the truth of you."

"Sayings of Chairman Donnelly," Pat muttered, "you and your simple answers." Uribe would despise her if she knew how little help she'd been in the tragic world of gay kids.

"The closet is simple," Warren contended. "It's gay people saying excuse me for living."

Donnelly nodded. "It's conceding there's something fundamentally wrong with you."

"No it's not, not for me," Querida said. "I just don't want to lose my grandfather."

"And so you sit with him in tacit agreement with his prejudice."

"Not today at least," Querida said calmly.

She deals so well with Donnelly, Pat thought. She said, "Butch as I look, I get grief enough in the school system. If I actually said I was a dyke, I'd have to think about every damn word that came out of my mind not to be accused of recruitment."

Bradley said, "What I publish has nothing to do with whether I'm gay. Telling people you're gay is a pain in the ass, and so damn much *work* — you have to sort out where they are about it, walk them through it till they get you assimilated again. It's a needless distraction."

Warren suggested mildly, "Distraction, or discomfort?"

Averill said harshly, "Asking people to burn themselves at the stake is asking too much, Donnelly. You don't have a family to lose, you don't even know what you're talking about —"

"You're right about a family," Donnelly said, her face, her voice subdued. "All the family I have is right here in this room. The four of you are all I have, you're why I needed to be here."

If Donnelly's answer mollified Averill, it was not apparent. She continued angrily, "You *have* to make exceptions for individual situations, you have no respect at all for my situation on the tour —"

"You're right, I don't, Averill. No way on earth could I hide and pretend I was your secretary or assistant or whatever damn thing it was you wanted me to be —"

Pat did not dare steal a look at Angela.

"You told me that," Averill accused, "but you never said I had to make a choice. You just walked away."

"I didn't have the time to wait and see if you'd work through it. And anyway, if I'd told you, would you have done anything about it?"

"That's beside the point. You never gave me a choice."

"I don't believe in issuing ultimatums about the closet," Donnelly said. "I still believe you should leave the closet for yourself, not because someone else wants you to."

Angela said, "But this veto's changed you."

"That, added to everything I know that's happened to people in this room, people I love. The closet suffocates everybody in it. The closet is death."

Angela said to Averill, "Martina's come out, taken all the up front heat. That has to make it easier now for other —"

Averill snapped, "Martina's made everything harder, not easier."

"You can't mean that. She's a *hero*, she —"

"She's not. All the notoriety she brought to women's tennis rubbed off on all the rest of us, opened all the doors for reporters to come sniffing through, there's all this curiosity about me —"

"There would be anyway."

"Don't be ridiculous, Angela."

"Oh Averill, everybody just pretends not to know

what everybody really knows. Nobody seriously believes I'm your assistant —"

Averill sprang from her chair. Angela raised an arm as if in defense, her eyes wide with dismay.

Looming over Angela, Averill shouted, "That's not true! I've been too careful!"

Warren held a hand in front of his mouth in a pretend-yawn. "Just one more queer discovering she's living in a glass closet."

Ebony and Ivory

As Averill, still on her feet, drew herself up for what looked to be an assault on Warren, Bradley rushed in. "It *is* true. The clues are always there. We can't really fool heterosexuals."

"Really, Mary," Warren said derisively.

"You can't seriously believe that," Averill said. Her stare an accusation of betrayal, she dropped back down into her chair. "You know it isn't true. You don't look or act the least bit gay."

Bradley thought of the boy on the bicycle so many years ago, of all the years spent in desperate fear of exposure. And Warren's accusing, grief-filled words were branded in his mind. The closet did kill. Killed hope, killed willingness to trust... "It *is* true," he said. "People who don't see the homosexual me aren't looking. The only time I really passed for straight was in high school — I did more sneering at fags than anybody else. To this day I believe the worst homophobes are the worst closet cases — normal heterosexuals just shouldn't care that much."

"If I came out," Averill asked him earnestly, "what do you expect me to do when my whole life comes crashing down in flames?"

"My life..." muttered Pat.

Bradley strained to hear her; her voice was pitched toward her Reeboks where her eyes were fixed. "My life...came crashing down in flames," she said with visible reluctance. "I got fired...from a job I loved because I was a lesbian. I went on."

He said, "I didn't know that, Pat." He realized that Donnelly had not told him about this because Pat must have told her not to, a measure of Pat's anguish. He said, hearing the strain in his own voice, "I loved teaching, but I quit the profession...because I couldn't handle it as a closeted gay man. I went on too."

"I didn't know that about you, either, Bradley," Pat said, looking up at him with a gaze that connected somewhere deep inside him. "I've always had trouble about my own teaching for the exact same reason."

"Denise in my office..." Querida began, and then trailed off, her eyes distant.

"I've got a buddy with a big career in the military," Warren said. "He's being investigated."

Let It Be

With Angela's face averted from her in a distress all too evident, Averill directed a thought at her: *None of this is my fault.* Too much wine on an empty stomach, having to justify how she had to live ... she'd lost control. Staring at her, Averill thought, *I'll prove it to you,* and voiced her most primal fear: "Coming out would mean quitting the tour. All I know is golf."

Bradley said, "Why wouldn't you just go on playing? No way they can kick you off the tour."

"It's not that easy. Golf is all mental, it's confidence and concentration. If I lose my concentration, I lose my game —"

"Of all the people I've ever known ..." Angela was culling her words, as if, Averill thought, she were accountable to someone for them. "Everybody I know who ever came out, all of them said it was the most ... freeing act. It made everything in their lives better, easier, not worse."

Averill announced her bottom line: "It's a huge gamble whether that will happen, isn't it."

No way would she be the one to bring scandal down on the tour. No way would she have this kind of focus on her.

She'd always made her own way, had never even heard about the riot of gay people at Stonewall until she met Donnelly, she was twelve when Stonewall began this whole thing of gay rights, and all that while she'd been expending everything in her to build something worth having and keeping.

Yes, she loved women but this gay community thing wasn't her business. There wasn't anywhere else she needed to be except on the proving ground of a golf course, gripped in the rigors of the game, dependent on no one else but herself. No one understood that. No matter how long she played, how much money she

made, she would never stop loving dew splashing on her
golf shoes in the crisp cool promise of a new day, the
feel of the grass crimping under her spikes, the rising
hum of insects, the chirps and songs of birds, the
smells...and that virginal scorecard to be filled in. The
growing heat of the day, the honest sting of sweat
trickling between her breasts, gathering under the rim of
her visor, the spectators adding their energy. And,
sometimes, the superhuman high of being on top of her
game and under the eyes of cheering witnesses...

There could be nothing else anywhere like the
camaraderie of the tour. On the practice tee, on the
course, in the scorer's tent, in the locker room, at
sponsor functions, dinners, exhibitions, charity games — the
glad-handing all done with gratitude to the purveyors of
what was beyond prize money — the opportunity to
agonize, despair and, sometimes, triumph over the game
they all loved...

"What about reaching the Hall of Fame," Pat asked,
"would you change your mind about coming out then?"

The question had not contained Pat's usual edgy
challenge; there was a note of genuine inquiry in her
voice that Averill had never heard before. She answered,
"That would make me more conspicuous than ever."

"What about when your playing days are over and
you leave the tour?"

"Maybe then. But...I might be able to go into
broadcasting, some of the girls have, like Donna Caponi
and Judy Rankin. Not a chance, though, if I've got
scandal attached to me."

"It didn't hurt Billie Jean King," Bradley said, "she still
does some broadcasting."

"Didn't hurt her?" she said incredulously. "It turned
her into a freak show. The endorsements she lost could

fill a Swiss bank vault. Look at Martina. Hardly any advertiser will come near her."

"Because no one knows our economic clout," Querida said. "Yet."

I'll tell you right now," Donnelly said, "the daughter of a Bush–Reagan cabinet officer will be coming out. A senator's daughter, actors and actresses will be coming out, and singers. Successful people from all walks of life, celebrities making it easier for other celebrities —"

Averill said, "So who are all these people?"

"They'll out themselves," Donnelly said. "In due course."

Oh sure, Averill thought. Nice bluff. If they did come out she felt sorry for their families. Easy for Martina — her parents were in Czechoslovakia, what did they care? Her own were right here in California.

She'd been in the newspapers since she was in college, notices that her parents faithfully kept in scrapbooks. Their delirium when she first won on the tour was still etched in her mind, their shy-faced pride when she made front-page headlines in her hometown _Gazette_, when they became famous in their own right as her parents, pointed out along the sidelines when they attended her tournaments by TV golf commentators. Their loins had produced this prodigy. Their golf champion daughter was the legacy of their lives ...

She spoke her thoughts: "What's wrong with not wanting to embarrass parents who've done nothing but support me and be proud of me?"

"Everything," Pat said, "when the support and pride don't apply to the person you actually are."

"You talked about coming out as a gamble," Donnelly said. "Gambling is courage —"

Averill looked out the window at two bluejays quarreling in the pine trees. These past three years she'd had the tendon damage in her wrist, a swollen knee drained twice. Only yesterday, it seemed, she'd thought the bright sweet days of youth and ambition would go on forever ... And now she was thirty-four years old, and Averill Calder Harmon, professional golfer, was who and what and everything she was ...

Joy to the World

Donnelly said, "Gay pride parades in the seventies and eighties — we got strong from just being able to see each other. Now, right now, we can make it safe or impossible for future gay and lesbian people to be out. Our enemies know it."

Angela said, "Young people — you look at them today, you can tell Warren and Querida have higher expectations and a lot more confidence than when we were growing up ..."

"Act up, fight back, old lady," Warren teased her, and then raised a fist high over his head.

"I can sure act up and fight back more than I have been," Querida murmured.

Pat said, "Older people always let the younger ones fight the wars, do the dying. This is one time we need to do better. We don't need to let our Warrens and Queridas be crippled the way we were. I hope to God we can all be in this together."

Angela was looking at Averill. "You were talking about courage," she said to Donnelly.

Donnelly too was looking at Averill. "If we ever want our lives to really make a difference, the time is right now."

And now the news . . .

"At the top of the news, Governor Pete Wilson has announced that he has vetoed —"

"Turn that damn thing off," Donnelly said, getting up from the sofa.

Leaping to his feet, Warren extended a hand to Bradley and pulled him up off the floor. "Let's get the hell out of here. We need to take care of that liar."

As Pat snapped off the radio and moved to the fireplace to spread the logs for quick safe burning, Warren checked his watch. "Querida, you and Donnelly get to West Hollywood. For sure there'll be a demonstration tonight —"

"There'll be one at the Federal Building in the morning," Pat said, "for any of us who can get there —"

"I'll be there," Angela said.

"Let's go down to L.A. for tonight's demonstration," Bradley said to Warren. "We can drive back to the City tomorrow."

"Great idea, Bradley. We can be in the Castro tomorrow night —"

"Call me Brad," Bradley said.

Warren slid an arm around him. "I actually prefer Bradley."

Donnelly stood with her arms crossed. "I still need to

know if the four of you will do what I called you here to do."

"Piss off," said Pat, "we're busy."

"Yeah," said Bradley.

"Si," said Querida.

Averill said somberly, "All I can say is I'll think about it."

"Averill," Angela said. "Would you finish up the packing? I want to give Pat a hand closing up here."

Averill looked disconcerted, then annoyed. Pat said, "I'm fine to—"

"Averill?" Angela said. "Please take care of the luggage."

Averill shrugged and moved off down the hallway.

Pat said, "I need to turn the water off outside the cabin. So the pipes don't freeze."

"Fine," Angela said, following her.

As Pat tightened the shut-off valve, Angela said, "I was hoping we could stay in touch."

"I'd love to. But Averill hates my—"

"About the kitten—I'd like to have him. Would you keep him for me?"

Pat said heartily, "You bet I will."

An hour later, Pat, about to climb into her pickup, looked up at the cabin one last time.

"Mother, we'll see," she murmured, "but I have in mind a particular plan for this place..."

Saturday
October 26, 1991

The House of
the Rising Sun

Pat answered the knock on the cabin door holding the kitten, a consciously planned maneuver, but one without any calculation that Angela would lean over and nuzzle the kitten, and clasp Pat's arms, bare in a polo shirt, in her warm hands as she did so.

Arms burning from the lingering touch, Pat said gruffly, "Glad you could come up."

"Me too," Angela murmured, pleasure in her face as she slowly surveyed the cabin.

"You've been a busy woman," Pat said, approving of the soft clinging lavender sweater and the black knit pants that emerged as Angela shrugged out of her car coat. Gently, Pat surrendered the kitten to Angela's arms, taking in exchange Angela's coat and hanging it in the closet. She strode off to the kitchen. "Make yourself comfortable, I'll get us some coffee."

She took her time filling two mugs, wondering how she would regain her composure around this woman.

This was the kind of lovesick mush she thought she had outgrown decades ago. In the month or so she had been seeing Angela, she seemed to be regressing ever further into it, old fool that she was. Her only hope could be that she keep this gracious young woman as a friend.

Accepting the mug of coffee and placing it on the coffee table, Angela kicked off her shoes and curled up on the gold corduroy sofa, tucking her feet up under her. Just as she had, Pat remembered, the very first time she'd sat on that sofa...

"My letter to Averill..." Angela gazed at Pat with clouded hazel eyes. "It came back this morning unopened. I've given up calling."

Seating herself in the recliner, Pat nodded acknowledgment. Angela had been updating her, phoning at least once and sometimes several times a day as Pat assisted her resettlement in Los Angeles.

"I talked to Toni, one of my friends on the tour. Averill's working on her game, and nothing else. When I first got to know her she was like that—absolutely driven. I thought she was the loneliest woman I'd ever known."

Pat said with genuine sympathy, "Think she'll ever come around?"

Her eyes on the fire, Angela traced the outside rim of her mug with a fingernail as she reflected. "Her view is so centered on how she thinks she has to live...it's all she sees. She's very, very convincing, Pat. I didn't realize how much I'd bought into her view."

Pat said quietly, "It's no different from what most of us have had to get through, me included. Some of us take a long time..." Like decades and decades, she thought. Like forever.

"The weekend all of us were up here was a

revelation, Pat. The closet's a completely justifiable place to her, she absolutely thinks she can afford the rent. She'd have kept me in there with her forever."

"Donnelly still talks to her all the time. Hasn't given up on her." Pat shook her head in vexation.

"I haven't either," Angela declared. "If Donnelly's in a corner of her life, there's at least a crack in her closet."

That silenced Pat. Donnelly had never given up on her, either. And could have, any number of times.

Pat chose her next words: "So how do you feel... about everything?"

"About Averill and me?" Faint frown lines appeared between Angela's eyebrows. "Concerned. For her. And that's all. She's where she wants and needs to be, I'm somewhere quite different. It's really terrible, but it's as if I woke up and she faded away like a vague dream."

Not so terrible, Pat thought. Take away Averill's trappings and she could be a wraith, so little of herself did she seem to give anyone.

She changed the subject. "Will you be working with Donnelly?"

Angela nodded. "We're to collaborate on a press release next week. I'm sure we'll brush shoulders all the time. Working in the Democratic Party should make an interesting 'ninety-two for us both." She asked, chuckling, "Do you think Wilson maybe regrets that veto?"

"Why?" Pat joked back. "Because raging gay demonstrators hound his every step?"

Angela laughed. "Every gay person I know is still in an uproar over it. People who've never ever been politically active before are out on the street. If Wilson's people thought this would be a minor brush fire, what a miscalculation. I really believe the veto was a flash point, and I'm not talking just about California. From everything

I see, it's spreading, waking up gay people clear across the country. The religious right, too. This election year's going to be some ruckus."

"Bradley called last night," Pat said. "Moaning how he hardly sees that smart-alecky snip he lives with. Warren's out every night in an ACT UP march." She added wryly, "I'm actually getting to be sort of friends with Bradley."

"I like him. What news from Querida?"

"Been thinking about her all day. This is the day she sees her grandfather . . ."

Higher and Higher

Querida listened to the song, then got out of her car and paused to straighten her shoulders, smooth her clothes. She had dressed carefully, unobtrusively, in beige pants and a turtleneck, her ⚨s around her neck for strength. She made her way to the private entrance to the basement apartment of her parents' house. They were both away this Saturday, her father to his repair shop, her mother baby-sitting her newest grandchild.

In these basement rooms where her grandfather lived, she had had insulation and paneling and carpeting installed, had added a small bathroom and kitchen, a free-standing wood-burning stove on a brick hearth — contributions to her grandfather's well being that gratified her, and in no way lowered the pedestal on which he stood.

"*Buenos dias, mi abuelo.*"

Miguel Quemada, clad in his usual baggy corduroy pants and denim shirt, returned her greeting with his customary kiss on her forehead and led her into the main room of his quarters. Sitting in the cane chair, his favorite, in front of a wall of hangings from Mexico, he stroked his chin with a thumb and forefinger, and settled his unwavering dark eyes on her in the scrutiny that never failed to intimidate her.

She arranged herself in the canvas chair facing him, prepared to accept her fate and anxious to know it. She came directly to her well-rehearsed point, speaking Spanish, as she always did with him: "Grandfather, there's something about myself I have decided to tell you —"

He abruptly raised a hand; but his piercing gaze had shifted away from her to the cluster of framed family photos taking up one entire wall; and she was not sure if the raised hand was meant to silence or acknowledge her. It did not matter; she was determined to go through with this.

"I have come to the decision to tell you —"

His eyes shifted back to her and seared her with their intensity. "*Why?*" The question was a lightning strike between them.

She said doggedly, "Because it's too vital a part of me to keep secret any longer. Because you are too important to me. Because keeping it from you diminishes me."

He nodded. "Speak."

But she was struck dumb by the pain filling his face, drawing down the corners of his eyes and his lips, until it seemed to pull down his very cheekbones. Could he be ill? Or — did he sense what she was about to tell him?

"Speak," he said again. And the command in his voice impelled her to go on.

"I need you to know..." Weak, dizzy, she expelled the words from lungs that seemed frozen. "I am a lesbian." He did not react. She further explained: "Homosexual."

As he lifted a hand to the chain at the neck of his

denim shirt, his dark eyes still did not change expression, did not waver from hers. He took in his fingers the silver locket he had never, to her knowledge, shown to anyone. She sat rooted to her chair as he ripped the chain from his neck, handed it to her.

"Open it."

Astonished, she accepted the locket and broken chain. What did this have to do with what she had just told him? *Mi abula,* she thought. My grandmother. Finally she would see her grandfather's wife, the shadowy Mary White. But how was this connected ... Fumbling with the locket, she managed to get a fingernail between the halves, and sprung it open.

The image in the locket was not her grandmother. She looked up in complete bewilderment. "It's you." The sepia-toned photograph was of a sensuously featured, aristocratic young man of perhaps twenty. Who was none other than her grandfather.

"Carlos." His hands gripped the arms of his chair, his eyes fastened on the locket. "Carlos. My twin. My brother."

"Your *brother?*" She had no knowledge of any brother. She would take an oath that no one else did either, not even her father.

"My sweet brother ..." The lines in his face seemed to deepen, darken. "He was twenty-two ..."

"I don't —"

"We came to San Diego for work." He spread his wiry hands over his thighs and continued as if his words would be uttered only once and must therefore be fully understood. "My brother loved ... and was loved by the only daughter of the woman whose property he tended. The woman discharged Carlos." His tone was austere. "Her foolish daughter could have nothing to do with a man who was only a gardener, and worse, a Mexican."

Miguel Quemada's gaze was again fastened on the locket Querida held in her palm. "Carlos came to my room to tell me his beloved carried his child, and they would go to Mexico. Carlos did not know something about me. He did not know about a young man named Pietro. That Pietro and I were ... had become ..."

The eyes he raised to hers were filled with dark, profound grief. "Pietro had three brothers, and they knew what Pietro and I had become to each other. They waited for me at my room. They did not know I had a twin brother. They beat Carlos with baseball bats. They killed him."

Pummeled by horror, and realization, she stammered, "You — then you're ..."

"I told la Blanca Maria ..." He spoke the Spanish term for Mary White with sorrowing affection, "I told her I should have died, not Carlos. She blamed only the hatred, the same hatred she endured for loving my brother. For the safety of us both, and her child, she said we should keep to Carlos' plan, go to Mexico for the child's birth, then return to another part of California. So we went to Tecate, to my family there. To all we were husband and wife, her child was my child. She loved Carlos, you see, and I had Carlos' face ... and I pledged myself to the life meant for Carlos ..."

She whispered, "She never came back ..."

"She hoped time would ... diminish the hate. When she fell ill, she wrote to her parents, and they replied that for them she had already died."

His eyes again shifted to the family photos on the wall. "After her death, I found she had burned every picture, every record, so that her son would have no image or knowledge of the grandparents who scorned his existence. I fulfilled her plan. I took my brother's child — your father — back to California."

Faintly, she asked, "And Pietro —"

"No," he said. And repeated slowly, as if she had not understood, "No. I should have died, not Carlos. I paid for his life with my life."

She closed her eyes for a moment, too wrenched to look at him.

He said, "I have always known... about you."

"Grandfather —"

"Your father chose a life below my hopes," he said. "You, of all my family, have the courage of your true grandfather and grandmother. I... willed you to come here and tell me this. I knew you had the strength to face the challenges of... a hard life."

"Grandfather," she said with all her heart, "I came here to tell you that I celebrate my life."

A smile began, became a brilliance pouring over his features. "You are my star."

I was right, she thought as she got up and went to him. I was *right* to adore him...

Best Of My Love

The night was colder than any of the weekend nights in September when Pat had been here last — the weekend of Donnelly and the veto — but the cabin was deliciously warm: the kitten dozed in a contented sprawl of silver-gray fur on a pillow in front of the fireplace.

Pat, sitting with Angela after dinner over coffee, in quiet talk, got up from her recliner to freshen the flames. The afternoon with Angela, the hours-long stroll along curving, tree-lined roads in the crisp chill of this sere, late October day, the easy conversation, the equally easy silences; then the leisurely dinner... The whole day had been so lovely, such an idyll that even though Angela would not leave until tomorrow, Pat was already melancholy with the loss of her.

She turned from the fire. "You don't know how much it means to me that you would come up here this weekend."

"From everything you've told me about your life . . ." Angela paused, and looked at her gently. So gently, Pat thought, that she could kindle warmth in a snowflake. Angela continued, "I know this weekend is hard for you."

"Not . . . hard, exactly," Pat answered. "What I'm doing feels exactly right. But it would be too hard to do it . . ." *without you,* she started to say, and instead said, "alone." She had needed — been compelled — to come here to make a formal farewell, a final closure; yet the fresh grief she felt for her mother would be insupportable if she had had to be all alone in this sepulchre so filled with the brooding presence of her mother. "It's very hard to explain."

"Pat, you're actually leaving the whole place intact? Not taking a thing from here?"

Reaching to the mantel, Pat caressed the ivory carving of the bird just launching itself into flight, the first object her mother had placed in this cabin so very many years ago. "Only this," she said. "Is there something you'd like to have?"

Angela shook her head. "Something about this place would make that seem . . ."

Angela did not finish, and again Pat was amazed by what seemed to be a near-psychic sensitivity. Removing anything else from here, from this eloquent statement of her mother's life, seemed a violation, and the circle containing her mother's life and her own needed to be completed, not continued. Someone would come in here, dismantle and transform this place utterly. Better that it be a stranger, better that she herself be gone and never come up here again, better to keep this place intact in memory...

Pat smiled then, as the oldies station began a new song. "How very appropriate," she murmured.

The Long and Winding Road

"My favorite Beatles song," Angela said. Getting up from the sofa, her body swaying to the slow rhythms of the song, she moved to where Pat stood at the fireplace. "Dance with me..." A question, but she slid her hands up over Pat's shoulders.

Pat's arms took possession of Angela, and in the act of taking this woman into her arms and holding her, restraint seemed to fall from her like molted skin.

She breathed in Angela, scents of peach that rose from her skin, and, as Angela rested her soft warm cheek against Pat's, almond scents from her hair.

Angela's throaty hum blended with Paul McCartney's gentle tenor in the words of the song, and Pat led her securely in its slow, sinuous rhythms.

And Angela became pure response to the direction of her hands on Angela's back, to her body pressing lightly against Angela's. Pat moved her hands in their own dance, slowly up over Angela's back, and then down into the curve that suggested the swell of Angela's hips. *I was born to perform this dance with this woman... I was born knowing this...*

Angela murmured, "I don't know why anyone would want to be a lesbian, do you?"

"I can't think of a single reason," Pat murmured back. "Why go through all this grief..."

Whatever Angela gave her, whatever they would have together, whatever time was left in her own life, nothing would temper this joy...

Angela whispered, "Everybody knows we don't even fit together... we're unnatural."

Pat held her closer, this woman whose body surely had been formed to fit perfectly in her arms. "Yes, God made Adam and Eve, not Adam and Steve..."

"Don't you mean Ada and Eve..."

Soft hands touched Pat's face, smoothing out all the pain she had ever known. Soft fingers touched the back of her neck, her hair, her ears, stroked her cheeks... This woman was an angel of healing.

"No, I meant Pat and Angela..." To this woman she would give all the love she had in her to give...

Angela said, "God knows we lesbians never have a happy day..."

Pat said, "Our lives are sheer hell..."

Angela sighed, "You are the most hellish butch woman..." She sang softly with the music, "The long and winding road..." And raised her face to Pat's. "I have a feeling this may be our song..."

Pat tightened her arms. "All the songs are ours." And her lips brushed, and then took possession of Angela's.

EPILOGUE

Tuesday
November 3, 1992

You Make Loving Fun

Emerging from the cab in heavy traffic on the corner of Market Street and Sanchez, Pat glanced at her watch, then hurried through the crisp San Francisco night, trotting the final block to the Castro, flanked by dozens of men and women all heading in the same direction. She heard, faintly, the music of Fleetwood Mac rocking in the distance, merged with shouts and cheering.

The Castro was closed to automobile traffic; yellow wooden horses and police cars barricaded its Market Street intersection. In the crush of pedestrian traffic she spotted Bradley, in jeans and a leather jacket, waiting, as promised, in front of Twin Peaks, the bar at the Castro Street intersection. Slinging her overnight bag over her shoulder, she sprinted through the crowd, captured him in a shoulder-pounding hug, and let loose her joy.

"He won he won he *won!*" she screamed.

"Yes yes *yes,*" he shouted back, and danced her in a spinning circle.

"Where's Warren?" she finally managed to ask.

223

"With the ACT UP group, he'll be along. Where's your peanut, woman?" he demanded, patting the pockets of her windbreaker.

"Here, right here," she bluffed, shoving her hand into a front pocket of her jeans. "You want I should roll it down this street with my nose and be trampled in two seconds?"

"I knew you'd use that excuse," he said, his broad shoulders heaving with an exaggerated sigh. "Okay, I concede the payoff. In consideration of what you did for the campaign."

She had been in the Castro several times in recent years, but as she turned the corner and saw the huge gay pride rainbow flags fluttering on poles from virtually every bay window of the Victorian buildings along the two-block strip that was the heart of the Castro, delight expanded in her chest. Seizing Bradley's arm, she buoyantly moved to join the crush of people streaming down the center of Castro Street, past the bold pink neon letters of the Castro Theater toward the sound stage set up in mid-street, just beyond the next intersection at 18th Street; its huge box-speakers poured Fleetwood Mac over the crowd of thousands that continued to flood the Castro.

I'm *part* of all this, she realized, I helped *do* this. She said, "I tried to reach Donnelly from the L.A. airport."

"She's with Roberta. In Little Rock."

"I figured. Querida —"

"Three guesses who she's with, and two don't count," Bradley said, and flung his arm around her shoulders.

Querida was in her apartment in Los Angeles, marching up and down the living room in her excitement, cheering "Olé!" as state after state fell into the Democratic column. "Did you hear that?" She dashed to her grandfather, exultantly seized his hand. "Gay people voted in a block, over seventy percent for him!"

Squeezing her hand, he gestured to the television where a color graphic of the United States showed the spreading tide of Democratic victories. "Si," he said simply, and turned on her the same brilliant smile of triumph and pride that he had bestowed on her just over a year ago.

As she leaned down to embrace him she thought: I could have gone to my grave, and he to his, without ever having had this together.

Go Your Own Way

"I talked to Querida this morning," Pat said. "She's still trying to persuade her grandfather to go with her to one of the gay Latino parties in West Hollywood tonight."

"Isn't he the most amazing story," Bradley said. "Anybody who thinks gay and lesbian people don't invent their lives should hear that man's life story." He asked, "How come your sweet Angela didn't come with you tonight?"

"My sweet Angela," she said with a gentle smile, "is at the Mixner party in L.A."

He grinned, shrugged. "Sounds reasonable. And Averill?"

Pat was the one to shrug. "Sitting on her laurels."

* * * * *

Averill was sitting in the den of the home she had built for her parents in Palm Springs. Sipping champagne, she watched a video tape of *The Terminator*.

Not a single other thing on television but the election, and her parents were glued to the set in the living room watching the returns. Fine, the Democrats were winning mostly everything, it appeared, and that would make Donnelly happy. And no one could say Averill Calder Harmon hadn't done her share.

After thirty-five years on the planet, from where she sat she agreed with her father that technology had made everything better, but the problems were always the same: the economy, crime, peace on earth. It didn't make any difference who sat in the White House. Daddy didn't understand the why of the check she'd written to the Democratic Campaign, but so be it. Politicians and their claims were all hot air, it was money that talked. And by God, Averill Calder Harmon had talked the talk.

It was all she could do. Her priority, more than ever, was to get herself into good mental shape for next year. Only one tournament she'd even had a chance at the whole of this year, and her concentration at Springfield so far in the toilet her putter had felt like a tree trunk and nothing but muscle memory had put that final six-footer in the hole for third place. Everybody, including her, had spent this year chewing on Dottie Mochrie's dust . . .

The math was absolute. Six more wins for the Hall of Fame, and she was thirty-five years old. Amy Alcott had been sitting on needing only one win for heaven knew how long, and her hourglass had about run out. If she herself ever got into that situation, she would die. She had a few good years left, she had to get it done. The Hall would separate her from everyone else forever, the

Hall would make every price — every price — she'd ever paid worthwhile...

Averill picked up the bottle of Taittinger's, topped up her glass. *Mattie Schroeder*, she thought in disgust. The final tournament of the year, and the first time since she was a rookie she wouldn't be going on to Florida for the Championship, she hadn't had a tournament win to qualify. So she'd relaxed and had a few — but she had not, not for one minute, needed help driving, not from anyone, much less butch-of-the-world Schroeder who all but wore DYKE stamped across her visor. The woman was playing head games with her, trying to mess her up for next season.

Okay, she'd fallen down a little on the money list, in the top twenty-five instead of the top ten... Big deal. She knew how to win, and she'd be back. Back on top as a winner. And in the Hall of Fame.

Angela... She wouldn't think about Angela. Trusting Angela had been a mistake. Angela was history.

Donnelly, though, must be very happy tonight, and the check for twenty-five grand hadn't been chopped liver in making this night for Donnelly possible.

Who knows, she thought, one of these days... she might... just might... take another look at what Donnelly really wanted her to do.

Never Going Back Again

Feet bouncing to the music, everyone around her dancing, Pat laughed her exuberance as the sound stage speakers, in between announcements of senate victories for Feinstein and Boxer, and defeats to challenges to gay rights in Oregon and Maine, poured music over the crowd that continued to fill the Castro. Toilet-paper streamers hung from the bus cables above the intersection of Castro and 18th Street, more toilet-paper rolls were being hurled upward to cheers or groans from the crowd.

On balconies overlooking the street, couples in tank tops and tights danced with abandon; a prancing Tipper Gore look-alike drag queen blew kisses to the crowd from her perch above Walgreen's Drug Store. Six young men and women, having climbed onto the plastic roof of a bus stop, performed their own energetic bump and grind dance routine.

Pat was grabbed in a one-armed hug by a woman in a 49ers jacket, a curtain of straight dark hair almost covering her face, who pressed an unopened ice-cold can of Budweiser into her hand. "On me! Celebrate!" And she went spinning off into the crowd.

"Let me buy you one," Pat said to Bradley, pulling him toward the Village Deli where bottles and cans of beer sat packed in barrels of ice on the sidewalk.

Bradley accepted her gift of the beer and clinked his can against hers. "For what you did."

"You too, my friend," Pat said, and laughed at a go-go dancer boogying on a balcony, at the people in a room overlooking Castro Street who danced and waved and shook bottles of champagne out the window at the thousands of gay and lesbian people dancing on Castro Street. "What a party!"

Taking her arm again, Bradley drew her through the throng toward A Different Light bookstore, open for business and jammed with customers.

"The one blight on the evening," he moaned, "my Valdez novel isn't in that store, won't be till January." But he had struck it rich this past year, finding a publishable first novel by a new Latino writer, and a promising African-American essayist whose first work he would soon publish... Not bad for a fledgling gay publishing house...

"I heard a rumor you're not retiring yet," he said to Pat.

"Only a rumor," she said, and did not elaborate. A counseling program for gay and lesbian teenagers at her school was in the works, but, lacking the determined calm of pioneer Virginia Uribe, she did not doubt that she would last about as long as it took to breathe fire all over the first member of the Traditional Values Coalition to cross her path.

"Olé, my favorite," Bradley said, pointing to a commentary on George Bush's defeat on a sign held up by a young Latino: HASTA LA VISTA, ASSHOLE.

"It has a certain directness," Pat agreed.

Don't Stop Thinking About Tomorrow

Bradley laughed at Pat's understatement. He had been here in the Castro long before Pat, had been at the Castro Street Station bar when ABC announced that Clinton's electoral vote had taken him over the top, when the jammed bar burst into "Happy Days Are Here Again" and the place became a bedlam of flashing lights, noisemakers, confetti, and cheering people spilling out onto the street in celebration.

"There's Warren," Pat said in a suddenly sober tone.

Wearing black jeans and a black ACT UP T-shirt, Warren was part of a procession marching as best it could through the crowd, bearing on its shoulders a huge papier mache black coffin on which was written a number: 150,000.

AIDS mortalities, Bradley knew. Other ACT UP members, carrying life-size cardboard caricatures of George Bush, Dan Quayle and Jesse Helms, also paraded down the street.

"How goes it with you and Warren?" Pat asked him.

"Better and better. He must regret what he said in the cabin about not finding a way into me. I'm a regular gabby Gertrude."

"He doesn't seem to mind," Pat observed as Warren spotted Bradley in the crowd and blew him a kiss.

No, he didn't, Bradley silently agreed. Channels were opening ever wider between them, including love-making . . .

In concert, the ACT UP contingent carrying the caricatures threw them to the ground, trampled on them; those carrying the coffin ignited it and danced around the funeral pyre as the entire crowd in the Castro burst into song.

Ding Dong the Witch Is Dead

Dancing and singing the song, Pat was grabbed and embraced by an emaciated young man. He said, "All I wanted — I just wanted to live to see this day . . ." He broke away from her and hugged another stranger.

A young man in an olive drab jacket faced her. "Where are you from?" he asked.

"Los Angeles. You?"

"Utah. Just got here. Say, what's going on, do you know?"

What planet had this guy been living on? "Clinton's won —"

"I don't know much about this, much about politics. I hear this new guy's promised to do something about the military. I got kicked out three weeks ago."

She was grabbed and hugged by another stranger, and another, and she began to hug people herself, and the street was filled with cheering people, people drinking toasts . . .

On the phone, from Little Rock . . .

As the music cut off, the crowd hushed only slightly as the young man at the microphone on the sound stage shouted, "Our own Roberta Achtenberg, national co-chair of the Clinton–Gore campaign! From Little Rock, our own . . . ROBERTA!"

Amid crescendos of cheers Pat could hear the clear firm tones only intermittently:

"Bill Clinton will be president because you elected him . . . The lesbian and gay community voted to make Clinton president . . . For twelve years we have had a president and vice president who have denied our existence and been willing to kill us. That time is over . . . You all understand that our work is just beginning . . ."

On the phone, from Capitol Hill . . .

The young man on the sound stage shouted, "From

the National Gay and Lesbian Task Force, calling us from Washington, DC — ROBERT BRAY!"

"*Every gay and lesbian on Castro now should claim credit for the national victory for gay people everywhere. It's a new era in politics and history, and we are not going back into the closet. We are finally part of the governing body of this country...*"

Don't Stop Thinking About Tomorrow

Then a new voice, breaking into the din of the crowd.

"Clinton," Bradley said from beside her. "His victory speech."

"*...my fellow Americans, we must face problems too long ignored — from AIDS to the environment to the conversion of our economy from defense to a domestic economic giant. And most important of all, to bring our people together as never before so that our diversity can be a source of strength, where everyone counts and everyone is part of America's family...*"

Bradley said, "If these people only knew, California's single biggest contributor to the Clinton campaign is standing right next to me."

"I don't know that I am, and neither do you," Pat protested.

"Send me a postcard from the inauguration," was Bradley's teasing response. "I wonder what your family would think about what you did with that cabin."

Pat shrugged. She only cared about what her mother would think.

Words echoed in her, the words Donnelly had spoken after Pat had sold the cabin, paid taxes on the proceeds, and presented the balance to the Clinton campaign: "I think your mother would be cheering."

Pat looked at her celebrating brothers and sisters spread out by the thousands over the Castro. And remembered how her journey here had all started with Bradley and Warren arriving at the cabin a year and one month ago. And how she had yanked out and tossed a ceramic flamingo, decorated with a sign they had brought, under the low-growing ferns fronting the cabin windows.

She remembered the day she and Angela had left the cabin for the final time. Remembered looking up at the place one last time, and then striding over to those ferns. And planting, with a single powerful thrust, that flamingo, the QUEER NATION sign plastered across its breast, deeply into the earth.

A few of the publications of
THE NAIAD PRESS, INC.
P.O. Box 10543 • Tallahassee, Florida 32302
Phone (904) 539-5965
Toll-Free Order Number: 1-800-533-1973
Mail orders welcome. Please include 15% postage.

FLASHPOINT by Katherine V. Forrest. 256 pp. Lesbian
blockbuster!   ISBN 1-56280-043-4 $22.95

CROSSWORDS by Penny Sumner. 256 pp. 2nd VictoriaCross
Mystery.   ISBN 1-56280-064-7   9.95

SWEET CHERRY WINE by Carol Schmidt. 240 pp. A novel of
suspense.   ISBN 1-56280-063-9   9.95

CERTAIN SMILES by Dorothy Tell. 224 pp. Erotic short stories
.   ISBN 1-56280-066-3   9.95

EDITED OUT by Lisa Haddock. 224 pp. 1st Carmen Ramirez
Mystery.   ISBN 1-56280-077-9   9.95

WEDNESDAY NIGHTS by Camarin Grae. 288 pp. Sexy
adventure.   ISBN 1-56280-060-4   10.95

SMOKEY O by Celia Cohen. 176 pp. Relationships on the playing
field.   ISBN 1-56280-057-4   9.95

KATHLEEN O'DONALD by Penny Hayes. 256 pp. Rose and
Kathleen find each other and employment in 1909 NYC.
                                                   ISBN 1-56280-070-1   9.95

STAYING HOME by Elisabeth Nonas. 256 pp. Molly and Alix
want a baby . . . or do they?   ISBN 1-56280-076-0   10.95

TRUE LOVE by Jennifer Fulton. 240 pp. Six lesbians searching for
love in all the "right" places.   ISBN 1-56280-035-3   9.95

GARDENIAS WHERE THERE ARE NONE by Molleen Zanger.
176 pp. Why is Melanie inextricably drawn to the old house?
                                                   ISBN 1-56280-056-6   9.95

MICHAELA by Sarah Aldridge. 256 pp. A "Sarah Aldridge"
romance.   ISBN 1-56280-055-8   10.95

KEEPING SECRETS by Penny Mickelbury. 208 pp. A Gianna
Maglione Mystery. First in a series.   ISBN 1-56280-052-3   9.95

THE ROMANTIC NAIAD edited by Katherine V. Forrest &
Barbara Grier. 336 pp. Love stories by Naiad Press authors.
                                                   ISBN 1-56280-054-X   14.95

UNDER MY SKIN by Jaye Maiman. 336 pp. A Robin Miller
mystery. 3rd in a series.   ISBN 1-56280-049-3.   10.95

STAY TOONED by Rhonda Dicksion. 144 pp. Cartoons — 1st
collection since *Lesbian Survival Manual.*   ISBN 1-56280-045-0   9.95

CAR POOL by Karin Kallmaker. 272pp. Lesbians on wheels
and then some!   ISBN 1-56280-048-5   9.95

NOT TELLING MOTHER: STORIES FROM A LIFE by Diane
Salvatore. 176 pp. Her 3rd novel.   ISBN 1-56280-044-2   9.95

GOBLIN MARKET by Lauren Wright Douglas. 240pp. A Caitlin
Reece Mystery. 5th in a series.   ISBN 1-56280-047-7   9.95

LONG GOODBYES by Nikki Baker. 256 pp. A Virginia Kelly
mystery. 3rd in a series.   ISBN 1-56280-042-6   9.95

FRIENDS AND LOVERS by Jackie Calhoun. 224 pp. Mid-western
Lesbian lives and loves.   ISBN 1-56280-041-8   9.95

THE CAT CAME BACK by Hilary Mullins. 208 pp. Highly praised
Lesbian novel.   ISBN 1-56280-040-X   9.95

BEHIND CLOSED DOORS by Robbi Sommers. 192 pp. Hot, erotic
short stories.   ISBN 1-56280-039-6   9.95

CLAIRE OF THE MOON by Nicole Conn. 192 pp. See the movie —
read the book!   ISBN 1-56280-038-8   10.95

SILENT HEART by Claire McNab. 192 pp. Exotic Lesbian
romance.   ISBN 1-56280-036-1   9.95

HAPPY ENDINGS by Kate Brandt. 272 pp. Intimate conversations
with Lesbian authors.   ISBN 1-56280-050-7   10.95

THE SPY IN QUESTION by Amanda Kyle Williams. 256 pp. 4th
Madison McGuire.   ISBN 1-56280-037-X   9.95

SAVING GRACE by Jennifer Fulton. 240 pp. Adventure and
romantic entanglement.   ISBN 1-56280-051-5   9.95

THE YEAR SEVEN by Molleen Zanger. 208 pp. Women surviving
in a new world.   ISBN 1-56280-034-5   9.95

CURIOUS WINE by Katherine V. Forrest. 176 pp. Tenth
Anniversary Edition. The most popular contemporary Lesbian
love story.   ISBN 1-56280-053-1   9.95

CHAUTAUQUA by Catherine Ennis. 192 pp. Exciting, romantic
adventure.   ISBN 1-56280-032-9   9.95

A PROPER BURIAL by Pat Welch. 192 pp. A Helen Black
mystery. 3rd in a series.   ISBN 1-56280-033-7   9.95

SILVERLAKE HEAT: A Novel of Suspense by Carol Schmidt.
240 pp. Rhonda is as hot as Laney's dreams.   ISBN 1-56280-031-0   9.95

LOVE, ZENA BETH by Diane Salvatore. 224 pp. The most talked
about lesbian novel of the nineties!   ISBN 1-56280-030-2   9.95

A DOORYARD FULL OF FLOWERS by Isabel Miller. 160 pp.
Stories incl. 2 sequels to *Patience and Sarah.* ISBN 1-56280-029-9   9.95

MURDER BY TRADITION by Katherine V. Forrest. 288 pp. A
Kate Delafield Mystery. 4th in a series. ISBN 1-56280-002-7   9.95

THE EROTIC NAIAD edited by Katherine V. Forrest & Barbara Grier.
224 pp. Love stories by Naiad Press authors. ISBN 1-56280-026-4   12.95

DEAD CERTAIN by Claire McNab. 224 pp. A Carol Ashton
mystery. 5th in a series. ISBN 1-56280-027-2   9.95

CRAZY FOR LOVING by Jaye Maiman. 320 pp. A Robin Miller
mystery. 2nd in a series. ISBN 1-56280-025-6   9.95

STONEHURST by Barbara Johnson. 176 pp. Passionate regency
romance. ISBN 1-56280-024-8   9.95

INTRODUCING AMANDA VALENTINE by Rose Beecham.
256 pp. An Amanda Valentine Mystery. First in a series.
ISBN 1-56280-021-3   9.95

UNCERTAIN COMPANIONS by Robbi Sommers. 204 pp.
Steamy, erotic novel. ISBN 1-56280-017-5   9.95

A TIGER'S HEART by Lauren W. Douglas. 240 pp. A Caitlin
Reece mystery. 4th in a series. ISBN 1-56280-018-3   9.95

PAPERBACK ROMANCE by Karin Kallmaker. 256 pp. A
delicious romance. ISBN 1-56280-019-1   9.95

MORTON RIVER VALLEY by Lee Lynch. 304 pp. Lee Lynch at
her best! ISBN 1-56280-016-7   9.95

THE LAVENDER HOUSE MURDER by Nikki Baker. 224 pp. A
Virginia Kelly Mystery. 2nd in a series. ISBN 1-56280-012-4   9.95

PASSION BAY by Jennifer Fulton. 224 pp. Passionate romance,
virgin beaches, tropical skies. ISBN 1-56280-028-0   9.95

STICKS AND STONES by Jackie Calhoun. 208 pp. Contemporary
lesbian lives and loves. ISBN 1-56280-020-5   9.95

DELIA IRONFOOT by Jeane Harris. 192 pp. Adventure for Delia
and Beth in the Utah mountains. ISBN 1-56280-014-0   9.95

UNDER THE SOUTHERN CROSS by Claire McNab. 192 pp.
Romantic nights Down Under. ISBN 1-56280-011-6   9.95

RIVERFINGER WOMEN by Elana Nachman/Dykewomon.
208 pp. Classic Lesbian/feminist novel. ISBN 1-56280-013-2   8.95

A CERTAIN DISCONTENT by Cleve Boutell. 240 pp. A unique
coterie of women. ISBN 1-56280-009-4   9.95

GRASSY FLATS by Penny Hayes. 256 pp. Lesbian romance in
the '30s. ISBN 1-56280-010-8   9.95

A SINGULAR SPY by Amanda K. Williams. 192 pp. 3rd Madison
McGuire. ISBN 1-56280-008-6   8.95

THE END OF APRIL by Penny Sumner. 240 pp. A Victoria Cross
Mystery. First in a series.   ISBN 1-56280-007-8   8.95

A FLIGHT OF ANGELS by Sarah Aldridge. 240 pp. Romance set at
the National Gallery of Art   ISBN 1-56280-001-9   9.95

HOUSTON TOWN by Deborah Powell. 208 pp. A Hollis Carpenter
mystery. Second in a series.   ISBN 1-56280-006-X   8.95

KISS AND TELL by Robbi Sommers. 192 pp. Scorching stories by
the author of *Pleasures*.   ISBN 1-56280-005-1   9.95

STILL WATERS by Pat Welch. 208 pp. A Helen Black mystery.
2nd in a series.   ISBN 0-941483-97-5   9.95

TO LOVE AGAIN by Evelyn Kennedy. 208 pp. Wildly
romantic love story.   ISBN 0-941483-85-1   9.95

IN THE GAME by Nikki Baker. 192 pp. A Virginia Kelly
mystery. First in a series.   ISBN 01-56280-004-3   9.95

AVALON by Mary Jane Jones. 256 pp. A Lesbian Arthurian
romance.   ISBN 0-941483-96-7   9.95

STRANDED by Camarin Grae. 320 pp. Entertaining, riveting
adventure.   ISBN 0-941483-99-1   9.95

THE DAUGHTERS OF ARTEMIS by Lauren Wright Douglas.
240 pp. A Caitlin Reece mystery. 3rd in a series.
          ISBN 0-941483-95-9   9.95

CLEARWATER by Catherine Ennis. 176 pp. Romantic secrets
of a small Louisiana town.   ISBN 0-941483-65-7   8.95

THE HALLELUJAH MURDERS by Dorothy Tell. 176 pp. A Poppy
Dillworth mystery. 2nd in a series.   ISBN 0-941483-88-6   8.95

ZETA BASE by Judith Alguire. 208 pp. Lesbian triangle
on a future Earth.   ISBN 0-941483-94-0   9.95

SECOND CHANCE by Jackie Calhoun. 256 pp. Contemporary
Lesbian lives and loves.   ISBN 0-941483-93-2   9.95

BENEDICTION by Diane Salvatore. 272 pp. Striking,
contemporary romantic novel.   ISBN 0-941483-90-8   9.95

CALLING RAIN by Karen Marie Christa Minns. 240 pp.
Spellbinding, erotic love story   ISBN 0-941483-87-8   9.95

BLACK IRIS by Jeane Harris. 192 pp. Caroline's hidden past . . .
          ISBN 0-941483-68-1   8.95

TOUCHWOOD by Karin Kallmaker. 240 pp. Loving, May/
December romance.   ISBN 0-941483-76-2   9.95

BAYOU CITY SECRETS by Deborah Powell. 224 pp. A Hollis
Carpenter mystery. First in a series.   ISBN 0-941483-91-6   9.95

COP OUT by Claire McNab. 208 pp. A Carol Ashton mystery.
4th in a series.   ISBN 0-941483-84-3   9.95

LODESTAR by Phyllis Horn. 224 pp. Romantic, fast-moving
adventure.   ISBN 0-941483-83-5   8.95

THE BEVERLY MALIBU by Katherine V. Forrest. 288 pp. A
Kate Delafield Mystery. 3rd in a series.   ISBN 0-941483-48-7   9.95

THAT OLD STUDEBAKER by Lee Lynch. 272 pp. Andy's affair
with Regina and her attachment to her beloved car.
                                                    ISBN 0-941483-82-7   9.95

PASSION'S LEGACY by Lori Paige. 224 pp. Sarah is swept into
the arms of Augusta Pym in this delightful historical romance.
                                                    ISBN 0-941483-81-9   8.95

THE PROVIDENCE FILE by Amanda Kyle Williams. 256 pp.
Second Madison McGuire   ISBN 0-941483-92-4   8.95

I LEFT MY HEART by Jaye Maiman. 320 pp. A Robin Miller
Mystery. First in a series.   ISBN 0-941483-72-X   9.95

THE PRICE OF SALT by Patricia Highsmith (writing as Claire
Morgan). 288 pp. Classic lesbian novel, first issued in 1952 . . .
acknowledged by its author under her own, very famous, name.
                                                    ISBN 1-56280-003-5   9.95

SIDE BY SIDE by Isabel Miller. 256 pp. From beloved author of
Patience and Sarah.   ISBN 0-941483-77-0   9.95

STAYING POWER: LONG TERM LESBIAN COUPLES
by Susan E. Johnson. 352 pp. Joys of coupledom.
                                                    ISBN 0-941-483-75-4   12.95

SLICK by Camarin Grae. 304 pp. Exotic, erotic adventure.
                                                    ISBN 0-941483-74-6   9.95

NINTH LIFE by Lauren Wright Douglas. 256 pp. A Caitlin
Reece mystery. 2nd in a series.   ISBN 0-941483-50-9   8.95

PLAYERS by Robbi Sommers. 192 pp. Sizzling, erotic novel.
                                                    ISBN 0-941483-73-8   9.95

MURDER AT RED ROOK RANCH by Dorothy Tell. 224 pp.
A Poppy Dillworth mystery. 1st in a series.   ISBN 0-941483-80-0   8.95

LESBIAN SURVIVAL MANUAL by Rhonda Dicksion.
112 pp. Cartoons!   ISBN 0-941483-71-1   8.95

A ROOM FULL OF WOMEN by Elisabeth Nonas. 256 pp.
Contemporary Lesbian lives.   ISBN 0-941483-69-X   9.95

PRIORITIES by Lynda Lyons 288 pp. Science fiction with
a twist.   ISBN 0-941483-66-5   8.95

THEME FOR DIVERSE INSTRUMENTS by Jane Rule. 208
pp. Powerful romantic lesbian stories.   ISBN 0-941483-63-0   8.95

LESBIAN QUERIES by Hertz & Ertman. 112 pp. The questions
you were too embarrassed to ask.   ISBN 0-941483-67-3   8.95

CLUB 12 by Amanda Kyle Williams. 288 pp. Espionage thriller
featuring a lesbian agent!   ISBN 0-941483-64-9   8.95

DEATH DOWN UNDER by Claire McNab. 240 pp. A Carol
Ashton mystery. 3rd in a series.   ISBN 0-941483-39-8   9.95

MONTANA FEATHERS by Penny Hayes. 256 pp. Vivian and
Elizabeth find love in frontier Montana.   ISBN 0-941483-61-4   8.95

CHESAPEAKE PROJECT by Phyllis Horn. 304 pp. Jessie &
Meredith in perilous adventure.   ISBN 0-941483-58-4   8.95

LIFESTYLES by Jackie Calhoun. 224 pp. Contemporary Lesbian
lives and loves.   ISBN 0-941483-57-6   9.95

VIRAGO by Karen Marie Christa Minns. 208 pp. Darsen has
chosen Ginny.   ISBN 0-941483-56-8   8.95

WILDERNESS TREK by Dorothy Tell. 192 pp. Six women on
vacation learning "new" skills.   ISBN 0-941483-60-6   8.95

MURDER BY THE BOOK by Pat Welch. 256 pp. A Helen
Black Mystery. First in a series.   ISBN 0-941483-59-2   9.95

LESBIANS IN GERMANY by Lillian Faderman & B. Eriksson.
128 pp. Fiction, poetry, essays.   ISBN 0-941483-62-2   8.95

THERE'S SOMETHING I'VE BEEN MEANING TO TELL
YOU Ed. by Loralee MacPike. 288 pp. Gay men and lesbians
coming out to their children.   ISBN 0-941483-44-4   9.95

LIFTING BELLY by Gertrude Stein. Ed. by Rebecca Mark. 104
pp. Erotic poetry.   ISBN 0-941483-51-7   8.95

ROSE PENSKI by Roz Perry. 192 pp. Adult lovers in a long-term
relationship.   ISBN 0-941483-37-1   8.95

AFTER THE FIRE by Jane Rule. 256 pp. Warm, human novel
by this incomparable author.   ISBN 0-941483-45-2   8.95

SUE SLATE, PRIVATE EYE by Lee Lynch. 176 pp. The gay
folk of Peacock Alley are all cats.   ISBN 0-941483-52-5   8.95

CHRIS by Randy Salem. 224 pp. Golden oldie. Handsome Chris
and her adventures.   ISBN 0-941483-42-8   8.95

THREE WOMEN by March Hastings. 232 pp. Golden oldie. A
triangle among wealthy sophisticates.   ISBN 0-941483-43-6   8.95

RICE AND BEANS by Valeria Taylor. 232 pp. Love and
romance on poverty row.   ISBN 0-941483-41-X   8.95

PLEASURES by Robbi Sommers. 204 pp. Unprecedented
eroticism.   ISBN 0-941483-49-5   8.95

EDGEWISE by Camarin Grae. 372 pp. Spellbinding
adventure.   ISBN 0-941483-19-3   9.95

FATAL REUNION by Claire McNab. 224 pp. A Carol Ashton
mystery. 2nd in a series.   ISBN 0-941483-40-1   8.95

KEEP TO ME STRANGER by Sarah Aldridge. 372 pp. Romance
set in a department store dynasty.   ISBN 0-941483-38-X   9.95

IN THE BLOOD by Lauren Wright Douglas. 252 pp. Lesbian
science fiction adventure fantasy   ISBN 0-941483-22-3   8.95

THE BEE'S KISS by Shirley Verel. 216 pp. Delicate, delicious
romance.   ISBN 0-941483-36-3   8.95

RAGING MOTHER MOUNTAIN by Pat Emmerson. 264 pp.
Furosa Firechild's adventures in Wonderland.   ISBN 0-941483-35-5   8.95

IN EVERY PORT by Karin Kallmaker. 228 pp. Jessica's sexy,
adventuresome travels.   ISBN 0-941483-37-7   9.95

OF LOVE AND GLORY by Evelyn Kennedy. 192 pp. Exciting
WWII romance.   ISBN 0-941483-32-0   8.95

CLICKING STONES by Nancy Tyler Glenn. 288 pp. Love
transcending time.   ISBN 0-941483-31-2   9.95

SURVIVING SISTERS by Gail Pass. 252 pp. Powerful love
story.   ISBN 0-941483-16-9   8.95

SOUTH OF THE LINE by Catherine Ennis. 216 pp. Civil War
adventure.   ISBN 0-941483-29-0   8.95

WOMAN PLUS WOMAN by Dolores Klaich. 300 pp. Supurb
Lesbian overview.   ISBN 0-941483-28-2   9.95

HEAVY GILT by Delores Klaich. 192 pp. Lesbian detective/
disappearing homophobes/upper class gay society.

                                          ISBN 0-941483-25-8   8.95

THE FINER GRAIN by Denise Ohio. 216 pp. Brilliant young
college lesbian novel.   ISBN 0-941483-11-8   8.95

HIGH CONTRAST by Jessie Lattimore. 264 pp. Women of the
Crystal Palace.   ISBN 0-941483-17-7   8.95

OCTOBER OBSESSION by Meredith More. Josie's rich, secret
Lesbian life.   ISBN 0-941483-18-5   8.95

BEFORE STONEWALL: THE MAKING OF A GAY AND
LESBIAN COMMUNITY by Andrea Weiss & Greta Schiller.
96 pp., 25 illus.   ISBN 0-941483-20-7   7.95

WE WALK THE BACK OF THE TIGER by Patricia A. Murphy.
192 pp. Romantic Lesbian novel/beginning women's movement.
                                          ISBN 0-941483-13-4   8.95

SUNDAY'S CHILD by Joyce Bright. 216 pp. Lesbian athletics, at
last the novel about sports.   ISBN 0-941483-12-6   8.95

OSTEN'S BAY by Zenobia N. Vole. 204 pp. Sizzling adventure
romance set on Bonaire.   ISBN 0-941483-15-0   8.95

LESSONS IN MURDER by Claire McNab. 216 pp. A Carol
Ashton mystery. First in a series.   ISBN 0-941483-14-2   9.95

YELLOWTHROAT by Penny Hayes. 240 pp. Margarita, bandit,
kidnaps Julia.   ISBN 0-941483-10-X   8.95

SAPPHISTRY: THE BOOK OF LESBIAN SEXUALITY by
Pat Califia. 3d edition, revised. 208 pp.   ISBN 0-941483-24-X   10.95

CHERISHED LOVE by Evelyn Kennedy. 192 pp. Erotic
Lesbian love story.   ISBN 0-941483-08-8   9.95

LAST SEPTEMBER by Helen R. Hull. 208 pp. Six stories & a
glorious novella.   ISBN 0-941483-09-6   8.95

THE SECRET IN THE BIRD by Camarin Grae. 312 pp. Striking,
psychological suspense novel.   ISBN 0-941483-05-3   8.95

TO THE LIGHTNING by Catherine Ennis. 208 pp. Romantic
Lesbian 'Robinson Crusoe' adventure.   ISBN 0-941483-06-1   8.95

THE OTHER SIDE OF VENUS by Shirley Verel. 224 pp.
Luminous, romantic love story.   ISBN 0-941483-07-X   8.95

DREAMS AND SWORDS by Katherine V. Forrest. 192 pp.
Romantic, erotic, imaginative stories.   ISBN 0-941483-03-7   8.95

MEMORY BOARD by Jane Rule. 336 pp. Memorable novel
about an aging Lesbian couple.   ISBN 0-941483-02-9   9.95

THE ALWAYS ANONYMOUS BEAST by Lauren Wright
Douglas. 224 pp. A Caitlin Reece mystery. First in a series.
                                                ISBN 0-941483-04-5   8.95

DUSTY'S QUEEN OF HEARTS DINER by Lee Lynch. 240 pp.
Romantic blue-collar novel.   ISBN 0-941483-01-0   8.95

PARENTS MATTER by Ann Muller. 240 pp. Parents'
relationships with Lesbian daughters and gay sons.
                                                ISBN 0-930044-91-6   9.95

MAGDALENA by Sarah Aldridge. 352 pp. Epic Lesbian novel
set on three continents.   ISBN 0-930044-99-1   8.95

THE BLACK AND WHITE OF IT by Ann Allen Shockley.
144 pp. Short stories.   ISBN 0-930044-96-7   7.95

SAY JESUS AND COME TO ME by Ann Allen Shockley. 288
pp. Contemporary romance.   ISBN 0-930044-98-3   8.95

LOVING HER by Ann Allen Shockley. 192 pp. Romantic love
story.   ISBN 0-930044-97-5   7.95

MURDER AT THE NIGHTWOOD BAR by Katherine V.
Forrest. 240 pp. A Kate Delafield mystery. Second in a series.
                                                ISBN 0-930044-92-4   9.95

ZOE'S BOOK by Gail Pass. 224 pp. Passionate, obsessive love
story.   ISBN 0-930044-95-9   7.95

WINGED DANCER by Camarin Grae. 228 pp. Erotic Lesbian
adventure story.   ISBN 0-930044-88-6   8.95

PAZ by Camarin Grae. 336 pp. Romantic Lesbian adventurer
with the power to change the world.   ISBN 0-930044-89-4   8.95

SOUL SNATCHER by Camarin Grae. 224 pp. A puzzle, an
adventure, a mystery — Lesbian romance.   ISBN 0-930044-90-8   8.95

THE LOVE OF GOOD WOMEN by Isabel Miller. 224 pp.
Long-awaited new novel by the author of the beloved *Patience
and Sarah*.   ISBN 0-930044-81-9   8.95

THE HOUSE AT PELHAM FALLS by Brenda Weathers. 240
pp. Suspenseful Lesbian ghost story.   ISBN 0-930044-79-7   7.95

HOME IN YOUR HANDS by Lee Lynch. 240 pp. More stories
from the author of *Old Dyke Tales*.   ISBN 0-930044-80-0   7.95

SURPLUS by Sylvia Stevenson. 342 pp. A classic early Lesbian
novel.   ISBN 0-930044-78-9   7.95

PEMBROKE PARK by Michelle Martin. 256 pp. Derring-do
and daring romance in Regency England.   ISBN 0-930044-77-0   7.95

THE LONG TRAIL by Penny Hayes. 248 pp. Vivid adventures
of two women in love in the old west.   ISBN 0-930044-76-2   8.95

AN EMERGENCE OF GREEN by Katherine V. Forrest. 288
pp. Powerful novel of sexual discovery.   ISBN 0-930044-69-X   9.95

THE LESBIAN PERIODICALS INDEX edited by Claire
Potter. 432 pp. Author & subject index.   ISBN 0-930044-74-6   12.95

DESERT OF THE HEART by Jane Rule. 224 pp. A classic;
basis for the movie *Desert Hearts*.   ISBN 0-930044-73-8   9.95

FOR KEEPS by Elisabeth Nonas. 144 pp. Contemporary novel
about losing and finding love.   ISBN 0-930044-71-1   7.95

TORCHLIGHT TO VALHALLA by Gale Wilhelm. 128 pp.
Classic novel by a great Lesbian writer.   ISBN 0-930044-68-1   7.95

LESBIAN NUNS: BREAKING SILENCE edited by Rosemary
Curb and Nancy Manahan. 432 pp. Unprecedented autobiographies
of religious life.   ISBN 0-930044-62-2   9.95

THE SWASHBUCKLER by Lee Lynch. 288 pp. Colorful novel
set in Greenwich Village in the sixties.   ISBN 0-930044-66-5   8.95

MISFORTUNE'S FRIEND by Sarah Aldridge. 320 pp. Histori-
cal Lesbian novel set on two continents.   ISBN 0-930044-67-3   7.95

SEX VARIANT WOMEN IN LITERATURE by Jeannette
Howard Foster. 448 pp. Literary history.   ISBN 0-930044-65-7   8.95

A HOT-EYED MODERATE by Jane Rule. 252 pp. Hard-hitting
essays on gay life; writing; art.   ISBN 0-930044-57-6   7.95

WE TOO ARE DRIFTING by Gale Wilhelm. 128 pp. Timeless
Lesbian novel, a masterpiece.   ISBN 0-930044-61-4   6.95

AMATEUR CITY by Katherine V. Forrest. 224 pp. A Kate
Delafield mystery. First in a series. ISBN 0-930044-55-X 9.95

THE SOPHIE HOROWITZ STORY by Sarah Schulman. 176
pp. Engaging novel of madcap intrigue. ISBN 0-930044-54-1 7.95

THE YOUNG IN ONE ANOTHER'S ARMS by Jane Rule.
224 pp. Classic Jane Rule. ISBN 0-930044-53-3 9.95

OLD DYKE TALES by Lee Lynch. 224 pp. Extraordinary
stories of our diverse Lesbian lives. ISBN 0-930044-51-7 8.95

DAUGHTERS OF A CORAL DAWN by Katherine V. Forrest.
240 pp. Novel set in a Lesbian new world. ISBN 0-930044-50-9 9.95

AGAINST THE SEASON by Jane Rule. 224 pp. Luminous,
complex novel of interrelationships. ISBN 0-930044-48-7 8.95

LOVERS IN THE PRESENT AFTERNOON by Kathleen
Fleming. 288 pp. A novel about recovery and growth.
ISBN 0-930044-46-0 8.95

TOOTHPICK HOUSE by Lee Lynch. 264 pp. Love between
two Lesbians of different classes. ISBN 0-930044-45-2 7.95

MADAME AURORA by Sarah Aldridge. 256 pp. Historical
novel featuring a charismatic "seer." ISBN 0-930044-44-4 7.95

CONTRACT WITH THE WORLD by Jane Rule. 340 pp.
Powerful, panoramic novel of gay life. ISBN 0-930044-28-2 9.95

THE NESTING PLACE by Sarah Aldridge. 224 pp. A
three-woman triangle — love conquers all! ISBN 0-930044-26-6 7.95

THIS IS NOT FOR YOU by Jane Rule. 284 pp. A letter to a
beloved is also an intricate novel. ISBN 0-930044-25-8 8.95

ANNA'S COUNTRY by Elizabeth Lang. 208 pp. A woman
finds her Lesbian identity. ISBN 0-930044-19-3 8.95

PRISM by Valerie Taylor. 158 pp. A love affair between two
women in their sixties. ISBN 0-930044-18-5 6.95

OUTLANDER by Jane Rule. 207 pp. Short stories and essays
by one of our finest writers. ISBN 0-930044-17-7 8.95

ALL TRUE LOVERS by Sarah Aldridge. 292 pp. Romantic
novel set in the 1930s and 1940s. ISBN 0-930044-10-X 8.95

CYTHEREA'S BREATH by Sarah Aldridge. 240 pp. Romantic
novel about women's entrance into medicine.
ISBN 0-930044-02-9 6.95

TOTTIE by Sarah Aldridge. 181 pp. Lesbian romance in the
turmoil of the sixties. ISBN 0-930044-01-0 6.95

THE LATECOMER by Sarah Aldridge. 107 pp. A delicate love
story. ISBN 0-930044-00-2 6.95

ODD GIRL OUT by Ann Bannon.   ISBN 0-930044-83-5   5.95
I AM A WOMAN 84-3; WOMEN IN THE SHADOWS 85-1;   each
JOURNEY TO A WOMAN 86-X; BEEBO BRINKER 87-8. Golden
oldies about life in Greenwich Village.
JOURNEY TO FULFILLMENT, A WORLD WITHOUT MEN, and   3.95
RETURN TO LESBOS. All by Valerie Taylor   each

These are just a few of the many Naiad Press titles — we are the oldest and
largest lesbian/feminist publishing company in the world. Please request a
complete catalog. We offer personal service; we encourage and welcome direct
mail orders from individuals who have limited access to bookstores carrying
our publications.